# SWEET CONFUSION
## ON THE PRINCES' ISLANDS

A novel by

## Lawrence Goodman

Islands Editions
ADALI YAYINLARI

**Publisher**

**adalı**

**Adalı Yayınları**
Tel:    0216 382 52 80
Fax:    0216 382 52 90
www.adalar-istanbul.org

**Text**
Lawrence Goodman

**Series Editor**
Mary Ann Whitten
islandereditions@yahoo.com

**Printed by**
Seçil Ofset
Matbaacılar Sitesi 4. Cad.
No: 77 Bağcılar - İstanbul
Tel: 0212-6290615

**Illustration**
Metin Çağlayan


May 2005

**ISBN: 975-9119-013**

For
Meryem Hanim

For

Meryem Hanım

# 1

As the Akdeniz approached Seraglio Point and sailed across the mouth of the Golden Horn, the city suddenly and magically revealed itself: a breathtaking introduction to Istanbul only to be had from an approach by sea. Standing at the ship's bow, two of the passengers watched passing before them the Blue Mosque with its six minarets, the rose-colored mass of the Haghia Sophia, and the dark outline of the Topkapı complex overlooking the point. On the hills in the distance heavy, dignified, gray mosques dominated a tangle of streets and red rooftops and at the water's edge stood airy wooden mansions and Italianate palaces of honey-colored stone. Then the ship moved rapidly past the Golden Horn and settled into its berth at the Karaköy docks. The two figures standing at the bow were, in descending order, Ed Wilkie, a young Californian in his early thirties, and his companion, Starleen, a white English bull terrier. Ed was slight and sandy-haired, with a dreamy manner and naïve blue eyes. He had somewhat impulsively taken a job as a teacher in a private Turkish high school in Istanbul, a city he was seeing for the first time.

As soon as the ship had docked, the spell of the journey was broken and there was a sudden chaos of activity. Ed saw gangplanks rattle down to the landing, as announcements were muttered incomprehensibly over the loudspeakers, and passengers spilled onto the decks clutching hand luggage, calling out for porters, shouting at the crew, and taking emotional farewells of each other. Porters pushed their way up the gangplanks and into the crowds on the deck, where they were led to cabins to collect baggage. Then they emerged loaded down with suitcases and trunks, plastic bags, and string-tied cartons and mixed in with the excited families pouring down the gangplanks.

According to arrangements made by the school, Ed was to be met by a member of the staff and taken to the island in the Sea of Marmara where his new school was located. Miss Bayraktar, with whom he had been corresponding, had written that he should look for a sign with his name on it when he landed, so he began anxiously staring down from the deck onto the mob of passengers disembarking onto the landing. They swirled around the piles of luggage and stacks of wooden crates and wicker baskets that checked their progress at every step, and the baggage carried on the backs of porters tossed in the crowd like the flotsam of a shipwreck in a roiling sea. A dignified old man's family had come to greet him, and they were one by one coming up to bow and kiss his hand; a little girl in a pink dress was running ahead of her mother shrieking "Baba, Baba!" to her father, who was kneeling on the pavement with his arms outstretched to her; a middle-aged couple seemed to be having an altercation about a piece of missing luggage, their porter standing patiently beside them. Turkish officials shouted, porters and taxi touts called to the passengers, and interested bystanders stopped to observe the spectacle, make comments, and give advice. The whole scene was pervaded by a rich aroma compounded of diesel oil, fish, and sweat.

Eventually, Ed's eye fell on a small man clutching a sign held upside-down with "E. Wilkie: Istanbul Collegiate Academy" printed on it. The man was intently scanning the deck where Ed was standing, so Ed waved to him and he immediately began to charge through the crowd leaving the ship and fought his way up the gangplank, ignoring the indignant shouts and curses of the descending passengers and porters. Eventually, continuing his ruthless progress through the crowd, he got to Ed, and then looked up and shouted, "Bay Vilkie?" He was perhaps forty years old, with a humorous, unshaved face and sharp, lively eyes, and wore an old and shabby suit, much too large for him, and a shirt buttoned up to the throat without a tie. On his head was a stained flat cap and on his feet he wore scuffed black shoes with the backs mashed down like slippers. When Ed nodded, the little man reached into his breast pocket and thrust a much-fingered envelope into his hand. Ed moved out of the stream of passengers, opened the envelope, and found a short note inside:

*Dear Mr. Wilkie,*

*Please accept my apology for not meeting you personally, but things are rather confused at the Academy today due to the approach of the new term. Mehmet Efendi will take care of your luggage and escort you to the ferryboat. That will bring you to the island, where you will be met by Mr. Yurtsever, one of your new colleagues. My father and I are looking forward to meeting you per-*

*sonally later today.*

    *Best wishes,*

    *Zeynep Bayraktar*

    *P.S.: Mehmet Efendi does not speak English, but has been told what he is to do.*

While Ed was reading the letter, the little man watched him closely, apparently waiting for Ed to signal that he was ready to place himself in his charge. Ed smiled at him and nodded, to indicate that he had understood the letter's instructions: "I am in your hands, Mr. Efendi." The little man looked up at him and shouted, *"Kamara, kamara!"* When Ed looked puzzled he thought for a moment and then barked, "Ka-been!" Ed led him through the now diminishing crowd to his cabin to collect his luggage. Mehmet Efendi then busied himself gathering together the baggage. When the two suitcases, train case, and string-tied cardboard box of books were assembled, he looked up questioningly: *"Başka?"* Ed looked at the expensive but worn luggage—rather feminine crocodile with the initials of his mother, whose property they had been, in gold script. He shrugged his shoulders and indicated with outstretched arms that this was it. Mehmet Efendi nodded and shouted, *"Hamal arıyorum!"* miming his intention to engage a porter.

Mehmet Efendi returned with a porter and directed the business of getting Ed's things off the ship. While he was engaged with this, Ed stepped to the gangplank, where he shook hands with the purser:

"So, Mr. Wilkie, you start your holiday now?"

"No," said Ed. "I will be working in a school here."

"Very interesting, sir. Well, good luck!" Several of his former shipmates were passing and he wished them good-bye. They smiled and passed on, anxious to disembark, and Ed was left alone to wait for Mehmet Efendi.

After a few minutes, he was joined by a fellow passenger, Mr. Agopian, a rug merchant in the Grand Bazaar: a bald, middle-aged man with very thick glasses and an ingratiating manner, who had joined the ship at Marseilles after having supervised the delivery of a consignment of carpets to dealers in Paris.

"Ah, Mr. Wilkie," he said, squinting up at Ed, his moist eyes oyster-like behind heavy gray-tinted lenses, and smiling toothily. "I was hoping that we would meet again before we left the ship. I have enjoyed our conversations during our cruise together and I hope that we will stay in touch when you are settled. Did you write any poems during our voyage?"

Ed smiled shyly. "No, Mr. Agopian. But I took some notes. Maybe later…"

"Excellent! You can read them to me someday. I would like to receive you in my shop. We will drink tea and I will show you some beautiful carpets!"

"Thank you, Mr. Agopian," said Ed. "I'll certainly give you a call."

"Excellent!" he replied, rubbing his hands and smiling. "So, are you going directly to your island or will you be staying in Istanbul first?"

"I am going directly to the island. The school has sent a man to take me there. He is with the porter right now. Then we'll go by ferry."

"Ah, then we will again be fellow passengers! I will take the ferry from Sirkeci also. It goes first to Kadiköy on the Asian side of the city, where my home is, and then continues on to the islands. So I will have your company for a little while longer." He seemed genuinely pleased by the prospect.

"I look forward to that, Mr. Agopian."

"Good. Well, now I must get my baggage together and pass through customs. My nephew is meeting me. I will meet you at the ferry landing. Good-bye till then."

Just then Mehmet Efendi returned with the porter and Ed said good-bye to Mr. Agopian.

The porter was an old man, if possible even more shabbily dressed than Mehmet Efendi, and was bent nearly double under the weight of bags and books. Ed carried the train case, part of the crocodile set, in which he had stored his valuables and personal papers: high school and college diplomas, Starleen's and his birth certificates, passport, his mother's death certificate, and a copy of her will. There was also a little blue velvet box containing an antique ring set with sapphires and diamonds that had belonged to her.

Mehmet Efendi led the little caravan through the still-crowded landing, shoving and shouting imperiously at rival porters and stray passengers. Several people called out to Ed and plucked at his sleeve, evidently proposing themselves for various services, but Mehmet Efendi contemptuously motioned them away. Starleen complicated matters by running ahead, sending one woman into hysterics by sniffing her legs and then joining a family group, causing the children to fly screaming in every direction.

Eventually, they arrived at the customs and immigration windows. Mehmet Efendi shouted, "Pasaport!" and thrust out his hand. Ed gave it to Mehmet Efendi, who immediately pushed his way through the untidy line waiting for the disembarkation formalities and jostled himself in front of the window. The crowd was remarkably indulgent, probably assuming that he was the courier for some important person, and contented itself with mild remonstrance: *"Çok kaba bir insan!" "Hay Allah!" "İnek!"*

When he had completed the formalities, occasionally gesturing in Ed's direction to indicate to the officials that Ed was the owner of the passport, he returned and shouted, "Gel!" and motioned that they could proceed.

They started to move toward the exit, and Ed was working his way through the crowd, when he was unexpectedly stopped by a young uniformed policeman wearing dark glasses and carrying an automatic rifle. As Ed started to speak, he unsmilingly motioned with his gun that Ed was to come with him. Mehmet Efendi came back and started to intervene, but the policeman shouted something at him in Turkish, silencing him instantly. Given Mehmet Efendi's reaction, Ed decided it was most prudent to accompany the policeman without protest, wondering uneasily what he could possibly be suspected of. Was there some Turkish regulation that he had unconsciously broken? Something to do with Starleen?

Sweat broke out on the back of Ed's neck and his heart beat more quickly as the policeman marched him back though the crowd to an office near the customs shed. Mehmet Efendi and the porter followed at a cautious distance. Starleen seemed to have taken a liking to the policeman and was nosing his boots, but he wordlessly gestured to keep her away, so Ed left her with Mehmet Efendi.

The room they entered was a large one, filled with cigarette smoke and containing battered desks at which more uniformed policemen sat. At the far end a dark man in a crumpled civilian suit seemed to be conducting interviews one by one with other people who had been plucked from the departing crowd. There were around twenty of them, and Ed noticed that they were all men in their early or mid-thirties. They were strangely silent and nervous, offering no protests or reproaches, watched over by armed policemen.

The interviews were conducted carefully, the questions asked in abrupt Turkish and the answers given respectfully and docilely. After some time Ed's turn came and he was brought over to the man in the crumpled suit. He was middle-aged and tired looking, with sagging, badly shaven cheeks and heavy bags under his eyes. There was a cigarette in the corner of his mouth and an overflowing ashtray before him. On the scratched surface of the desk were some typed pages that he referred to from time to time. He looked up and said sharply, *"Kimlik!"* Ed had no idea what he wanted, so he replied, "I'm sorry. I don't speak Turkish. I think there has been some sort of mistake."

"Ah, you are a foreigner. From which country?" he asked in heavily accented English.

"From America. The United States." Ed handed him his passport.

He looked at it briefly and then raised shrewd dark eyes. "And you boarded the ship at Marseilles?"

"Yes. I came to Marseilles on a ship from the United States."

"And you are in Turkey for...?"

"I will be teaching at a school in Istanbul—a boys' school."

"Do you have some proof of this?"

"Well, I guess this…." Ed gave him the note from Miss Bayraktar.

He read it over and handed it back. "Who brought it to you?"

Ed told him about Mehmet Efendi's having met him and the man gestured to one of the policemen to go out and verify the story. In a few moments the policeman returned and nodded to Ed's interrogator, who referred again to the passport.

"Well, everything seems to be in order Mr....Wilkie. I am sorry you have been delayed."

"Can you tell me why you were interviewing me?" Ed asked, now feeling calmer. "Was I acting suspiciously or something?"

The policeman thought for a moment and then said, "We had information that a criminal—a narcotics courier—would be here. We had only a description of him, which might have fitted you—in some ways." He exchanged glances with the young policeman, who grinned back. "I won't detain you longer. Good-bye."

Ed thanked him for the explanation and went outside, where he was glad to find Mehmet Efendi and the porter waiting with Starleen. But it seemed to Ed somehow an ominous sign that his first step into Turkey should involve an encounter with the police.

The old man who was carrying the baggage was standing like a block of stone, but he moved forward in response to Mehmet Efendi's command and, with Mehmet Efendi in the lead, they pushed through to the exit gate and emerged into the street. Mehmet Efendi stepped to the curb and flagged down a passing taxi, into which he loaded Ed's bags and carton. The driver was reluctant to admit Starleen, but Mehmet Efendi shouted him down and he agreed to take her. Mehmet Efendi then paid the porter, who accepted the money with ill grace and, telling the driver, "Sirkeci. Adalar Iskelesi," they drove off.

The taxi was an old American car that seemed to hold together only through the will of the driver, a resigned-looking man who guided his machine through the traffic with shuddering gear shifts. Ed was still too disoriented to take in his surroundings, being aware only of swirling crowds, gray buildings, and a series of unnerving near-death encounters with other cars and pedestrians. They crossed the Galata Bridge, over the Golden Horn, and into the old city, Stamboul, with Starleen sitting in Ed's lap, her head out the window.

After some time they made a wild left turn against three lanes of oncoming traffic, shaved the side of a tramcar, and, with the tram diver shouting after them, pulled up to the ferry landing. There was a ticket booth marked Adalar to which Mehmet Efendi proceeded, after unloading the taxi and arguing briefly with the driver. He quickly engaged another porter and then went to the ticket window, where he bought two tokens for the turnstile admitting them to the landing. Ed looked around for Mr. Agopian, but he seemed not to have arrived yet.

The ferry was a white two-decker, its funnels, marked with the crossed red anchors of the Turkish maritime services, billowing black smoke. The crew was casting off the lines and it appeared to be nearly ready to sail, so they rushed to the gangplank, where the porter quickly unloaded Ed's property onto the deck, leaping back on the landing as the ferry began to move away.

Since it was a sunny day, they sat on a bench on the outside of the upper deck, Starleen narrowly eyeing the seagulls that were following in their wake. They had been sailing for several minutes when Ed heard a voice behind him.

"Ah, Mr. Wilkie, I thought you had missed the ferry." Mr. Agopian came up smiling, shook hands, and patted Starleen. "My nephew seems to have stood me up, so I was a bit late getting to Sirkeci myself. I see you have been enjoying looking at the city. The most beautiful city in the world!" he said, gesturing dramatically with a hand on which a rather grubby fraternal ring sparkled dully.

All around them the shipping was passing through the Sea of Marmara: freighters from all over the Mediterranean, the Aegean, and the Black Sea. They seemed to Ed strangely small—almost like toys—at least to one used to the ocean-going ships of Los Angeles harbor.

Mehmet Efendi bought them little glasses of tea from a vendor and then sat stolidly smoking cigarettes as they moved toward the Asian shore. Ed notice an odd-looking little towered building that took up most of a tiny islet several hundred yards from the Asian coast.

"What's that, Mr Agopian? An old customs house or something?"

"Ah yes, among other things. That is the Kız Kulesi—the Maiden's Tower. Not so old—18th century. There is a legend that in ancient times a princess was put on that island by her father after a prediction that she would die of a snake bite. But a snake was smuggled in, hidden in a basket of grapes. It bit her and she died."

"So, she was murdered!" Ed's eyes widened.

Mr. Agopian looked up at Ed with amusement. "Maybe, Mr. Wilkie. But it's just a legend. Maybe it is telling us that you can't escape your kısmet—your fate—by human means."

"Yes. I suppose that's it," Ed replied, feeling a little abashed.

"Well, maybe you'll find your kısmet—but a happier one—on your island, Mr. Wilkie." The engines of the ferry began to shudder as it slowed down. "So, Mr. Wilkie, we are almost to Kadıköy, where I get off. Once again, I do hope you will visit me in the Grand Bazaar."

He seemed anxious, so Ed nodded and said, "Of course, Mr. Agopian. Soon."

"Good." He seemed relieved, and then added, "I have already had the pleasure of meeting one of your colleagues from your school. A foreign lady—from France. Very nice, but a little… nervous. Maybe she thought I would cheat her." He seemed momentarily depressed. "But she bought a good little kilim—very cheap. My God, how she bargained! She also looked at a lovely Saruk, which I could see she wanted very much. But so cautious! It will be interesting to see if she came back and bought it. My nephew, Ari, who is looking after the shop for me, is very persuasive!" He seemed entertained by the thought. "She came with a Turkish man. Also from the school. You will meet them later, I guess. Ah, we are here. And there is my rascal of a nephew," he said, pointing at a figure waving to him from the dock. He shook hands and then quickly joined the people moving towards the gangplanks being shoved onto the ferry from the shore and was soon lost in the crowd passing through the gates of the landing.

The ferry stayed at the landing only a few minutes before casting off and proceeding once again out into the Sea of Marmara and toward the little archipelago called the Princes' Islands. From his guidebook Ed had learned that these islands are part of the municipality of Istanbul. Several are large, with year-round populations in the thousands; others are small and uninhabited; and at least one is privately owned. In the Byzantine period the archipelago was called Papedonisia, because of the monasteries that were there. Later, when Justin II built a palace on Megale, the largest of the islands, it became known as Prinkipo—the Island of the Prince—and the archipelago was eventually called the Princes' Islands. Until the mid-19th century the islands were inhabited primarily by monks and nuns and by small fishing communities. Then, a ferry service was established between the city and the islands and they became a retreat for summer visitors, who built houses where they could escape the heat of the city. Eventually, however, the islands fell out of favor with wealthy Istanbulites, who preferred to vacation on the Mediterranean or Aegean coasts, or travel abroad for their holidays, leaving behind the great wooden summer houses and hotels. The most famous of the islands is Büyükada, "the Great Island," as Prinkipo is now called; it is the one most often visited by tourists wanting to see a remnant of old Istanbul. Ed's island had a year-round population of four thousand, with perhaps twice that number in the summer months.

They stopped at several of the islands, but each time Mehmet Efendi shook his head to show that they had farther to go. At last, he pointed to an island that lay ahead. Ed jumped up and leaned against the railing to take in his first view of his new home. From the sea it rose gradually, a smooth, round shape, with a little harbor and seafront and roads rambling up the hillside. Houses were thick on the lower slopes, thinning out as the roads went higher, and finally giving way to a forest of pine trees. As they sailed into the harbor, he could see the ferry landing with its little ticket office and waiting room. There were many small boats darting back and forth and two large, battered-looking ships at anchor. As they drew closer, he could see the seafront promenade, with tiny figures moving along it. The sun was shining and the sky was a clear blue, with the water sparkling and the sounds of seagulls crying around them.

# 2

Mehmet Efendi sprang to his feet and motioned to Ed that they should hurry to get the luggage off the ferry before it continued on to the next island. Ed helped him put the bags on the landing and then Mehmet Efendi bounced away, presumably to find another porter. As Ed stood waiting for him to return, he felt a hand touch his sleeve.

"Mr. Wilkie, is it not?" He turned and found standing beside him a plump man of medium height, with a round, smooth face, dressed in a lightweight summer suit and pink shirt. Smiling, the man held out his hand. "I am Yurtsever. I am a teacher of English at the Academy, come to welcome you. *Hoş geldiniz!*"

They shook hands and he continued, "Zeynep Hanım—Miss Bayraktar—sends her regards. Your rooms at the Academy are not quite ready, so she has arranged for you to stay at the Grand Otel—the island's premier hostelry—until they can receive you. I will take you there now and later we will go together to the Academy." For some reason that he couldn't identify, Ed had the feeling that Mr. Yurtsever was uneasy with his task and, while perfectly polite, he seemed somehow hurried and anxious to be done with it.

Ed thanked him. "Mr. Efendi has been very helpful. I already feel very welcome."

"Mr. Efendi?" Yurtsever looked puzzled.

"Yes. Mehmet Efendi."

He smiled. "Ah, I see. Efendi is not his name, Mr. Wilkie. His first name is Mehmet and we call him Mehmet Efendi—Mr. Mehmet. You will call Turks by their given names that way."

"And I should call you...?"

"Kemal Bey. My given name is Kemal."

"Not Kemal Efendi?"

"No. Efendi is used for servants." He shrugged his shoulders and spread his hands. "Not very democratic, but…" He paused, then continued, "For ladies you use hanım. Miss Bayraktar is Zeynep Hanım."

"I see. Thanks. By the way, um, Kemal Bey, I seem to have had a little brush with the police when I arrived."

He seemed startled. "A brush? They were sweeping something?"

"No. I mean they interrogated me."

Ed went on to describe his adventure on the Karaköy dock, and when he had finished Kemal Bey said, "Well, I am very sorry that this happened. It must seem so inhospitable. But Turkey has a terrible problem with drugs. The police must be very vigilant." He seemed to dismiss the matter from his mind. He then gestured to two bright-eyed little boys standing behind him, each wearing a blue blazer with "I.C.A." and a symbol that Ed later learned was a stylized tulip on the breast pocket.

"These boys are two of our pupils. Cevat, Bülent! This is your new teacher: Mr. Wilkie."

They smiled shyly and said, "Good morning, sir!" Then they looked at Starleen and began shouting, "*Domuz! İpteki Domuz! Hay Allah!*"

Ed looked inquiringly at Mr. Yurtsever, who said, "Ah, they think your dog is a pig: *domuz.* A pig on a leash: *ipteki domuz.* They think it is strange for a foreigner—a Christian—to keep a pig as a pet."

"Well, please explain to them that she is a dog. An expensive dog!"

The boys looked surprised by Mr. Yurtsever's explanation, but apparently accepted it.

Mehmet Efendi returned with a porter, who was pushing a small handcart and greeted Mr. Yurtsever with a bow, *"Merhaba, hocam."* The boys helped load Ed's things on the handcart and they made their way from the landing to the seafront promenade. This ran around the semicircular natural harbor in which several fishing boats and three sailboats were anchored. In an earlier era it must have been quite smart, but now it seemed rather shabby, with a broken stone balustrade and cracked sidewalk.

Toward the middle of the promenade it opened into a square with shops, restaurants, tea gardens, and other buildings. There were also several palm trees, and some effort had been made to brighten things up by adding concrete planters filled with red and orange geraniums that relieved the gray of the weathered buildings. A number of people were seated on benches in the square and under the awnings of the tea gardens, drinking little glasses of tea and smoking cigarettes. Several women were picking over figs in a fruit stall and talking with the owner. Overall, Ed thought, the place had the same sort of raffish Mediterranean charm as Marseilles or Naples or New Orleans.

A surprising number of seemingly stray dogs lay on the ground around the square, taking in the morning sun. Ed pointed them out to Mr. Yurtsever and said, "I thought Muslims didn't like dogs."

"We don't keep dogs as pets so much as you do," he replied, "but dogs are always welcome in Turkish towns. People feed them."

Ed noticed an alert-looking small man who seemed to be taking an interest in their progress as he sat over his glass of tea. Mr. Yurtsever followed Ed's gaze and nodded to the man.

"*Günaydın*, Osman Bey." Then he whispered to Ed, "An important official. Must keep on good terms!"

Ed's feeling of excitement and adventure grew as he looked at all the sights of his new home, and he found himself burbling, "I can hardly believe that I'm here. You know, everyone told me I was making a mistake, but it's as though fate…"

Mr. Yurtsever smiled. "The dog barks. The caravan moves on!"

Ed waited expectantly, involuntarily glancing at Starleen, but there seemed to be no more. "Ah yes! The dog and the caravan!" *What on earth was he talking about?* he wondered.

The boys were in a high state of excitement, bouncing around them, laughing and pushing each other. "Can we pat her, sir? Will she bite us?"

Ed said that Starleen liked boys and they skittishly patted her head, hopping back as she tried to lick their hands.

They had reached the end of the square and, turning a corner, Mr. Yurtsever announced, "Behold! The Grand Otel. Your home from home!"

The island's "premier hostelry" was a wooden building the size of a large private house, with a flight of steps leading to the front door and a verandah running around the second floor. It had a rather run-down and deserted appearance.

"Many years ago," said Mr. Yurtsever, "the island was considered a good place to cure those suffering from consumption. Many private sanatoria were established for their treatment, and this was one. They have all closed now, but this one was converted into a hotel."

All this did not, somehow, seem very encouraging, and Ed had a sense of unease as he passed into the former pest house. The room they entered looked like the lobby of an Edwardian hotel in some provincial English sea resort, though Ed was pleased to see that it was cleaner than he had been led to expect from the hotel's exterior. It was fitted with old, dark, heavy furniture and worn oriental carpets, and potted plants in brass pots stood on little wooden stands. A reception desk ran across one end of the room, with pigeonholes for room keys behind it. The room was dim and silent, with an aroma of mothballs and furniture polish.

Mehmet Efendi and the boys brought in Ed's luggage while Mr. Yurtsever walked back and forth rubbing his hands and calling out, "Mustafa Bey, Mustafa Bey! Ha! There you are. I have brought Mr. Wilkie."

Ed followed his glance toward the reception desk, but saw no one. A voice replied, *"Hoş geldiniz, hocam!"* Looking closer Ed saw a face emerge from behind the desk and rest its chin on the counter. The face was swarthy, with lively black eyes and a drooping black mustache. It disappeared again and a bent figure came around the side. Mustafa Bey was a dwarf, who rounded the corner with a listing motion, looked up at them smiling, and extended his hand first to Mr. Yurtsever and then to Ed.

"Welcome, Mr. Wilkie, to the Grand Otel."

Ed had recovered from his initial surprise and returned his firm grip. "I'm sure I'll be very comfortable."

Mr. Yurtsever then said, "I will leave you with Mustafa Bey, so that you can settle in and have a rest. Zeynep Hanım invites you for dinner, so I will return this evening at 8:00 to escort you to the Academy."

He shook hands with Ed, and the boys, who had been playing with Starleen, came up and shook hands also. Ed was somewhat surprised by Mr. Yurtsever's sudden departure, and by the fact that Miss Bayraktar had seemingly changed her mind about seeing him when he arrived; however, he dismissed these misgivings from his mind and turned his attention again to his new surroundings.

"I understand you will be with us for only a short time," Mustafa Bey said, looking up and smiling. "I have put you in a nice room with a sea view. I heard that you would be bringing a dog with you." His eye strayed to Starleen, who was straining at her leash with the evident intention of investigating him more closely. "A very unusual dog. Almost not like a dog. He doesn't bite, I hope."

"Not at all," Ed assured him. "She is very well mannered."

He seemed relieved. "Good. My other guests are not very used to dogs."

Then, listing from step to step, he led Ed up the stairs to a bright, airy room with the same sort of dark, old furniture and worn rugs that Ed had seen below.

"I will have your bags sent up, sir," said Mustafa Bey, though Ed suspected that he would undertake the job himself. "Let me know if you need anything," he said as he departed with another smile and clumped jerkily down the stairs.

# 3

Ed sat down on the lumpy bed with Starleen's muzzle on his knee, his head spinning slightly from the rush of new experiences. As he sat, he became gradually aware of music playing somewhere nearby:

Such a night,
Such a night
Sweet confusion under the moonlight...

Dr. John! Curious about who The Doctor's fancier was in the middle of the Sea of Marmara, he rose and opened the door of the room and looked up and down the hall. The music seemed, however, to be coming from the floor above. He started to close the door to go and investigate, but Starleen bounded over to him, determined not to be left behind. So he put her leash on her collar and they went up the creaking steps to the next floor. They stood on the landing while Ed tried to hear where the music was coming from—The Doctor had now moved on to "Iko Iko."

As Ed was hesitating, the door opposite was flung open and a slim man wearing a dazzling Hawaiian shirt appeared.

"Dr. Wilkie, I presume?"

"Yes. I mean, no," said Ed, startled by the sudden apparition. "That is, Mister Wilkie. Ed Wilkie."

"Lovely! Come on into my cage, Doc. I thought it might be you. Not too many strangers find their way to the island's answer to the Georges V."

"Yes. I just got in a little while ago," said Ed.

"I saw the glass of fashion from the school on his way to the landing and thought he might be going to fetch you," said his new friend. "Had a couple of the boys with him. My name, by the way, is Brown. Come in and take a pew."

As he was ushered into the room, Ed saw that Brown was a little over medium height, slim and graceful, with sharp gray eyes and closely cropped gray hair. His voice was a light, amused baritone, with a foreign accent Ed didn't recognize.

Brown's room was actually a suite, furnished with the same sort of dark wood pieces as Ed's, but with a number of personal touches that suggested a long residence. Ed noticed a great many books, and there were prints and photographs on the walls that didn't accord with the Grand Otel's other decorative features. An expensive-looking music system in a wooden case was now playing Glenn Miller.

"Grab a seat, Doc, and we'll have a bit of a chin-wag. What say to a welcome drink?"

"Well, perhaps just one. I have a dinner engagement this evening."

"Fine. Plenty of time for a snifter—or two—before you are summoned to your evening's jollifications. What say to a *rakı*—try the jolly old national drink, eh?"

Ed agreed to a *rakı*, which Brown went off to prepare. It turned out to be a clear spirit that turned an opaque white when mixed with water and ice. While Brown was busy with the drinks Ed observed him more closely. In addition to the striking shirt—a medley of palm trees and hibiscus—he wore crumpled cotton trousers and soft suede shoes. His foreign accent, combined with his out-of-date British slang, suggested an English learned more from books—specifically, works by P.G. Wodehouse. Ed suspected his name was not really Brown.

Starleen had taken advantage of Ed's abstraction to slip her leash and was eagerly moving around the room, investigating Brown's possessions. Finally, she came up behind him and leaned against his legs. He looked down with a smile.

"A beautiful bull terrier. Very unusual in Turkey. What's her name?"

"Starleen."

"Unusual name for an unusual dog, eh?"

"I named her for a lady of my acquaintance. A lady living in Houston, Texas. Her name was Starleen. But she called herself Star."

"But everyone knew her as Nancy!"

"Sorry?"

"Nothing. An affair of the heart, eh?"

Ed nodded. "Sort of. She was very kind to me at a difficult period of my life."

"I'm sure she must have been very flattered," he said, glancing down at Starleen and then looking up and winking at Ed.

"Yes, indeed." In fact, Ed could still see Star looking at him, her little cracker face lit up with fun, saying, "Shit-fire, boy! I sure's hell hope you don't think that I look like that squint-eyed little bitch!"

"Well, chin-chin," Brown said, lifting his glass. Ed gingerly tasted the *rakı*, which had a strong anise flavor, rather like Pernod, but less sweet and complex. The evening being warm, he followed with a long swallow. In the meantime, Brown had brought out some green olives and nuts in little bowls, which he placed on a low table between them.

"So, you'll be at the school all this year?"

"Yes. I've signed a contract for nine months. Then, I guess we'll see."

"Should be interesting. I believe the new owner has pretty much ditched the former staff and started fresh."

"Really? Do you know Dr. Bayraktar then?"

"Not to speak to. Seen him about."

"What, if I may ask, brings you to the island? Are you in business here?" asked Ed, hoping to find out more about his host.

"You may indeed, old boy. In fact, I..."

Just then the phone rang and Brown interrupted himself to answer it.

"Efendim? Oh yes. He is here." He turned to Ed. "It's for you. Someone from the school."

Ed took the phone. "Yes? This is Ed Wilkie."

"Mr. Wilkie," said a forceful feminine voice, "this is Zeynep Bayraktar. I hope you are settled in and that Mustafa Bey has made you comfortable."

"Yes, thank you very much, Miss Bayraktar. I have been making the acquaintance of my fellow guest. Right now I am..."

"So Mustafa Bey told me. Mr. Wilkie, I must once again apologize, but I will not, after all, be able to invite you to dinner this evening. As you know, we are refitting the Academy and the electricians have just blown out the electrical power. It will be restored by tomorrow, but not, I fear, in time to complete the dinner preparations. I hope you will forgive us for this lack of hospitality. Such are the vicissitudes of Turkish life."

"Please think nothing of it, Miss Bayraktar. I quite understand. In fact I..."

"How kind of you. Mustafa Bey can take care of you for the evening and will show you a restaurant. Tomorrow Mr. Yurtsever will call on you at 9:00 in the morning and bring you to the Academy. Once again, I must thank you for your understanding. We will meet at last tomorrow. And now I must rush off to deal with this electrical business. Good evening," she said, hanging up rather abruptly.

Ed turned to Brown. "I guess I no longer have a dinner engagement. Some emergency at the school."

"Excellent!" said Brown, taking Ed's now empty glass. "Now we can make an evening of it. Here's another snootful."

The evening turned out to be a long one. Brown poured the *rakı* with a liberal hand, and in the warmth of the night Ed found himself drinking it steadily. At one point Brown called down to Mustafa Bey, who brought them two plates of sliced roast lamb on flat bread—*döner*, he called it—from a nearby restaurant.

"So, Doc, how do you happen to be joining our happy island family?" asked Brown with an encouraging smile.

Ed thought for a moment. "Well, it's not easy to explain logically, I guess. My mother died earlier this year. I'd been living with her in Los Angeles—in California. And, um, writing poetry. When she died I guess I just wanted a change, so..."

"I see. Complete change of scene, and all that. And poetry, you say?" Brown seemed doubtful.

"Um, yes," said Ed shyly. "Two books: *The Pond in Winter* and *A Burning*

*House.* I don't suppose that you've heard…"

"I don't think so. I must have missed them," said Brown evasively.

"That's all right," said Ed smiling. "Most people did." He thought regretfully of the unsold pile in the Poetry Bookshop in West Los Angeles.

"Ah yes. So, poetry not being such a lucrative profession…"

"So, an old teacher from college—Ray Collins—suggested the school here. Seems that he knows Dr. Bayraktar from somewhere. I wrote, and well…"

"So, hey presto! You're now a former of the youth of the nation!"

"Well, at least an instructor in English language and literature, according to my contract."

As the evening wore on and the *rakı* began to take its effect, Ed became uncharacteristically loquacious. With only a little encouragement from Brown, he began to talk about himself:

"I grew up on a little citrus ranch in Southern California, where my father made a living for my mother and me. At about the time I was to enter junior high school, the housing boom sent the price of my father's property sky high and he sold out at a big profit. He invested his profits in more extensive orchards, but was followed by the developers, who offered him even greater rewards to sell out. After several efforts to continue as a rancher, he gave up to the inevitable, invested his profits, and retired to become a gentlemen. Unfortunately, he didn't have the education or temperament for leisure, and time hung heavy on his hands. So, he took to drink in a big way and managed to kill himself in a short while. My father wasn't an affectionate or communicative man and I didn't much miss him. My mother, after the first shock of widowhood, didn't seem to miss him much either. After my father's death I went to Occidental College, so that I could live with my mother, and I started to write poetry.

"Once my mother got used to having the management of money, she acquired a taste for spending it on an increasingly large scale. We moved to Beverly Hills, joined a country club, and traveled to Europe. She made a lot of what passed for friends and entertained largely, becoming quite a well-known hostess in the stratum of society we moved in: Southern California country club. Not old money, but plenty of it.

"My mother was pretty, fun, high-spirited, and ready for any new experience. She loved pretty clothes and I can still see her now coming home excitedly from a day in the smart shops with piles of boxes, which she opened for me in her bedroom, spilling out dresses, shoes, lingerie, until the room was draped with her purchases and scattered with empty boxes and tissue paper. She would look up at me, her face pink with pleasure and her lovely blue eyes shining, and exclaim, "Oh, Eddy! Isn't being rich fun!"

"Unfortunately, the only thing my mother really understood about money was how to spend it, and I have to say I didn't know much more. Inevitably, my father's fortune melted away. There were men who cheated her and there were bad investments, and her final folly was getting involved with a religious cult that drained away the last of her money. Though I knew that things were getting bad, I had no idea how bad until her death from a heart attack. I remember her just before she died, lying on her big bed in a peach-colored nightgown, looking at me with her beautiful blue eyes. 'Darling,' she said, 'I'm afraid there's not much left, but we did have a good time, didn't we?' In fact, there was nothing left, plus there were debts. So, by the time I got clear, I found myself an unemployed former loafer in need of a job."

Conscious that he had been running on, Ed came to an abrupt stop. He looked at Brown, whose eyes were closed. "Sorry, I didn't mean to monopolize the conversation."

Brown's eyes snapped open: "Don't worry, old cock. I helps to get things off your chest." Brown helped Ed rise from his chair. "Upsy-daisy, old boy," and walked with him and Starleen to their room. Ed lay down in his clothes and was instantly asleep.

# 4

The next morning Ed felt remarkably good, considering the amount of *rakı* he had drunk the evening before, and remembered Brown's saying, "Never a headache in a bottle. Like mother's milk—a mother lion's, that is!" He looked at his watch, which, such is the power of habit, he had carefully placed on the night stand, and saw that it was only 7:30. Plenty of time to prepare himself to meet Mr. Yurtsever. He put on his dressing gown and went down the hall for a shower— the island's answer to the Georges V not running to attached baths—and soaked for twenty minutes, then changed into a blazer and slacks, with a striped shirt, dark blue tie, and brown loafers, and took Starleen out for a morning stroll.

When he returned, Mustafa Bey had laid breakfast for him in the hotel's little dining room: white cheese and bread, accompanied by black olives, sliced tomatoes and cucumbers, and a little glass of tea. While Ed was breakfasting, a fashionably dressed middle-aged lady entered the breakfast room, accompanied by her two teenage daughters, modest-looking pretty girls, also nicely turned out.

The lady noticed Ed looking at them, so he nodded and said, "Good morning, I'm Ed Wilkie. I'm staying at the hotel for a few days."

After a moment's hesitation, she nodded also and said, "Good morning, sir. My name is Mrs. Akkaya." The girls looked at each other and giggled and the lady said sternly, "Tamam, Rezan!" A nice family, Ed thought. If they are residents, perhaps I'll get to know them better.

At 9:00 sharp Mr. Yurtsever arrived, looking very smart in a light gray suit, colored shirt, and bow tie. It occurred to Ed to wonder how he afford such outfits on a teacher's salary, but reflected that he was, after all, a bachelor and perhaps had a little private money.

"Good morning, Mr. Wilkie. You are looking very well. I'm afraid we were all at sixes and sevens yesterday. Zeynep Hanım was frantic! But today things are in order." He seemed much calmer and more relaxed. "Let us go whenever you are ready."

Ed said that he was at his service and they departed. He left Starleen with Mustafa Bey, who had agreed to take her out during Ed's absence. Outside the hotel stood a little carriage with two horses to draw it. Ed looked questioningly at Mr. Yurtsever.

"I didn't know if you are a walker, so I thought you might enjoy a ride in one of our *faytons*. There are no automobiles on the islands."

The *fayton* was a simple conveyance, consisting of an open body with two two-person wicker seats facing each other and a light canopy roof with side curtains to let down when it rained. The coachman nodded politely as they climbed into his carriage and then whipped up the two horses.

As they made their way up the hill, Mr. Yurtsever pointed out the mosque, the Armenian church, the tiny synagogue, the market just being set up, and some of the more notable private houses. "The Gazi stayed there in the big pink mansion just before he departed for Erzurum."

Much of this was lost on Ed, but he found the atmosphere delightful—a feeling of calm, with the peacefulness of the surroundings and no noise but the sound of the horses' hooves, the chatter of Mr. Yurtsever, and the occasional cries of the gulls wheeling above. They climbed steadily and the houses became larger and less numerous, set in unkempt gardens that rioted with flowers—roses of all colors, geraniums, nasturtiums, carnations, the walls draped with honeysuckle and wisteria. At last, they stopped before a huge stone house. At the gate was a new-looking brass sign: "Istanbul Collegiate Academy."

The house was an impressive one—very tall, with mansard roofs and a central tower with a stopped clock in it. It looked, in fact, like those houses outside of provincial French cities, built in the 19th century by proprietors of small, now obsolete or closed, factories, and sited by their proud owners near the works.

"This was originally the home of a great Greek merchant," said Mr. Yurtsever. "He departed Turkey after the War of Independence and it became a school for Turkish boys. Later, it was bought by Ali Bey—Dr. Bayraktar—who is now the director. Shall we?"

They dismounted and passed through the gate and into the garden. It was much like the gardens that Ed had seen around the other big houses, with a circle drive and a mass of vegetation, which included a number of fruit trees and a magnificent grandiflora in full bloom. The house itself was festooned with wisteria, giving it a romantic and faintly sinister appearance. From the back of the house he could hear the shouts of boys at play. As they approached the front door, it was flung open and Mehmet Efendi rushed out to greet them.

*"Merhaba, hocam! Hoş geldiniz!"* He slapped Ed on the arm with the force of a kick—they seemed in his mind to be old friends now. *"Zeynep Hanım bekliyor. Gel!"* Ed looked at Mr. Yurtsever, who explained, "Miss Bayraktar is waiting."

Mehmet Efendi led them through the main hall, which was furnished rather like the Grand Otel, though looking much more rubbed and kicked about, and down a long hallway, smelling slightly of mildew, insufficiently masked by bleach, with a light overlay of cold mutton. Three boys rushed by them at that moment on their way to the front door, brushing Ed in their haste—*"Pardon, hocam!"*—getting away before Mr. Yurtsever could rebuke them.

"Little devils are so excited by the opening of the term," he explained.

They arrived at a double door marked "Assistant Director." Mr. Yurtsever knocked softly and they entered. The room was large and airy, with a high ceiling and tall windows giving onto the garden. Ed noticed that the furniture was very different from that in the hall: good quality antiques, well cared for, rather delicate and feminine. A woman seated at a handsome writing desk near the windows rose to greet them. She was, Ed guessed, in her late forties, of medium height, and solidly built—not fat, but very well nourished and cleverly dressed to conceal it. Her face was broad and pale, with large, dark, almond-shaped eyes, and her dark hair was gathered back severely into a bun. She looked to Ed like a striking example of what his mother used to call "a strong-minded woman." She took his hand in a firm grip and smiled economically, showing small, very white teeth.

"Welcome, Mr. Wilkie. We meet at last." The smile was switched off. "Thank you, Kemal Bey," nodding at Mr. Yurtsever. "Mr. Wilkie and I have much to discuss." Mr. Yurtsever quickly took his cue and withdrew.

They sat down in a pair of pretty little armchairs and Miss Bayraktar crossed surprisingly good legs with, Ed noted appreciatively, very slim ankles.

"Mr. Wilkie, I once again apologize for the contretemps of last night. I appreciate your understanding. You will come to see that everything does not always go smoothly in Turkey, but I am mortified that you should think us inhospitable."

Ed assured her that he quite understood, but her tone implied that behind her polite words she didn't actually much care whether he did or not. Her voice was clear and controlled, and her manner showed that she was fully in charge and used to getting her own way.

"We will go to see my father in a few moments, Mr. Wilkie, but I wanted to speak to you first about your duties. As you know, my father counts on me for the day-to-day administration of the Academy. He has many interests and responsibilities outside the school."

He waited to hear what these might be, but she added nothing further on the subject.

"Classes start next week. As you know, the language of the Academy is English, and all lessons but Turkish language and history are taught in English. We have Turkish teachers who give the boys basic instruction in English; you will teach language and literature to the advanced classes. Your colleague, Kemal Bey—Mr. Yurtsever—will discuss the English curriculum with you and show you around the school. We are not yet very numerous, but we expect to grow quickly. We thought that, being a bachelor, you would like to live at the Academy. We are completing work on your rooms and you should be able to move in a few days time."

"Thank you," said Ed. "I..."

"I think that will be all for the moment, Mr. Wilkie. Let us now go and see my father." She smiled again briefly, indicating that their discussion was over. Ed was a little surprised that their conversation was not more extensive, but nodded and followed her to the door and up the stairs, her generous behind, under severe restraint beneath her smooth, well-cut skirt, swaying before his eyes. "This way, Mr. Wilkie."

Without knocking, they entered a second double-doored room, somewhat larger than Miss Bayraktar's—perhaps originally an upstairs parlor for the wealthy Greek merchant's wife and daughters. Like hers, it was well furnished with leather chairs and heavy bookcases filled with serious-looking books. There was an aroma of Havana cigars, rather like an old-fashioned gentleman's club. Standing by the window was an immense brass naval telescope. Ed later learned that it had originally come from Yıldız Palace, where the last great Turkish Sultan, Abdül Hamit II, had lived in mysterious and paranoid seclusion. It was said that he used the telescope to survey his capital, where, for fear of assassination, he himself seldom went.

Dr. Bayraktar was on his feet and came forward to meet Ed. He was Ray Collins' contemporary, so, Ed guessed, in his late sixties, very tall and thin, with wise, deep-set eyes, a large high-bridged nose, and white hair. His black suit, though well made, hung loosely on sloping shoulders. On his lapel Ed noticed the rosette of some order or decoration that he didn't recognize. His thin lips were set in a smile of greeting.

"Welcome, Mr. Wilkie. *Hoş geldiniz.*" He shook Ed's hand and patted his sleeve. "A pleasure to meet you. And how have you left my dear old friend Major Collins?"

He listened politely as Ed described his last meeting with Collins and then looked thoughtful. "Who would have imagined that he and I would end up as schoolmasters? A mad idea everyone would have said. Ah, *'İt ürür. Kervan yürür.'*" He glanced at Ed. "The dog barks. The caravan moves on."

"I know. Mr. Yurtsever told me."

"Excellent! Your Turkish grows apace." He turned to Miss Bayraktar. "Why have you not offered our guest tea, my dear?" She looked a little put out and replied, "I didn't know how long he would be with you."

"We must never forget the courtesies due to a guest, my dear." His soft voice had a slight edge, which she clearly felt, for she rose quickly and went off to attend to the tea. Ed was not actually very anxious for tea, especially since it appeared to have created a rift between his new employers.

Dr. Bayraktar spoke about the aims of the school. "We need modern Turks for a modern Turkey. The purpose of our school is to provide a thoroughly modern education in the Western tradition, and when I say the Western tradition I mean the American tradition—the most advanced and liberal Western nation. Like America, Turkey is made up of many nationalities, coming down from Ottoman times, when our empire included North Africa, the Levant, Arabia, the Balkans. The Gazi, Atatürk, showed the way, but died too soon. We lost our way somewhat, but schools like this one will take up the task he set us. We teach in English because this is the international language our boys must have to complete Turkey's modernization and integration into the Western world..." and much more to this effect. He spoke easily and fluently, but Ed had the impression that he was slightly abstracted. Finally, he concluded his harangue.

"Well, Mr. Wilkie, you must excuse my enthusiasm. You can tell Major Collins what a thorough pedagogue I have become."

Miss Bayraktar had brought tea during her father's exposition, a fine Darjeeling that they drank from porcelain cups, rather than little glasses. Dr. Bayraktar took out his watch.

"But forgive me. You must be anxious to see more of your new home. Please do not let me detain you."

This was clearly the sign for them to move on, and Miss Bayraktar, who had been sitting rather impatiently on the edge of her chair during her father's measured and unhurried musings, rose to her feet and said, "Yes. Let's be going."

Ed said good-bye to his new employer and followed Miss Bayraktar out of the room. She flounced along the corridor, her high heels clicking on the bare floorboards in an irritated sort of way, and finally stopped at an open door, where Ed saw Mr. Yurtsever seated with several other people.

"Kemal Bey, would you please introduce Mr. Wilkie to his new colleagues and show him around?" Turning to Ed, she added, "You must excuse me now. We will meet again soon," and then clicked away down the corridor.

Mr. Yurtsever looked after her for a moment and then said, "Do come in and meet some of the people you will be working with," leading Ed into the room, where two men and a women sat drinking tea and smoking.

"First, let me introduce you to Mademoiselle Leblanc, who teaches French and German." Mlle Leblanc was a hot-eyed little woman with short blonde hair and an abrupt manner. She was nervously smoking a gunpowder-smelling cigarette, which she removed from her mouth long enough to say, "Enchantée, Monsieur Wilkie."

"*Bonjour*, Mlle Leblanc," Ed said in his best accent. Then reverting to the safer ground of English, "I believe that I have already heard of you from Mr. Agopian. He said that you were a very keen bargainer."

"Ah yes?" she looked up suspiciously and then smiled briefly. "One must take great care not to be cheated! I have bought several nice things. I find his nephew, Ari, very sympathetic." She glanced at one of the men she had been talking with. " Erol—Mr. Demiray—first showed me the shop, but he is no good at bargaining like me. Well, I must be off. We shall meet again. *Au revoir.*"

Mr. Demiray, an alert-looking man wearing glasses and a white lab coat, taught science and invited Ed to visit his laboratory ("a model modern facility"), and the other man, Mr. Bozkurt, a colorless person in a rumpled blue suit, taught history. Mr. Yurtsever then invited Ed to join him in a tour of the school, saying, "Do call me Kemal. Perhaps I may call you Edward. We are informal here."

"Yes, of course. Call me Ed."

He took Ed over the premises, which, for all of Dr. Bayraktar's eloquence, consisted of old-fashioned classrooms filled with wooden desks and smeared blackboards, and an annex with dormitories for the boys, fitted with individual cubicles containing iron bedsteads—all in contrast to the air of near luxury in the Bayraktars' offices. A playing field behind the school was laid out for football and several boys were kicking a ball among them. They looked up as Ed and Kemal passed and said, *"Merhaba, hocam!"*

Ed turned to Kemal. "Why are they calling you hocam, when your name is..."

"Ah," he replied, *"hoca* means teacher. *Hocam* is the possessive, 'my teacher.' A term of respect. They will call you *hoca,* too."

On their wanderings they met one further member of the staff, Miss Agi, an untidy lady who taught "progressive" social sciences and doubled in math. Ed gathered from Kemal that she was one of Dr. Bayraktar's innovations to bring modernity to the curriculum. She had rather mad eyes that Ed found disturbing.

Kemal indicated that Ed would be taking the two upper classes in English and gave him copies of the textbooks and the photocopied course schedules. The books appeared to be leftovers from the previous administration—straightforward surveys of language and literature edited by well-known pedants. It looked like something that he would be able to handle with a little preparation.

Kemal then invited Ed to join him for lunch in the school canteen and they went to a hall set up with long tables and benches. A dozen or more boys were already there, eating a kind of meat stew—*güveç,* he called it—which turned out to be quite good. The boys looked at Ed furtively, where he sat with Kemal at a table reserved for teachers, and someone apparently said something funny, as they all snickered among themselves.

"English, please!" shouted Kemal and the noise stopped instantly. "The boys must speak only English while in the building. It helps implant the language," he explained.

After lunch Kemal said he had some work to do and suggested that Ed might want to explore the island a little, so Ed said good-bye and told him that he could find his own way back to the Grand Otel. As he passed through the front garden he saw Mlle Leblanc in urgent conversation with the scientist, Mr. Demiray, standing beneath the great grandiflora, but they were too busy with their own concerns to notice his departure.

Over the following weeks Ed continued his rambles and eventually came to know the whole island. Since the Princes' Islands are part of Istanbul, they have all the modern services available elsewhere in the city, but their remoteness from other neighborhoods and their lack of motor transport or industry mean that they have none of the noise or pollution that blight the rest of Istanbul. The island has a year-round population of fishermen and day laborers in ramshackle cottages or crowded into floors of large old houses, as well as affluent old families living in their mansions. During the summer months there are also middle-class families renting houses and flats for an inexpensive holiday. Most of the older structures are made of wood brought from Romania in the 19th century; their prevailing colors are shades of gray, as the paint has faded and peeled, revealing the weather-beaten wood beneath. But on the upper slopes, some of the big houses are well-maintained and painted white or pastel colors or a sort-of reddish-brown. The island is humid all year round and very green, with a variety of plants and flowers all growing mixed and uncontrolled, with vines and climbing roses growing exuberantly up fences and the walls of houses. At the top of the island are natural pine forests and along its coast, many little secluded beaches where Ed and Starleen could swim.

# 5

That weekend Ed began to make some preparations for the classes he would be teaching. It was still not clear to him what the full extent of his responsibilities would be or how many pupils he would have, but he decided that, having stepped on this train, he would just relax and see where it took him.

On Sunday, Ed saw his new friend Brown, who suggested that they dine together that evening at a restaurant he liked. Ed had eaten several more *döner* and was ready for something else, so he readily agreed. That evening they set out at 8:00 and Brown led the way across the main square and past the restaurants on the promenade. They continued on for some time through side streets, eventually moving up and out of the main town, until they reached a sort of alley called Hamit Sokağı. This appeared to be a rather forlorn little residential road, made up of old houses leaning against each other. One, however, was lit up and bore a sign reading "Güven Lokantası."

"Doesn't look like much, old boy," said Brown, "but the food's good."

They entered and Ed was surprised to see that there were already many customers. Despite the unprepossessing exterior, the inside was bright and cheerful, consisting of several large rooms furnished with simple wooden tables at which the customers were eating from a variety of interesting-looking little dishes of salads and platters of grilled fish. There was a lively buzz of conversation and a pervasive aroma of rakı and cigarette smoke. The customers were mainly men, but there were also families. Ed noticed the lady from the Grand Otel with her two daughters. He pointed them out to Brown, who looked over at them and nodded, "Ah yes, Mrs. Akkaya and her girls. Our dear neighbors."

They were greeted by the owner, Nesret Bey, who was apparently expecting them. He took them up a flight of stairs to another set of rooms, also with customers, but not so crowded as the floor below, and ushered them to a table set in a sort of bay window. From this height they had a fine view of the harbor and the sea beyond.

"*Ne içersiniz, efendim?*" asked their host, and Brown ordered *rakı* and drank to Ed's success in his new career: "Good luck, old man. Better you than me!" A waiter brought them a large tray stacked with the little dishes Ed had seen on the other tables and they selected a variety of them: white cheese, melon, little salted fish, white beans in vinaigrette, pureed eggplant, fried eggplants, artichoke bottoms, a big mixed salad. For some time they concentrated on these—*meze*, Brown called them—and talked in a random way. Brown asked Ed about his impressions of his new colleagues at the school and seemed especially interested in his description of Mlle Leblanc.

"I've heard of her. Hot stuff, these mademoiselles!"

Ed asked him more about his profession, and Brown said vaguely that he was a "sort of business consultant." It appeared that Brown had been living on the island for some time, but why he conducted his consulting business from there was unclear. What did seem clear, however, was that he didn't care to talk about it, so Ed let it go. One thing he did mention was that the hotel was owned by Ali Bayraktar, who owned other properties on the island, and perhaps elsewhere in Istanbul. This helped to explain the rather luxurious appointments Ed had seen in his and his daughter's offices.

After the *meze* Brown ordered grilled fish and after that they had a bowl of fruit on ice. As they were ordering coffee, a man got up from a table nearby, where he had been dining by himself, and came over to them.

"Good evening, Mr. Brown. May I join you and our new island resident? Mr. Wilkie, is it not?"

Ed recognized the alert little man whom Kemal had addressed as Osman Bey—the "very important official"—when he first arrived on the island. He was trim, neatly dressed in dark clothes, with dark hair turning gray, and a dark mustache. He accepted Brown's offer of coffee with a grin and proposed brandy to go with it. He seemed relaxed and somehow a little amused. Brown, on the other hand, became edgy.

"Let me introduce myself, Mr. Wilkie," said Osman Bey. "I am Osman İlik. I am in charge of security for the islands." Ed wasn't sure what all was encompassed by this description, whether he was a simple policeman or had more extensive responsibilities, but Osman Bey didn't elaborate. "Ali Bey applied for your residence and work permits some time ago. The application was rather late, but we were able to accommodate him. You will, however, need to bring your passport to the police station for an endorsement within the next three days. Mr. Brown knows where to find it. I am sure he will be glad to show you the way. In any case, I don't think that this will be your first encounter with the Turkish police, Mr. Wilkie," he said with a knowing smile. Obviously, he kept himself well informed.

"Quite right, Osman Bey, I'll bring him right over," said Brown quickly.

Osman Bey seemed in no hurry to leave, and they had several more coffees and brandy, or at least what the waiter called brandy, and discussed various aspects of the ever-present crises in the Mediterranean area. He spoke knowledgeably and invited Ed's opinion, but Ed quite truthfully denied all knowledge of the issues involved. Brown sat silent, drinking his brandy and only occasionally adding a brief comment.

At last Osman Bey looked at his watch. "I see that it is rather late. I'm afraid I kept you up on a 'school night,'" he said with a smile. They said goodnight, shook hands, and Osman Bey left them. Brown seemed ready to go also, so they paid their quite modest check and walked back to the Grand Otel.

# 6

On Monday Ed called Brown to ask if he could go with him to the police station, as Osman Bey had requested. Brown said he was free the next day and they agreed to meet at the ferry landing to take the boat to Büyükada.

"All the administrative stuff for the islands is on Büyükada," Brown explained. "Pay your taxes, get trade licenses, dog tags, whatever, the offices are there."

It was a fifteen-minute ride by ferry from their island to Büyükada. The moment they got off at the elegant Ottoman-style landing Ed felt the difference between the two islands. While his had a kind of shabby charm, Büyükada was quite grand: large, stately 19th-century mansions, heavy with carpenter's gingerbread, sitting in big gardens, the streets tree-lined, well-maintained and dignified. It was easy to imagine the island in the late Ottoman times, say 1910, with the wealthy Turkish, Jewish, Armenian, and Greek families taking their ease on their verandahs, strolling on the seafront, drinking coffee in the little cafes—the ladies chatting together, perhaps arranging marriages for their children; the men talking business, smoking cigars or nargiles, during the long twilight of the Ottoman Empire.

Today there were modern cafes selling ice cream and pop to young people in jeans and shorts, a cinema showing an American film, courting couples with no mama's eye on them. But still the *faytons* plied their dignified way. At Brown's suggestion, they walked to the police station, which was located in a charming stone building on a little square not far from the seafront. It looked as though it had at one time been a private house, perhaps, like the Academy, abandoned by Greeks after the War of Independence.

They entered the building and found themselves in a large, rather dim room smelling of disinfectant. A police official was seated behind a desk, and several dejected-looking men in shabby clothes were sitting on chairs along the wall. In the background there was the sound of a typewriter being worked with two fingers and someone shouting orders. They approached the desk and Brown explained in very halting Turkish that Ed was there to have his passport endorsed. The official smiled and said, "Yes, Mr. Wilkie, Osman Bey told us that you would be coming in. This will take a few minutes. Please sit down."

They sat down on one of the benches and Brown muttered in Ed's ear, "Good Christ! A few minutes! Who does he think he's kidding? He won't get the sodding passport open in a few minutes."

Ed composed himself for a long wait and studied the photograph of Atatürk on the wall behind the official's desk. In this picture the Gazi was in white tie and tails, as though on his way to the opera. Unlike most of the rather stern-looking official portraits, in this picture he was smiling—perhaps he was going somewhere more interesting than the opera. Ed then shifted his attention to a printed notice on the other wall and tried to pick out words he could recognize from the Turkish grammar he had begun to study. Many things seemed to be yasak, "forbidden." Then the official called, "Your passport is ready, sir!" Brown muttered in amazement as Ed collected the document and thanked the official.

"Is Osman Bey's office here? Perhaps I could say hello."

The policemen looked shocked. "Oh no, sir. Osman Bey has his own offices. Not here."

Ed thanked him again and they departed.

"You must have made a big hit with Osman Bey, Doc!" said Brown. "I had calculated the whole morning for this little job. Must be your pretty blue eyes!"

Having time on their hands, they hired a *fayton* and took a tour of the island. Brown pointed out the house where Trotsky lived from 1929-33 and wrote much of his *History of the Russian Revolution*—now a picturesque ruin in an abandoned garden by the sea. Also the home of Izzet Pasha, head of Abdül Hamit's secret police. Ed thought about Ali Bey's telescope and wondered if Izzet Pasha had also studied the city through it.

# 7

During the next few days, parents arrived with their boys, on foot or in faytons, to enroll them in the school for the next term. The process—though it must have been conducted every fall for many years—seemed to catch everyone by surprise: teachers, parents, and pupils. There was much milling around: heavy fathers disputing fees, mothers calling their sons to order in a hopeless sort of way, the boys wild and out of control with the excitement of meeting their friends. An exhilarated Kemal called it a "genuine *anababa günü*."

"What's that?" Ed asked.

"Literally, 'a mother-father day.' It means a big confusion."

"Sorry? A sweet confusion?"

"A big confusion. A mess. Registration à la turca!"

At last, the registration was completed, the boys assigned to their dormitories, the class rolls made up. There was a convocation and Ali Bey spoke to the boys along the same lines as he had to Ed about the new generation for a new Turkey. Zeynep Hanım supervised the proceeding with a sharp eye for any lack of attention or indiscipline.

On Ed's first day of teaching, Kemal led him to his classroom through corridors filled with boys of all sizes, frantically looking for their classes, yelling at friends, running after each other, and generally getting under foot. They stopped in front of a scarred door with a frosted glass panel. Kemal threw it open and Ed was startled to see the whole roomful of pupils jump to their feet when they entered. He had the momentary sensation that the boys were going to fling themselves on him in their rage at being forced to start their lessons again, but Kemal said, "Sit down boys. I want you to meet your new teacher, Mr. Wilkie, from America. I expect you to treat him with the same courtesy that you would show to me and make him feel at home at our school." He then shook Ed's hand and left him standing in front of thirty boys, staring at him silently, with wide, unblinking eyes.

Ed's mind suddenly went blank and could only think *My God! What am I doing here?* Then, he recovered sufficiently to croak, "Well, boys, I'm delighted to be here in, um…Turkey. I look forward to being your teacher and I hope that we will be good friends." He saw them relax and glance significantly at each other.

Ed called the roll, providing comic relief by his mispronunciation of their names, and then went over the syllabus and made the reading assignment for the next meeting. He then realized that he had shot his bolt and could think of nothing else to do. How much time had passed? Probably only a few minutes. He knew that it would be fatal to look at his watch, with thirty pairs of eyes on him.

"Are there any questions?" he asked hopefully.

After a long silence, a fat little thug in the back row raised his hand. "Please, sir. Where are you from in America?"

"From Los Angeles—in California."

Another long silence, while they digested this information. Then: "Please, sir. Have you ever met a movie star?"

Ed thought for a moment and remembered the disgusting old pederast with marcelled hair who had once specialized in playing cowboy heroes in B pictures. Fallen on hard times, he had cadged many an invitation to his mother's not very discriminating parties.

"Why, yes! I know a very famous movie star."

"Oh, sir! Tell us!"

They were in business. After a few days, the boys and Ed had taken each other's measure and arrived at an accommodation. The boys were generally lazy but good-natured and needed only to be interested to keep their attention. Ed didn't overload them with work and they treated him with a slightly condescending courtesy. Thus, they settled into a routine, ambling through the set syllabus and the anthologies, discussing stories and poems.

Ed began to meet his other colleagues on the teaching staff, a rather odd mix of the traditional teachers who had been retained from the former administration and the new staff, which, like him, tended to be less experienced and orthodox in their methods. He also moved from his temporary accommodation at the Grand Otel to a bachelor apartment in an upper floor of the Academy, a large and airy sitting room and a small bedroom. He bought Starleen a cushion that he put under the window to catch the sun and she became fully domesticated quickly—indeed, she paid regular and unauthorized calls on the boys' dormitories, where she got to roughhouse and eat forbidden sweets.

# 8

Ed found that the Academy had a remarkably good library, of a rather eclectic sort. Its foundation was a wealthy businessman's private collection, which had been bought at auction by the school's former owner, together with many items donated by a British Council branch library that had been closed several years ago. The wealthy bibliophile had collected widely in several languages, mostly history, archaeology and literature, and the British Council library had supplied standard works of English literature. Some books on the United States bore bookplates indicating that they were gifts from the U.S. Information Service and the U.S. Agency for International Development. To these had been added some newer works, mostly textbooks and anthologies, and a few subscriptions to magazines, such as *Time* and *The Economist*. The library was situated on the second floor in a large, high-ceilinged room that might originally have been a ballroom. It had a faded decorated ceiling and clattery parquet floor, free-standing steel bookcases of an army surplus aspect, and long library tables of stained and scratched golden oak. There were few visitors, except the occasional boy on detention or a faculty member asleep.

The librarian was a very old man, a holdover from the earlier ownership, who had once been a teacher but was now kept on at a minuscule salary, as he had nowhere else to go. Vural Bey had been, Ed was told, a good teacher, and even something of an authority on Byzantine numismatics, but now he spent his time pottering around the library and cultivating a small patch of garden that he had been allotted. He was a cheerful old man and Ed enjoyed talking with him. He told Ed that he had been sent to the school as a little boy from Izmir by his father, who had ambitions for him to join the civil service.

"When I first came to the school," he said, "I didn't know a word of English. I had learned French. But my father knew that English would be the important language. So I had to start all over again." From the school he went on to Istanbul University, where he heard lectures by famous German professors, who had earlier left their homeland for sanctuary in Turkey: "They were Jews, but very good men. One wore a monocle and had spats on his shoes." There had not been enough money for Vural to complete his education, so he returned to the school to teach Turkish history and language, and he had been there ever since.

One of Vural Bey's passions was making *turşu*, Turkish pickles. In his brine and vinegar-smelling office there were benches and shelves under the windows loaded with glass jars filled with pickled vegetables: cucumbers, tomatoes, carrots, garlic, and complicated stuffed pickles made with eggplants, all glowing like jewels as the sunlight streamed through the jars. On Ed's first visit he made him a present of a jar of mixed *turşu*, which were, in fact, delicious—only lightly salted, with a clean taste and crunch. Later, he showed Ed some of the secrets of his hobby and Ed made some in his room, though they were never as good as Vural Bey's.

Vural Bey had a kind of obsession about the new administration of the school and occasionally harangued about Ali Bey and his daughter, whom he suspected of sinister intentions and activities: "They don't care about the school," he would say. "They will bring it to grief!" Ed paid little attention, since the old man was clearly unhappy about the changes that had been made and the new faculty that had been introduced.

"The women are the worst! Gülsen Hanım—Miss Agi—with her dirty talk about Oedipus complexes and anal-compulsive behavior. What kind of thing is that for young boys to hear? And the French woman! Canoodling with Erol Bey in the library, shrieking at him because he doesn't treat her like a heroine in one of her disgusting French novels. She even tried to smoke in here! I soon told her...." He probably suspected, quite accurately, that his days in his post were numbered.

One day several weeks after Ed had begun teaching at the Academy, he was in the library reading *The Economist* and Vural Bey came up for a chat. After discussing a recent government flap for a few moments he began again on Ali Bey and Zeynep Hanım.

"Mr. Wilkie, you're a good man—young, not like me. You should get away from this place. They are some sort of criminals! No one thinks I see anything, but I see more than they know. You must..."

Ed heard a sound behind them and gestured to Vural Bey to stop. It was the clicking of high heels on the old parquet. Just then Zeynep Hanım rounded the corner and nodded briefly to Vural Bey, who lowered his eyes.

"*Merhaba*, Zeynep Hanım. *Hoş geldiniz*—welcome."

"*Hoş bulduk,* Vural Bey." She looked at Ed. "I hope you and Vural Bey have been having an interesting conversation. He is a learned man."

"Yes, thank you, Zeynep Hanım. We have been discussing *turşu*."

"Ah, I have heard about Vural Bey's hobby," she said, turning to him. "Perhaps I may sample them one day."

"With great pleasure, Zeynep Hanım."

Turning to Ed she said, "Still, be sure that you aren't led into a pickle."

"Yes. Ha ha! Very good!" Ed replied. Vural Bey looked confused.

"Mr. Wilkie, I have come from my father, who requests you to call on him in his office, if it is convenient." Her manner clearly indicated that his convenience was consulted in a purely formal way, so he replied, "Of course, Zeynep Hanım, I'll go right now.

"Good day, Vural Bey."

"Good-bye," he replied. "Good-bye, Mr. Wilkie. We will meet again, God willing."


Ed left the library and went directly to Ali Bey's office, where Ali Bey welcomed him with his usual old-fashioned courtesy. Tea was already laid out on a tray, so there had been little doubt in his mind that Ed would respond quickly to his summons.

"Greetings, Mr. Wilkie. Please sit down and have a cup of tea with me." He politely poured a cup and then settled back, crossing his long legs. "You have been at the school now for some time and I wanted to take the opportunity to discuss your progress and find whether you are happy with your work."

"I enjoy my work very much, Ali Bey, and I think the boys are learning."

"That is excellent. You may be interested in knowing that I have been in correspondence with our dear friend, Major Collins. In my next letter to him I will remember you to him. Shall I?"

"Oh yes, please, Ali Bey."

"Major Collins in recommending you to me said that eventually you might be interested in moving from teaching into more managerial work. I have a number of interests in Istanbul, and even beyond, in which I might be able to use a good man. What do you think?"

"I don't exactly know, Ali Bey. When my mother died I thought at first of going into some sort of business, but it didn't work out..."

"So Major Collins recommended you to me. He is a very discerning man— a great judge of character and temperament. Well, let us see."

He kept Ed for some time, during which he discussed a variety of topics of current interest and he also asked him a number of rather probing personal questions. Finally, he concluded the interview.

"Excellent! I am so glad that we had our little talk. We must meet again in the not too distant future." He rose. "Oh, by the way, Mr. Wilkie, this postcard addressed to you was brought to me by our mailman. Though he delivered it, he said that he really should not have done so. I am not sure how, in fact, it got as far as the island without being confiscated. You should tell your friends that this type of card should be placed in an envelope."

He glanced down at the card and then handed it to over with a smile. Ed shook hands and left the room. Then he looked at the card, which bore the legend "Howdy from Tex-ass!" and portrayed a comic drawing of a woman wearing a cowboy hat and nothing else, leaning over a gate, her back to the viewer: Star!

He took the card into the garden and found a secluded bench set next to the building. He turned over the card and read: "Dear Ed, Thinking of you. I hope you are thinking of me. Maybe this picture will help! Love, Star." The card was pure Star. The idea of Ed's receiving so compromising a picture and message en clair at what she thought of as his "snooty school" would certainly appeal to her sense of humor and general fondness for raising hell and deflating dignity.

# 9

Ed had met Star in Houston. Following his drive from Los Angeles to meet the ship bound to Marseilles, he had allowed a week to explore the area, which he had never visited. The manager of the Motel Six had recommended the Tijuana Cantina as the spot where he could taste the most authentic Tex-Mex food and see some nightlife. At the Cantina, Ed had been seated at the bar before dinner and had drunk four margaritas in fairly rapid succession. He was experiencing that false sense of well-being, almost of elation, that is the sure—and usually ignored—sign that the drinker is moving past the point of no return, when he heard a rather harsh female voice say, "Look here, mister, you gonna just sit there staring at me all night? Haven't you ever seen a girl before?"

When he refocused his eyes, he realized that he had been staring unseeing-ly into the mirror behind the bar at the woman seated two stools away from him.

"Oh, I beg your pardon. I didn't mean to…"

In his flustered condition he did what normally he would never have done, being somewhat shy with women: he found himself offering her a drink. She did-n't seem to be a shy girl, but replied, "Don't mind if I do!" and shifted to the stool next to his. He signaled for two more margaritas.

"I'm Star," she said. "What about you?"

"Me? Oh, I'm Ed. Star, you say?"

"Well, Starleen. But who needs a hillbilly name like that?"

His companion was a skinny little woman, with red hair piled untidily on her head; round, inquisitive brown eyes set in a triangular face; and a wide, humor-ous mouth, painted with plenty of orange lipstick. She was dressed in a bright-aqua dress with lots of sparkly costume jewelry. Her powerful perfume, she later told him, was "Evening in Paris."

"So, what do you do? Teacher or something?" Her bright eyes looked him over.

"Why, yes. I guess I am now," said Ed. "How did you know?"

"I dunno. I guess it's the way you talk—refined. You just passing through?"

"Yes. I'll be leaving in a week for Marseilles."

"Say again. Mar-say?"

"In France."

"Oo-la-la! Love 'em and leave 'em, huh?"

They had more margaritas and then moved on to another place that Star said was "not so high-class and stiff," where she taught Ed to drink tequila straight, with salt and lemon; then they had dinner at a rib house she favored, followed by more drinks at a country and western place, where she sang "Your Cheatin' Heart" along with the band.

"That was great, Star," he said as they left. "I've had a wonderful evening."

She laughed. "What makes you think it's over, buckaroo?"

The next morning he awoke in a strange bed with Star next to him. This had not been his first experience with a woman. There had been a girl in college, whom his mother didn't like, whom she called "that damned little beatnik—tell her to wash her hair before she comes back here again!"—and there were a couple of listless affairs with country club girls, with their blonde hair, pointy noses, and calculating eyes. But with Star it was as she herself said, a whole 'nuther thing: "Just home cooking, honey, but with raisins in it." The ultimate comfort food.

Over the next week they spent most of their time together. They ate out, cooked in, went to a rodeo, and spent hours in her bed. Another thing they did was go to a dog show, where he saw his first bull terriers—his mother had liked angora cats. He bought one from some people who were showing their dogs and decided to name her after his new friend.

Star took the day off to say good-bye when Ed sailed.

"It's been super, honey. You're a real gentleman, and a girl appreciates that. Not like some o' these jerks you run into! You write when you get to wherever that place is you're goin' to!"

She stood on the wharf as Ed sailed away, a small, skinny figure in a cowgirl dress, smiling and waving and wiping her nose with the back of her hand. From Istanbul he sent her a postcard with a chaste view of the Haghia Sophia, giving his new address. This was her reply.

As Ed sat lost in his thoughts of Star, he became aware of a conversation in Turkish in the background. He looked up and saw that he had seated himself near the French doors of Zeynep Hanım's office, which were open to admit the afternoon breeze. She was speaking urgently and increasingly loudly. Her interlocutor, a man, was apparently temporizing, or reasoning with her. After a moment Ed realized that it was Ali Bey and he remained where he was, reflecting that at least he couldn't be accused of eavesdropping, since he couldn't understand what they were saying. A moment later, Mehmet Efendi came by with a watering can. He waved at Ed and entered through the doors without knocking, saying, *"Merhaba, hocam!"* and indicating that he was going to water the plants in the office.

Zeynep Hanım started to protest, but Ali Bey said in English, "Please go on with what you were saying." After a moment's hesitation, she resumed, also in English.

"So the old fool in the library has got to be gotten rid of."

"Relax, my dear. No one pays any attention to Vural Bey. There are other things more important than this. We must not let ourselves become distracted."

"Still, we've got to get rid of him!"

"Very well, *canım*. We'll discuss it later. Good-bye. *İyi günler*, Mehmet Efendi."

Ed waited a few minutes, but heard nothing else. Presumably Zeynep Hanım was brooding alone. So he crept quietly away and returned to his apartment.

Later, Ed was in his sitting room in his armchair by the window, communing with Starleen, her muzzle on his knee and her tail thumping on the floor, when Mehmet Efendi knocked and came in with the mail—minus the postcard that Ali Bey had delivered personally. Among the out-of-date magazines and bills was a card showing a scene in the Grand Bazaar of Istanbul. The signature on the back was one that he didn't recognize, but the message ran, "Dear Mr. Wilkie, I hope you have now settled into your new home, and look forward to receiving you in my shop. Perhaps next Saturday, if you are free. Your shipmate, A. Agopian." Ah yes, thought Ed, his friend the rug merchant from the ship. In the excitement of starting his new classes, he had completely forgotten his invitation to visit the shop. Ed knew little about oriental carpets, though they were one of his mother's passing enthusiasms. Still, it might be interesting, and the sitting room could use some personal touches. Maybe a colorful kilim wouldn't be too expensive.

It struck him that he hadn't seen Brown for some time, so he gave him a call to see if he would be interested in joining an expedition to the Grand Bazaar.

"Love to, old boy! What say you come to your former home from home and I'll blow you to a good breakfast chez moi."

Ed agreed to meet him at the Grand Otel the following Saturday at 9:00.

# 10

On Saturday Ed regretfully bid Starleen good-bye, feeling that she would not be welcome in the crowds of the Grand Bazaar. Her by now fast friend, Mehmet Efendi, agreed to take her for a stroll mid-day and feed her later. When Ed arrived at the Grand Otel, Mustafa Bey popped up from behind his desk and lurched over to grab his hand and pump it energetically. As he started across the lobby, Ed saw Mrs. Akkaya, looking as usual very chic, at the foot of the stairs and stopped to pay his respects.

"Mrs. Akkaya, how are you this morning? I hope your lovely daughters are well?"

She looked uncertain for a moment and then smiled delightedly.

"Ah, dear Mr. Wilkie, you Americans have such a witty way with you. I have met a number of American gentlemen and they all loved to 'kid'!"

Ed smiled in reply and started to move on, but she touched his arm.

"Mr. Wilkie. Mr. Brown tells me that you are a teacher. A teacher of English. Is this so?"

"Yes, Mrs. Akkaya. I teach English at the Academy."

"Excellent. I wonder if you would ever consider taking private pupils?" She looked up at Ed and cocked her head.

Ed had not previously considered the possibility, but it struck him that it might, indeed, be a useful supplement to his Academy salary.

"Perhaps. Did you have anyone specific in mind?"

"Yes. My dear girls. They speak only Turkish and a little French, but I think English would very much improve their prospects."

"I certainly think that I would be interested," Ed said, remembering the delicious girls he had seen with her. "I would teach both of them together, I suppose."

"Yes, of course. There might even be several more—a little class!" She clapped her hands together playfully.

"Your daughters' friends?" This was getting better, thought Ed.

"Ha, yes! You silly man! I see that you are engaged now, but I will call you soon and see if we can come to an arrangement. *Au revoir*, Mr. Wilkie."

Brown was in a lively mood. "So, how's tricks at Dotheboys Hall, Doc?"

Ed assured him that he was keeping ahead of things and they settled into an excellent English breakfast of eggs, sausages, French fried potatoes, and good coffee, followed by a glass of pear-flavored kirsch.

"What the hell, old boy, it's not a school day! So, how did you get to know this rug peddler we're going to see?"

"He was my shipmate on the boat from France. He had been there on business."

"He takes his rugs to France by ship?"

"Yes. He said that several times a year he ships large consignments of cheaper rugs for the European market and delivers them to the Paris dealers. I take it that he sends the more valuable rugs by air."

"But, still, I wouldn't think he'd need to go personally with the shipment."

"Oh, I don't think he usually does. He told me he has a nephew in the business who mostly handles the shipments. This was partly a holiday, I believe."

"Better he than I. Stuck on some Turkish rust-bucket for four days! Doesn't sound like much of a holiday to me."

"By the way, Brown," Ed said, his thoughts reverting to the conversation he had overheard between Ali Bey and Zeynep Hanım. "What does *canım* mean?"

"*Canım?* Well, *can* means soul—'my soul'—like we say 'my dear.'"

Ed told him about his conversation with Mrs. Akkaya and he agreed that it sounded like a good idea.

"After all, Doc, it's always a good thing to expand the range of your teaching experience. Not only will you teach them, but doubtless you will learn from them."


They took the ferry to the Sirkeci landing. Ed had been so engaged in teaching and class preparations that he had come to the mainland only a couple of times, and was always amazed and confused by the transition from the calm and quiet of the island to the noise, dirt, jostling crowds, and honking horns when he stepped off the boat.

They then rode the tram to the Beyazıt stop and plunged into the bazaar, a vast stone labyrinth, with high domed ceilings pierced by openings from which dim light filtered through colored glass. Antiques, precious textiles, and windows piled with harshly lit gold jewelry were interspersed with stalls offering household wares, clothing, tiles, and souvenirs of all kinds. There was an odor of leather, perfumes, and spices, and a cacophony of voices in numerous languages. They found themselves in a mob of eager shoppers: stolid, middle-aged Germans somberly contemplating the windows of gold jewelry; backpackers fingering cheap souvenirs; intense, noisy Italians trying on leather jackets; slow-moving Arab women in enveloping cloaks; Japanese, camera at the ready; Americans finding everything "real cute—and so cheap!" Hands grabbed at his sleeve.

"Hey, buddy. Come in and see my rugs!"

*"Merhaba. Buyrun!"*

"Good leather. Cheap!"

*"Güten tag, mein herr!"*

"Change money. Best rate!"

They had been searching and stopping for directions for some time when Ed saw someone he thought he knew moving through the crowd in a determined manner. "Mlle Leblanc!" he called out and she stopped and looked around her anxiously, running a hand through her short blonde hair. He waved and they went over to join her, moving out of the hustling crowds, and stood together in front of a leather shop.

"Hello, Lucie, this is a pleasant surprise. Please let me introduce my friend Brown, who also lives on the island. We were just looking for Mr. Agopian's shop."

"Hello, Ed. Mr. Brown, *enchantée.*"

"Delighted, Mademoiselle. Ed told me that he had a charming French colleague. It's a pleasure to meet you at last," he replied with a look of interest.

She seemed a little startled, but not displeased. "You are too kind, Mr. Brown."

"Well, I hope we'll meet again, soon."

"I also, Mr. Brown. Unfortunately, I am in a great rush right now or I would take you to Mr. Agopian's shop. I am just returning from there. You have only to walk down this path, back from where you were coming, and turn left at the little fountain. Walk fifty meters and he is there." She seemed anxious to be on her way, so Ed said, "Thanks very much. I'm sure we can find it. See you later." She nodded briefly and walked quickly away.

---

"Not bad!" said Brown, looking after her. "I'll have to follow up on this one."

"She has a Turkish boyfriend on the faculty. A chemist."

"Tough luck for him. I think I could provide a little chemistry of my own. She looks like a right little piece."

Following Lucie's directions, they at last found a shop with a sign reading "L. Agopian and Son: Fine Carpets and Kilims." They entered and were welcomed by Ed's erstwhile travel companion, who shook hands and invited them to sit down on low stools. The shop was small, stacked floor to ceiling with folded carpets. On the walls hung more rugs, together with framed, possibly authentic, signed testimonials from famous customers. There was also a signed photograph of a minor European royalty and grinning snapshots of what Ed assumed were well known Turkish personalities.

Mr. Agopian, in his workaday costume of cardigan sweater and wrinkled slacks, rubbed his hands and invited them to take tea with him.

"It's a pleasure to see you—and your friend, Mr. Brown. I so much enjoyed our conversations on the ship. I'm sure I'll make a rug lover of you!"

He called his helper, Kadri, who began unfolding rugs one by one, Mr. Agopian naming the style and commenting on it.

"Caucasian. Maybe fifty years old. Good shape. But I repaired the fringe—see here. This one is a Hereke. New. As you can see, a Persian design. Not really my kind of rug, but some people like them."

They placed the rugs they liked in one pile and Kadri put aside the rejects. Then they looked again at the ones they had liked, Mr. Agopian giving more details and mentioning the price. In the end Ed had winnowed the rugs down to a small Caucasian tribal, which cost—needless to say—more than the upper price that he had set himself. He said that he would cash a check and come by to pick up the rug later, but Mr. Agopian brushed this aside.

"Take it now. You will pay me whenever you wish. And I will sell you another rug!" He gestured at the sign in the window. "I am the son. We've been in this business many years. I know when I can trust a man." Business finished, Mr. Agopian grew more relaxed. "Tell me, Mr. Wilkie, how are you enjoying your island? You like the teaching?"

"Oh yes. I love the island, but you know it's always hard to make friends in a new place—at least for me."

"Well, Mr. Wilkie, I wanted to mention to you a friend of mine who lives on your island: Mrs. Balian, a very nice lady, *çok hanımefendi*—very polite, cultivated. I will give her a call. Maybe she can telephone you at your school."

"With great pleasure, Mr. Agopian."

They were just about to leave when the door opened and a young man entered. Mr. Agopian smiled and said, "Ah, Ari, you're just in time to meet Mr. Wilkie, my shipmate from Marseilles, and his friend, Mr. Brown. This is my nephew, who works with me in the business."

Ari was in his early thirties, very slim and elegant, with an expression of studied boredom. He was informally but modishly dressed in tight jeans and an expensive-looking yellow turtleneck sweater, with a lot of gold jewelry, including some sort of astrological medallion on a chain around his neck, and dark glasses. He shook his hair out of his eyes, looked Ed over and then smiled and shook hands.

"Yes, Lucie—Mlle Leblanc—from your school told me about you. In fact, she was here earlier today. I hope we'll see much more of you, too."

"Ah, I'm sorry I missed her!" said Mr. Agopian. "Did she buy anything?"

Ari shrugged his shoulders listlessly. "No, she just looked in to say hello."

"Ari has such a way with the young ladies," Mr. Agopian said chuckling. "He can sell them anything! Though always good quality, of course," he added quickly. "Especially French ladies. He speaks wonderful French. You should see him charm the French customs officials. They love him..."—Ari winked at Ed— "...Me, they hate!"

Ed said good-bye, receiving an attenuated handshake and lingering glance from Ari. They left, Ed carrying the neat parcel that Kadri had made up.

"I think you did rather well," said Brown, "but remember, it can become an obsession. Agopian seemed like a nice old bird, but I can't say I cared much for the fairy with the gold dog tag. I'd keep my back covered with that one. Anyway, let's stretch the legs a bit and pop in on the book market."

Brown's interest in books proved to be perfunctory, and they walked rather quickly through the passages where dealers in books and prints traditionally carried on their trade. Ed paused to look at some framed engravings of Ottoman

Istanbul, but Brown led the way into a small shop that displayed a jumble of dusty objects, old copper and brass, bits of jewelry, broken toys, an old-fashioned gramophone with an enormous horn. Brown greeted the owner and asked, "Anything new?"

The owner smiled and opened a drawer, taking out two sets of worry beads—*tespihs*, Brown called them. "I collect these in a small way," he said, "and this old thief keeps his eye out for good antique ones for me." The owner smiled politely.

Brown looked over the two *tespihs*. "This one's not too bad. Real amber. Nice color. Mid-19th century. All the beads original. The *imame*—the part where the tassel comes out—is a bit chipped. How much, old cock?"

The proprietor named a sum only a little less than Ed had just paid for his rug. Brown expressed indignation and outrage. "None of your tourist prices for me, Hasan!"

Hasan smiled and assured him that this was a price only for his dear friend, Mr. Brown—the last possible price. Any less would mean taking bread from the mouths of his children. Brown demurred, counter offers were made; at one point Brown threw up his hands and started for the door; was recalled; new negotiations began, and a final price—still high, to Ed's mind—was agreed upon. Brown paid—he seemed to have had the cash ready in advance—and they departed with much ceremony.

"Not a bad price," Brown said. "This will fit nicely in my collection. I have nearly a hundred of these, some quite rare and old."

Well, to each his own, thought Ed. It seemed like a hell of a price to pay for thirty-three beads on a string. Brown, however, seemed elated.

"Let's go celebrate our purchases, Doc!"

He took him to a small cafe tucked into a wall of the market and ordered *rakı* and a dish of olives. They sat talking together over several drinks, with Brown running his new *tespih* through his fingers.

"Always stroke the beads," he advised. "They shouldn't click."

Brown had some other business to take care of before returning to the island, so they agreed to meet later at the landing. He moved on, and Ed was just finishing his drink and wondering about the advisability of another one, when a man approached and said, "Mr. Wilkie? Osman Bey asks if you could join him."

He gestured in the direction of a table some distance away and Ed saw Osman Bey sitting with a glass of beer and grinning at him. "Of course," he replied and, taking his nearly empty glass, went over to join him.

Osman Bey seemed to be in an excellent mood. They shook hands and he invited Ed to have another drink and ordered another for himself. His companion was a Mr. Kuvvetli, a plump, nondescript man in an ill-fitting suit.

"Tekin Kuvvetli is my right hand," said Osman Bey. "I hope I am not interrupting you, Mr. Wilkie. I was in the neighborhood on business and spotted you with Brown. When he left you I thought I would give myself the pleasure of a few moments of conversation. If you are free."

"Of course."

"I see that you have become a rug buyer. Mr. Agopian is a very well-knowing—knowledgeable—man about rugs. Very honest, I believe. How did you meet him?"

"Actually, he was a fellow passenger on my ship…"

"From Marseilles?"

"Yes."

"A delightful city. Very historical."

"Did you visit Marseilles on holiday?" Ed asked, hoping to learn more about his acquaintance.

"No. I was on business. But enough about me! You are enjoying your work at the Academy? Ali Bey is a very interesting man. Do you talk with him about his interests?"

"Actually, Zeynep Hanım seems to direct the day-to-day business of the school. Though I have talked with Ali Bey. He tells me that he has other businesses besides the school."

"He told you that? Well, he's a man of many talents. Very well connected. I think you are quite friendly with Mr. Brown?"

"Yes. He's been very nice to me—showing me around, and everything."

"Brown is a man of great charm and ability." Ed started to speak, but Osman Bey concluded, "Well, Mr. Wilkie, I must be going." They shook hands and he departed, leaving Ed still unclear about the purpose of their conversation.

Later, when Ed met Brown at the dock, he mentioned his encounter with Osman Bey. "He seemed very interested in knowing how I'd met Mr. Agopian."

"On the good old *Akdeniz?*"

"Yes. How did you know the name, Brown?"

"I guess you must have mentioned it, Doc," said Brown with a grin. Perhaps, thought Ed, but he didn't think he had.

# 11

"When it came night, the waves paced to and fro in the moonlight, and the wind brought the sound of the great sea's voice to the men on shore, and they felt that they could be interpreters," Ed quoted dramatically to his senior English class. He paused to let these closing words of "The Open Boat" have their effect.

"Well, boys, what do you think of that?"

A profound silence. Thirty pairs of eyes looking at him for guidance. *Allah! Why the hell doesn't he just say what he thinks it means?* written clearly on their faces. Then finally:

"Please, sir. What kind of a ship was it?"

"Ship? What ship? It was a boat. A lifeboat," Ed explained.

"No, sir. I mean what kind of a ship was it that sank?"

"Well, really, Ibrahim! What does it matter? This is a symbolic story!"

Thirty pairs of eyes stared at him: *He doesn't know!*

Ed paused. "Well, OK. Let's look." They looked at the beginning of the story. "Ah yes, here it is. The scene of the sinking ship. I had forgotten: '...later the stump of a top-mast with a white ball on it that slashed to and fro at the waves, went low and lower, and down.'" He looked up. "So there it is, boys, a sailing ship. Just look at the text, as I always tell you."

"Was it a whaling ship, sir?"

"What? Why do you think that?"

"Well, sir, one of the men in the boat was an 'oiler,' so I thought..."

"No. Not at all," Ed explained patiently. "'Oiler' here doesn't mean whale oil; it means that this man worked in the engine room of the ship. He oiled the engine. See?"

"The engine of a sailing ship, sir?"

*Gotcha!* Ed recovered. "Good point, Ibrahim. Excellent observation!"

Thirty pairs of eyes exchanged glances.

"Well," Ed glanced at his watch. "I see our time is nearly up. You all think about this and we'll discuss it more next time."

The boys clattered out. "Very interesting story, sir! Very symbolic!"

Ed was walking along the corridor, reflecting on the pitfalls of great literature, when he came upon Erol Demiray, the science teacher he had met the first day of school. Erol had been cornered by Mlle Leblanc, who was as usual in a high state of excitement, running her hands through her short hair—the style that intellectual French women seem to like best, making them look like collaborators after a recent encounter with the Resistance—and sucking on one of her gunpowder cigarettes. Ed said hello and Erol, seeming glad of an excuse to terminate the discussion, said, "Ah, Ed! I had promised to show you over the science department of our school."

He had, indeed, suggested this several times, but they hadn't found a mutually convenient moment; in any case, Ed had no interest in the natural sciences. Still, to help him out, he replied, "Ah yes. I've been looking forward to that," seeming to suggest a prior arrangement. Erol looked at Ed gratefully and Mlle Leblanc glanced at him with irritation.

"Very well, Erol, we'll continue later! *Au revoir*, Mr. Wilkie." she said as she marched off. Erol looked after her.

"A charming person, but, you know, very passionate. Very emotional. The Latin temperament. I tell her to try and keep a more balanced, more scientific point of view."

"But not successfully?"

"No," he sighed. "In any case, do let me show you over my little kingdom." He took Ed downstairs into the basement of the building. "These rooms were originally the kitchens, pantries, laundry—you know, the service areas when this was a private house. We converted them into a tip-top set of labs. Here the boys get a first-class scientific training. We cultivate the scientific method—rational thinking!"

The rooms really did seem well equipped. The lighting was good, showing long counters with scientific equipment on them, sinks, jars with gruesome exhibits in spirits, some sort of experiment that involved growing green beans under an eerie white light. Ed was becoming a little light-headed in this atmosphere, particularly since he was now being shown an experiment the boys were working on that involved taking frogs to pieces.

Fortuitously, the lights dimmed and then went out, the school's ever-fragile electrical plant seemingly suffering from a new hiccup. Ed thanked Erol and said that he would have to be getting along. Erol seemed disappointed not to be able to show him more, but told him to come back any time.

"I'll put a scalpel in your hand and you can give it a try with a frog of your own!"

# 12

That evening Ed was writing a letter to his old teacher, Ray Collins. After describing the school and his new island life he added,

*Ali Bey sends you his regards. He has mentioned that you were working together at one time. All rather mysterious—what was it, smuggling, white slavery, espionage? I have met with him twice and he seems to be a very cultivated and intellectual person. I understand that he has extensive business interests beyond the school—which is, I guess, a kind of hobby with him. He has hinted that there might be something for me. Do I owe this to your recommendation? It appears that I may be getting some private tutoring in English. A lady at the hotel where I stayed has suggested a little class for her daughters and some of their friends. The daughters are knockouts—I can wait to see the friends!*

As he was finishing, the telephone rang and a woman's voice said, "Mr. Wilkie? My name is Mrs. Balian. I am calling you at the suggestion of my old friend Mr. Agopian." Her voice over the telephone was polite and well-bred; not exactly welcoming, not exactly not.

"He thought that you might enjoy meeting some people on the island not associated with your school—though, in fact, I am well acquainted with Ali Bey and, of course, Zeynep Hanım. Perhaps you would care to join me for tea some day soon?"

"That would be delightful, Mrs. Balian," said Ed with pleasure. "I really appreciate your kindness. It is not always easy to get to know people in a new place."

"Good. Then shall we say next Saturday at, let me see, 5:00? My house is on Yeni *Hamam* Street, number 37—a large white house."

"I'll be there, Mrs. Balian. Thank you again."

"Till then, ta-ta, Mr. Wilkie."

He had hardly hung up when there was a knock at the door and Mehmet Efendi entered smiling. He patted Ed's arm with his usual vigor and gave Starleen a quick neck rub.

*"Bay Wilkie, Zeynep Hanım seni bekliyor."*

He wondered what she might want with him. Maybe something about semester break or next term. Not wanting to keep her waiting, he went quickly to her office, knocked, and entered. She looked up from where she was sitting at her desk.

"Merhaba, Mr. Wilkie. Please sit down."

"Thank you." He waited expectantly, but she seemed, uncharacteristically, rather indecisive. "Mr. Wilkie, I must speak to you on a rather delicate matter."

"Yes, Zeynep Hanım?" *What on earth could this be*, he wondered.

"I understand that you are undertaking private tutoring in English."

"Not yet, Zeynep Hanım. I have been approached about the possibility. Is this a problem? Doesn't the Academy permit its teachers to give private lessons?

I'm sorry—I probably should have asked, but I didn't..."

"It would have been well if you had, Mr. Wilkie. Though we have no objection to the staff giving private tuition, in a limited way, we are more concerned with the nature of your intended pupils." She gave him a hard look and then dropped her gaze.

"I don't think I quite understand. It would only be Mrs. Akkaya's daughters and maybe a few of their friends."

"Mrs. Akkaya's daughters!" she said, her voice rising. "Mr. Wilkie, if you want to make a joke of this, we won't continue. But I think you should have some respect for the reputation of the school!"

Suddenly, Ed's mind cleared. Those lovely girls were actually…

"Zeynep Hanım, please forgive me! I didn't realize...," he stammered.

She looked curiously at him. "That was a possibility that had been suggested, but I had considered it remote. Now it seems…" She smiled. For the first time a real smile, rather than the mechanical, official one.

"Well, we won't say anything more. Please just drop this idea."

"Yes, indeed." He got up and found his way to the door. "Thank you. Good day."

"Good-bye, Mr. Wilkie." As Ed closed the door he heard her laughing.

Ed explained to Mrs. Akkaya that his terms of employment at the Academy would, he found, not permit him to teach privately. She seemed disappointed and said that her girls, particularly the beautiful Rezan, had been looking forward to it. When Ed spoke to Brown about it and said that he thought he might have warned him, Brown's only reply was, "Better you should learn for yourself, old cock. Part of your education."

# 13

Ed spent the next Saturday morning at the harbor with Starleen. They looked at the fishing boats, already back with their early morning catch displayed in buckets and baskets. Housewives, looking critically at eyes and gills for freshness, were discussing prices. Cats sat staring purposefully at the fish, their patience occasionally rewarded with scraps tossed to them as the fish were cleaned for the customers. Ed and Starleen walked out on the jetty and looked at the few pleasure craft, small sailboats, and boats with outboard motors, and continued on to inspect the big battered ships that lay in the harbor.

"Interesting, isn't it?" said a voice behind Ed. "These are tankers that bring water from the mainland."

He turned and found the science teacher, Erol Demiray, for the first time without his white lab coat.

"As you see, Mr. Wilkie, I am also taking advantage of a sunny Saturday to have a stroll. To get away from the aromas in the laboratory that you like so much." He smiled, and they continued on together.

"Tell me," Ed asked, "Why do they need to bring in water? There must be wells on the island."

"A few, but not enough. Many houses have a *sarnıç*—a reservoir for rainwater—but that isn't enough for our modern conceptions of cleanliness and hygiene. These ships bring in the water, which is pumped through these big pipes, up to the top of the hill," he pointed upwards, "and collected in a large reservoir. It's a rather interesting operation that I sometimes come to watch. Then the water feeds by gravity down to the houses."

"Interesting," Ed nodded, looking up.

"From time to time in the summer, when there are more people on the island, the water pressure goes down, or even stops, until another shipful can be pumped up."

Their conversation was interrupted by the arrival on the scene of Lucie Leblanc accompanied by Ari from Mr. Agopian's shop. After greetings were exchanged, Ed smiled and asked if Ari's visit to the island involved a rug purchase. Ari fingered his medallion.

"No, Mr. Wilkie, this is a social call. Lucie invited me over for lunch. Perhaps you will be joining us? I believe we are meeting your friend Mr. Brown for drinks afterwards."

So Brown had made his move to improve his acquaintance with Lucie, thought Ed. Lucie looked at Ed with obvious irritation and he quickly said, "No, I'm afraid I have made other plans." There was an awkward pause, during which no one urged him to change his mind, so he said, "Well, if you'll excuse me, I'll be on my way. Good morning." He saw the three of them looking after him for a moment and then they began speaking together.

For lunch Ed continued on to an outdoor place where Starleen was welcome—an old fishing boat, permanently tied to the wharf, that served as a little restaurant. Its menu was of the simplest: fish filets cooked on a small charcoal grill and placed on a half loaf of bread with tomato slices and red onions.

Ed put in his order to Cavit, the proprietor, and went across the road to buy a cold Efes beer, Cavit serving only soft drinks. When lunch was ready he sat at an unsteady little table provided for customers and shared bites of his sandwich with Starleen.

In the late afternoon Ed prepared himself for the tea party with Mrs. Balian. He put on his "good" gray flannel suit—it dated from a trip to London with his mother, and had been made by Anderson and Sheppard—and added a white shirt and the tie of a tennis club he had belonged to at one time in California. As he passed through the garden he picked a pink rosebud and placed it in his lapel.

He had looked up Yeni Hamam Street, which was on the other side of the island from the Academy. It was in a neighborhood of large, old houses, in what he learned was a traditionally Armenian part of town. Mrs. Balian's house was similar to the others on the street, looking as though it had seen better days: the wrought iron fence around it was choked with honeysuckle and the garden was filled with old-fashioned roses and lavender.

Mrs. Balian greeted him with the same restrained courtesy that she had shown on the telephone.

"Welcome, Mr. Wilkie. Please come in," she said with a formal smile. She was a tall, slim, rather austere woman, Ed thought probably in her mid-fifties. She had large dark eyes, a long sallow face, and dark hair unmarked by gray. She wore a silk print dress with a discreet pattern and some equally discreet jewelry. He noticed that she used a scent that he recognized: Habanita, a perfume that his mother had liked, and which she had discovered when they visited Grasse, in Southern France.

Mrs. Balian led Ed into the salon, which was, like her, a little old-fashioned, but well maintained and distinguished. There was a light aroma of potpourri and lemon polish; dark furniture glowed in the late afternoon light; and large dark green Boston ferns stood in brass planters. A table with tea things for two had been laid. Apparently he was the only guest.

"What a lovely room, Mrs. Balian," Ed said by way of conversation.

"Thank you, Mr. Wilkie. The house belonged to my late husband's family. You may know that at one time many Armenians lived on the islands. But most have, do you say 'emigrated' in English? My English is not good. I was educated in a French convent school in Istanbul."

"Your English is excellent, Mrs. Balian."

"Thank you. My late husband worked at one time with Ali Bey. When Ali Bey started to plan his *retraite...*"

"Retirement?"

"Exactly. My husband suggested this island."

"So your husband—passed on recently?"

"No. Some years ago. I lead a lonely life. We had no children."

There seemed no reply to this, so he remained silent.

"But I am a bad hostess, Mr. Wilkie. Let me offer you some tea. Or perhaps you would prefer a drink—sherry or a whisky soda?"

He hesitated a moment and she said, "A drink, then! I will join you."

An elderly maid entered. She was dressed in Turkish village clothes, with a scarf over her hair.

*"Evet, efendim?"*

Drinks were organized and Mrs. Balian and Ed both had whisky and sodas. Once she had the drink in her hand, Mrs. Balian became less formal and more animated. The first drinks were soon finished and she called for refills. She was very interested in knowing how he happened to come to the island and, stimulated by her questions and the several additional refills, Ed eventually told her most of the story of his life, his mother's death, his trip to Houston (omitting mention of Star), journey to Marseilles, and eventual arrival at Istanbul. He concluded with a review of his first term at the Academy.

"A life filled with incident!" said Mrs. Balian, finishing her latest drink and wiping her lips with the back of her hand. *"Tres chargée!* So you have had the tragedy to lose your dear mother, and I my beloved husband. Nothing ever seems to work out as expected or predicted—it is fate. The Turks say, 'The dog barks. The caravan moves on!' But enough of the past. Tell me, what do you think of my old friend Ali Bey? Do you see much of him?"

"I think he is a fine man—very distinguished—but I don't see much of him. I gather that he is involved in various other business ventures besides the school."

"Yes. The school is really a distraction—a hobby."

"He seemed to think that one day I might be helpful to him in some of his other enterprises," Ed said, missing the side table as he attempted to set down his drink. "Oops, sorry! Ah, it was empty."

"Very interesting, Mr. Wilkie. Well, I would listen very carefully to any proposal he makes to you if I were you. He was very helpful to my late husband in his investments. Thanks to him, I now own several houses on this island."

They sat in silence for a few moments. He noticed that it had grown dark during their conversation and when he glanced at his watch he was surprised to see that it was nearly 8:00.

"Please forgive me, Mrs. Balian, I didn't realize how late it was. I am afraid I have pomop—monopolized the conversation." He rose and for a moment found his head spinning. Recovering quickly he thanked his hostess for a lovely afternoon. She rose stiffly and led him to the door.

"Good evening, Mr. Wilkie. I can't tell you how interesting I found your conversation. *Au revoir."*

At the gate he looked back and saw her still on the porch looking at him. He waved and, turning, tripped over a loose paving stone. As he passed through and into the street, he thought he heard her laughing.

When Ed got back to the school he found the lights out again. He lit a candle from an emergency reserve on a table in the entry hall and found his way to his room. Starleen was looking rather desperate, so he took her out for a breath of fresh air and gave her a bite to eat. Then they settled down by candlelight and he poured himself a glass of *rakı*. He was thinking over the events of the day, and especially his somewhat unusual tea party with Mrs. Balian, when he noticed an invitation card on his writing desk. Mehmet Efendi must have delivered it earlier in the evening. It proved to be an invitation to dinner with Ali Bey to mark the end of the term, two days later. He noticed that his glass was empty and poured himself another *rakı*, spilling a little on the floor. Starleen got up and lapped at the puddle and then stared at him accusingly. Looking at her, his thoughts turned to her namesake in Houston. Who was she with now? He looked at his empty glass. "I can't make a habit of this," he said out loud, as he refilled it.

# 14

The day of Ali Bey's party, Ed happened to meet Brown, who invited him to his place for a "preprandial tightener." As he said, "You probably won't get much to drink at a faculty bunfight like this one—catch Zeynep Hanım wasting money on booze for the poor sodding teachers!"

That evening Ed and Starleen visited Brown in his suite at the Grand Otel and settled in for *rakı* and Stan Kenton. Ed was wearing his "good" flannel suit in readiness for the dinner party and Brown commented on his tie, which was from a riding club he had formerly belonged to ("Good for the posture and for meeting classy girls," his mother had said, though neither had proved to be true.).

"Looks like something the dog's been sick on. No offense, Starleen," commented Brown.

"Too loud?" said Ed, looking down at it doubtfully.

"A little sudden."

"I'll change it before dinner."

"So, how are things at Charles Addams Manor? Any more hot dates with Mrs. Balian?"

"Fine. Not yet. I think I may have offended her by drinking too much and running on about myself."

"Could be. Wait and see. Any more from Ali Bey?"

Ed said no and they moved on to other topics, refilling their glasses from time to time. Ed noticed regretfully that the copy of *A Burning House* that he had given to Brown appeared not to have moved from the spot where Brown had first put it down. He glanced at his watch.

"Yikes! It's nearly 8:00. I must get going to Ali Bey's party."

"Right. Look in afterwards and give me the grim details. I'll be up late."

The dinner was given in a dining room that formed part of Ali Bey's suite, perhaps formerly a salon, or morning room, or smoking room, or billiard room, or some other specialized haunt that the Ottomans provided to separate the two sexes. In any case, it was a large room with flowered wallpaper and good lighting. There was a full bar, despite Brown's predictions, and a buffet supper was laid out on a table against one wall. The guests included members of the teaching staff, as well as several strange men introduced by Ali Bey as his "business associates"; these other guests probably explained the relative luxury of the arrangements.

The party was in full swing when Ed arrived—after stopping off at his apartment to park Starleen and change his tie. The teachers and the strangers formed two separate groups and everyone was talking animatedly. The teachers had clearly taken full advantage of the unexpected alcoholic offerings and were speaking rather louder than they usually would have in Ali Bey's presence. The business associates were smoking cigars and being more restrained with their drinks. Ali Bey stood in the middle of the room, clearly enjoying the rather odd mix he had assembled, while Zeynep Hanım, wearing a cocktail dress in an attractive shade of Nile green, made introductions and chivvied the servants around. At one point she nodded and smiled at Ed, perhaps recalling the recent scene in her office.

Ed found himself standing near a small, dark man with very shiny black hair and an expensive suit and decided it was time to "mingle."

"My name is Wilkie. I teach at the Academy. Are you an educator or a business associate of Ali Bey's?"

"My name is Farouki. No, I am not an educator." He seemed amused by the idea. "I am, as you say, a business associate."

"In Istanbul?"

"No. In Damascus."

He didn't seem inclined to elaborate on this, so Ed moved on and was stopped by Miss Agi, the teacher of social sciences. He noticed that her eyes seemed unnaturally bright that evening and her face was flushed and damp.

"How are you this evening, Ed? Not such a bad party, eh?" She gestured around her expansively, spilling some of her drink on his sleeve.

"So, what will you be teaching next term, Gülsen?" he inquired, discreetly dabbing at his sleeve with a paper napkin.

"Psy--kogoly! Ali Bey has agreed to introduce a unit on psychology for the little urchins. This is my field, you know. I studied in Vienna. Never thought then that I'd end up in a dump like this!" She took another swig of her drink and dribbled some on her chin. Ed began to suspect why it was that she had ended up in a "dump like this."

They were joined by Erol and Lucie, who said, staring around her defiantly, "I, too, do not find this place satisfactory. After one more term I leave."

Ed opened his mouth to reply, but they were invited by Zeynep Hanım to go to the buffet. There was, even more surprisingly, wine with dinner and brandy to follow, and by the end of the evening everyone, including Zeynep Hanım, was looking distinctly elevated. Even the old librarian, Vural, was on hand and enjoying himself. He caught Ed's eye, smiled and, after one false try, placed his finger beside his nose, glanced at the business associates significantly and waggled his eyebrows. He saw Zeynep Hanım looking at him and quickly used the finger to scratch his cheek. At last, Ali Bey thanked them for coming and the teaching staff filed out with thanks and expressions of enthusiastic loyalty. The business associates, however, remained behind.

Ed was now at a crossroads. He had, he felt, already had plenty to drink, but Brown was waiting for him. The smart move was for Ed to give him a call and say that he couldn't join him for drinks. Ed didn't make the smart move.

Brown was in an excellent mood and had also apparently been drinking steadily. Dave Brubeck was on. Ed asked for a brandy.

"So how did it go?" Brown asked, sitting back and looking at Ed a little blearily.

"Not bad at all. Ali Bey broke loose with drinks, wine with dinner, brandy after. Cheers!"

"Cheers! Here's looking up your kilt!"

Brown was, Ed noticed, dressed rather elegantly for an evening at home, with silver gray flannels and a dark blue silk shirt. He continued, "So, was it just your fellow sufferers tonight?"

"No. Ali Bey had invited some of his business associates. A strange group of men. I talked to one of them. A Mr. Farouki."

"From Damascus?"

"Yes, I think so. Do you know him?"

"What? No. Just a guess. Name sounds Syrian, maybe."

Brown said no more, so Ed let it drop. Brown noticed Ed's empty glass and refilled it. Brubeck was finished, so he chose an old Charlie Mingus. They talked in a desultory way, sipping their drinks and occasionally topping them up from the bottle on the side table. Brown began a long monologue about some woman he had been friendly with in Nairobi, but Ed found that he couldn't follow what he was saying. When Ed tried to look at him Brown seemed to swim before his eyes.

"Brown, maybe I should..." Somehow, he couldn't remember what it was he should do, but sat in a kind of trance.

Brown didn't seem to notice, but also sat staring into space. "Well, there it is!" he said suddenly. "I guess we should get a bit of shut-eye, eh?"

Ed found himself moving towards the door, but didn't remember getting up from his chair.

"Thanks, Brown. Must be going—dizzy bay tomorrow!"

Ed's next memory was of walking up the hill from the hotel. The air felt very cold, but he was sweating steadily, and he had to stop frequently to lean against a fence or tree. His heart was pounding and his breath came in short gasps. At one point he lost his bearings and had to make his way back to familiar territory. Finally, he saw the Academy floating before him and gratefully slipped through the front door—after some trouble getting his key into the lock. He tiptoed upstairs and at last got to the refuge of his apartment. Starleen looked up briefly from her cushion, thumped her tail on the floor, and went back to sleep.

He sat down in his armchair with a heavy sigh of relief. Safe home, at last. After a few moments, he dragged himself to his feet and took off his clothes, draping them over a chair, and slipped into his dressing gown. Later he could put on his pajamas. For this effort he thought he would reward himself with perhaps just one last *rakı*.

He awoke some time later, with the *rakı* glass still in his hand. It was empty, though the front of his dressing gown was wet. He had a terrible thirst and a most urgent desire to visit the lavatory—perhaps something from Ali Bey's dinner party was doing its work. As at the Grand Otel, the rooms at the Academy had shared bathrooms, so he stole to his door and peeked out—nothing moving. Gathering his dressing gown around him, he went down the corridor, bumping on the walls in his passage, and found his way to the toilet. Gasping with relief, he tried the door. Locked! He stood baffled for a moment, but the situation grew suddenly more urgent, as molten lava seemed to rage through his bowels. Remembering that there was another toilet in the other wing, he decided to make a run for it. After several false turns, he found sanctuary and locked himself in. Just in time.

# 15

When Ed came to, he found that he was still seated on the toilet. Orienting himself after a few moments, he got up unsteadily, regained the hallway, and was retracing his steps when, as often happened, the electricity went off and the hall was plunged into darkness. He found the wall and felt his way along it for several minutes, but became increasingly disoriented and giddy. At that moment, he heard the sound of a door closing and a woman's high heels coming towards him.

As the steps continued to approach, he reached behind him and encountered a doorknob. Instinctively, he turned the knob and slipped quietly into the room.

As soon as he had closed the door behind him, the lights came back on and he became dimly aware that he was in a furnished sitting room. He was reflecting on how fortunate he had been to avoid an embarrassing encounter, when the steps stopped in front of the door. The woman was going to come in! He spotted a folding screen standing against the wall opposite him and dashed across the room and behind it, nearly knocking it over in his stumbling passage, just as the door opened.

Ed had been lucky in his hideout, since the screen turned out to conceal a shallow alcove used as a sort of wardrobe, with various items of feminine clothing hanging from rods. He nestled among the clothes, trying to control his panting, and thought his heartbeat must be audible throughout the room. In the meantime, the owner of the room was moving around, humming to herself. After a few minutes of this Ed had grown sufficiently calm to notice that by moving over slightly he could peek between two of the sections of the screen and survey at least a part of the room. He did this by inching slowly over, careful to avoid stepping on the shoes that were neatly lined up on the floor, and eventually placed an eye to the crack. The woman was just out of range of his gaze, but he could hear her continuing to move around. Some dishes clattered, a chair creaked as she sat down for a moment. Then she got up and moved across the room and into his line of vision: Zeynep Hanım!

With an increasing sense of horror, Ed saw her walk to the door—she was now in her stocking feet—lock it, and bring the key back with her, passing by the screen and out of sight again. Her movements were leisured as she passed and repassed, fussing with books and papers, emptying an ashtray, and opening the window wide to let in the brisk night air. Then she stopped moving around and he strained to hear what she was doing. She backed again into view and he saw that she was starting to undress. He stood frozen as she quickly removed her dress—the same one that she had worn at the party—pulling it over her head with a silken rustle and laying it over a chair. She stood revealed in a kind of corset, which he remembered that Star had called a "merry widow" (though, as Ed couldn't help reflecting, on Star's slim body the garment's purpose was purely erotic, whereas with Zeynep Hanım its function was clearly structural). She sat down on a chair, unfastened her garters, and rolled down her stockings. Then she rose, struggled briefly with the corset's complex system of closures, and all at once it fell to the floor. Ed was surprised to see how round and pillowy her body was, unrestrained by rubber and wire.

He had only a moment for these reflections before she moved away and into an adjoining room, which proved to be the bathroom—no hall toilets for Zeynep Hanım, he thought bitterly. He heard a toilet flush, and the sound of gargling, and after another few minutes she moved across the room, this time wearing a remarkably feminine flame-colored silk nightdress, with her long dark hair down her back. There seemed to be something puzzling about her expression, until he realized that she must have left her teeth in the bathroom.

She turned out the light and he heard her move into her bedroom, leaving the door to the sitting room open, apparently to take advantage of the cool breeze from the window. The bed springs creaked and the light from the bedroom went off.

He was now well and truly trapped, unable to move a muscle for fear that she would hear him in the now complete silence. Was she an insomniac, a light sleeper, or could he hope that she would fall quickly into a heavy slumber?

Now that the immediate crisis was over, he began to realize how cramped he was and his muscles ached with standing still so long. The dust in the wardrobe was starting to irritate his nose and he worried that he would suddenly have an uncontrollable urge to sneeze. He could hear the night sounds coming through the window, seagulls settling themselves on the roof, the rustle of the wisteria against the side of the house, a dog barking in the distance. Then, suddenly, the best sound of all, the sound of snoring from the next room. Not tentative, fitful snoring, but full-bodied, serious snoring.

He was still, however, not home and dry. The door, he knew, was locked and the key removed, so that means of escape was closed to him; and obviously he could not explore for the key in a darkened room with a sleeping woman only a few steps away. The only solution seemed to be the window. He couldn't recall what sort of a drop it would be to the ground, but he thought that he might be able to climb down the vines, or perhaps there was a ledge that he could work his way around the house on. Whatever lay before him, however, was obviously more desirable than remaining where he was for the night, only to be discovered in the cold light of morning.

He began inching his way softly from behind the screen, again remembering to avoid kicking the shoes lined up on the floor. Fortunately, moonlight showed through the window, bathing the room in a dim light, so he was able to keep clear of any disastrous encounters with lurking pieces of furniture. There was also a thick oriental carpet on the floor, so the dry old floorboards didn't squeak as he moved stealthily over them

Everything seemed to be working in his favor, if only the window exit did not involve dropping himself into the darkness. He now moved more quickly towards his goal, passing the open bedroom door, and reached the window. He started to put his head out to survey the situation, when a voice said, "I thought you'd never make up your mind to come to me. Hurry up and come to bed!"

Ed found himself literally incapable of thought, and stood stock still with his hand on the windowsill.

The voice continued, "Stop standing there! You've kept me waiting long enough!"

Ed moved as in a dream. Did she know that he had been in the room all along, or did she think that he had just arrived? He staggered into the bedroom and found his way to the side of the bed, stubbing his toe on a chair. He stood there indecisively.

Now she said, in a much softer voice, "There, there, dear, I didn't mean to sound cross. I was just lonely for you."

With horror he felt her put out her hand and reach up under his dressing gown. The fingers grasped him and then suddenly her hand froze. He gulped and whispered, "I'm terribly sorry, Zeynep Hanım. I didn't..."

She seemed to reflect for a moment—not having as yet removed her hand—and then replied, "Get in, Mr. Wilkie. You are frozen stiff. I'll warm you up," pulling aside the blanket as she spoke.

Ed didn't fully remember the events of the night, except that they were many and varied, and that after a particularly strenuous effort he actually rolled out of bed and was helped back in by an hysterically giggling Zeynep Hanım. A few minutes later, there was a tapping on the door. She motioned him to keep quiet and went to the door, then came back laughing under her breath.

"My maid wanted to know if anything was wrong. I said that I had knocked over a chair."

At one point he left her to go to the toilet. When he turned on the light in the bathroom, he was startled to see, in the eerie fluorescent glow, her teeth smiling at him, Cheshire cat-like, as they floated in their bowl of light blue glass. Without them her kisses were very soft and deep.

The next morning Ed was awakened very early by Zeynep Hanım shaking him. "Mr. Wilkie, you must get back to your own room. The servants will be stirring shortly."

He noticed that she had replaced her teeth and put her nightdress back on. Her hair hung down loose on either side of her face. She could feel him start to get excited again, but said, "No. That's enough for now. Get going!"

Obediently, he crept out of bed. He went to the door, looked furtively each direction, and scurried away to his own room, where he spent the rest of the morning recovering and reflecting: *"For now?"*

Despite Zeynep Hanım's parting words, there was no recurrence of their romantic encounter. She treated Ed with her usual rather distant courtesy, and he didn't feel bold enough to go tapping on her door at night without some sort of encouragement.

# 16

Several days later Ed was daydreaming in his sitting room, with Starleen's head on his knee, when Kemal knocked and came in.

"Greetings, my dear Ed. I hope you are now all recovered from the big night!" Ed started guiltily. "Ali Bey gave a nice party, no?"

"Very nice. I enjoyed the night thoroughly," Ed agreed.

"Wonderful. I have come to you because I thought you might find it amusing to attend this evening a little performance—a sort of circus—on another of the islands. No, not a circus, a theatrical performance, al fresco."

"Why not? But what is it exactly? A play?"

"Exactly so! A little theatrical troupe. It performs in the open air around Istanbul. Mostly Turkish plays, but tonight the divine Shakespeare! *Othello!*"

"*Othello!* In English?"

"Ha! No, of course not. Who would understand but us? In Turkish. It is called *Arap'ın Intikamı*—the black man's revenge."

This seemed promising, so Ed agreed to experience this rare cultural treat. The plan was to go over to the other island for an early dinner and proceed to the "circus."

When they arrived at the other island Kemal took him to a favorite restaurant of his located on the promenade by the ferry landing. The owner greeted Kemal warmly and they ordered *rakı* while waiting to be shown the *mezes*. "*Şerefinize!*" said Kemal, raising his glass, "Ah! Everett Bey. Lily Hanım!"

Ed followed his gaze and saw a middle-aged couple waving from the promenade. They came over and Kemal introduced them:

"This is Everett and Lily Blum!" said Kemal enthusiastically. "Countrymen of yours! Americans! This is my friend Ed Wilkie, who teaches at the Academy." They sat down at the table and ordered *rakı*. The Blums were tall, tan, and relaxed-looking. Everett had gray hair and was wearing dark glasses. He had on a dark blue shirt buttoned at the throat and a tweed jacket, and as he said "How do you do?" in a soft Southern California accent, there was a rich aroma of *rakı*, which may have partly explained his air of calm detachment. Lily was a good-looking, slim woman with long, dark hair; she was dressed in a soft woolen dress that reached her ankles and a padded jacket.

"Are you going to the performance after dinner, Mr. Wilkie—Ed?" asked Lily. Her accent was also West Coast, but somehow not the same as her husband's. He later learned that she was a San Franciscan. She had a steady gaze and a friendly, encouraging smile. He said that he and Kemal would be going.

"So are we. What brings you to the islands? How did you happen to join Kemal's school? Tell all."

Over more *rakıs* he told his story and when he finished, Everett, who had seemed rather abstracted during the recital, looked up and said, "Well, the wolves howl and the caravan moves on!"

"The dog barks—*İt ürür...*" Lily corrected, "though I'm not sure it's quite apt."

"The Blums were in the foreign service," Kemal explained, "and when they retired they moved to this island. They teach English language at one of the universities now. And they have a beautiful house. An old Greek house."

Ed also learned that they loved terriers and had owned several wire-haired fox terriers.

"We'll have to meet Starleen!" said Lily enthusiastically. Everett and Ed talked about Southern California. Both of them had grown up in Los Angeles and they had many memories in common.

After dinner they went up the hill and finally reached a wide, flat, empty area where the performance was going to take place. Everett pointed out their house, farther up the hill, a pretty Greek house, painted a reddish-brown and set in a terraced garden.

"American tax dollars at work!" he said with a satisfied smile. Ed had the feeling that he said this often, and liked saying it.

Despite the chilly evening, the performance was surprisingly well attended, though the arrangements were of the simplest. A wagon was drawn up on the vacant lot and a horse was tethered nearby, cropping the grass. A natural grassy slope on one side provided amphitheater-like casual seating for the spectators. Ed and his friends sat on a blanket provided by Lily. The troupe consisted of five people, one of whom doubled as a rope dancer to attract and entertain the crowd before the performance. He also provided musical interludes on a concertina between scenes. The actor playing Othello was, in fact, very dark-complexioned, and Kemal explained that he was an "Arab-Turk" from the East. Desdemona was a blonde, a Greek girl from Izmir.

Ed was able to follow the action, having refreshed his memory in the Academy library. It was spirited and highly dramatic, with much posturing and striding back and forth by the male actors, and much wringing of hands and batting of eyes by the women. Lily listened intently, moving her lips with the actors' recitations:

*"Sana bir mendil vermiştim ben. Sen gidip bir yüzbaşıya verdin o mendili, kahpe kadın!"*

*"Ve sen ne diyorsun? Ben kimseye mendil falan vermedim."*

She looked puzzled. "It doesn't seem quite right. A very free translation." Later, she told Ed, she had mentioned this to a writer friend on the island, who said that, in fact, the words had been changed extemporaneously by the actor playing Othello, who thought that the Greek girl, Despina, was being unfaithful to him with a naval officer.

There was scattered applause and the actors took their single curtain call. Their party did its best to swell the sound, cupping their palms as Lily showed them to create more volume. "Very useful if you're attending your child's school play," she explained. During the applause, Ed glanced over to the edge of the audience and saw Brown. Ed tried to catch his eye, but he didn't see him and shortly afterwards mixed in with the departing crowd. Ed reflected that he wouldn't have thought that Brown was a devotee of the Elizabethan theater.

The Blums asked them to have a drink at their house, but they had to catch the last ferry for their own island. "We'll consider it a rain check," said Everett.

# 17

The semester break was coming to an end and Ed was starting to prepare his new classes. Having survived one term, he was in fact looking forward to the next one. The boys seemed especially to like their lessons on American literature, so he was selecting readings for them. He was in the library looking at some reference books when Mehmet Efendi came in and poked him in the arm. *"Zeynep Hanım seni bekliyor!"*

Could this be it, he wondered? He went to her office, knocked at the door and entered hopefully. She was seated at her desk, however, and he could sense from her attitude that this was to be a business meeting.

"Mr. Wilkie, *merhaba*. Please be seated."

He sat down and waited to hear what she had to say.

"Mr. Wilkie, as you know, we provide living accommodation at the school for bachelors, but we can also make available a housing allowance for those who would prefer to live in private residence on the island. My old acquaintance Mrs. Balian tells me that she has a small, furnished house that she is prepared to rent to a member of our staff. I think you have met Mrs. Balian?"

"Yes, indeed, Zeynep Hanım. I..."

"Good. The Academy would be willing to pay the rent on this residence for you, if you think you would be more comfortable in your own place."

"That is very kind of you. I think I..."

"Frankly, I think it might be best." For the first time, she seemed rather embarrassed, and glanced down at the surface of her desk.

"If you think so, Zeynep Hanım, I..."

"Then it is settled." She looked relieved. "I think it is for the best."

As Ed departed she pressed his hand and looked at him for a moment, as if she would say something more. She seemed, however, to change her mind and gave him a smile of dismissal.

Ed called on Mrs. Balian, who confirmed the arrangements. The house was, indeed, small: a bedroom, sitting room, kitchen, bathroom, and storage area. It had, however, a nice little garden with a grape arbor to sit under in the afternoons. "One additional good feature," Mrs. Balian pointed out, "is that there is a *sarnıç*— its own reservoir, under the floor. It catches the rainwater that runs down the spouts from the roof. You can pump it up and use it in your garden."

Ed and Starleen moved in without much ceremony. He had acquired nothing except his rug from Mr. Agopian, so his possessions were quickly stored away. The furniture was rather old and shabby, but he found it quite comfortable. There was even a little bit of a sea view—what Southern California realtors call a "filtered view"—but enough to remind him that he was an islander.

After the first sense of rejection at having been pushed out of his rooms at the Academy, Ed began to feel the advantage of his new situation. The little house was cozy, with its peeling wooden walls and its roof of pink tiles, and the garden, though small, was full of flowers and herbs. The evenings under the grape arbor, listening to the seagulls and the distant clip-clop of the horse carriages, were very restful after a day matching wits with the boys. A few days later, a young woman presented herself at his door and handed a folded piece of paper to him, a note from Zeynep Hanım:

*Mr. Wilkie,*

*I hope you are comfortable in your new home. In a bachelor establishment you will probably need someone to clean house for you. Balkiz is a very reliable person whom I can recommend without reservation. I suggest that you engage her for two or three days a week to clean and wash, and perhaps prepare some meals for you. This is up to you, of course, but I think you would find it convenient. She speaks a little English.*

The note also mentioned a daily rate, which seemed reasonable and afford-able. Balkiz stood waiting, looking at Ed expectantly as he read Zeynep Hanım's note. When he had finished he said, "Please come in. Would you like to work for me?"

*"Evet.* Yes, *efendim."* She was a small woman, plump and merry-looking, dressed the Anatolian way, with kerchief and wide trousers.

At this point he seemed to be at a loss as to what to say next. In California, his mother had dealt with the undocumented Mexican girls who came to clean their apartment and he had only a dim idea of what her duties should be.

"So, you will come three days each week?"

"Yes, *efendim.* Clean, wash, cook."

"OK. I mean, *evet.* Start today?"

OK, *efendim."*

And the deal was done.

Balkiz was a hard worker and, after some initial reservations, came to be good friends with Starleen, who supervised all her activities. She came and went on an irregular schedule—though Ed had the impression that he got more than the three days worth of work each week—and prepared excellent dinners, which she left for him. Sometimes, when Ed was at home while she was working, they had halting conversations. He learned that she had an "old husband" and an only child, a boy, whom she was very proud of.

"*Harika!* A miracle!" she said, rather obscurely, showing Ed her son's picture. "Very handsome, no? Very smart. He will go to university. Be a teacher, like you!"

When she was sixteen, she had come to Istanbul from Eskişehir, in central Anatolia, to marry and had never returned to her old home. Ed enjoyed her lively, smiling manner and her active bustle about the house.

Ed decided to give a small housewarming party several weeks after he moved into his new house and Balkiz prepared a table of meze for his guests: "Good Turkish food. Not American fast food!" she pointed out. Ed invited several members of the staff: Kemal, Erol, Lucie, Gülsen, the old librarian, Vural Bey, and several others including, of course, Brown. Zeynep Hanım declined.

The party was fairly subdued, but Ed had a feeling as he showed his guests around that he had become a solid citizen, a householder. Brown accused him of being "a real boor-jo." Gülsen Agi recounted again her plans to introduce her pupils to the mysteries of Freudian psychology—dribbling her glass of *rakı* on his new carpet as she did so. Starleen played hostess, passing among the guests, getting underfoot, cadging snacks, and graciously accepting pats. Lucie, who was in one of her moods of exhilaration, aided by plentiful lashings of *rakı*, had been talking animatedly to Brown; he seemed definitely to have made progress with her. Now she came over to where Ed was standing with Starleen and made over her extravagantly.

"It makes me so sad, Ed, when I see your dog. I love dogs!" She looked at him owlishly. "My own doggie died last year. An old friend—ten years together! He went everywhere with me, slept on my bed at night. Here, I will show you his picture!" She handed Ed her glass to hold, while she found her purse and pawed through it. "See, here he is," she said, taking out a little folding picture holder and opening it to show a color snapshot of a black and white French bulldog sitting on a blue armchair. "This is Pompom," she said, looking at Ed with a slightly out-of-focus tragic expression. "Such a beautiful, so intelligent a dog." She gave the picture a kiss. "I always carry his photograph with me."

"That is very touching, Lucie."

"I knew you would understand, Ed. You are so sympathetic a man." She took a last look at her picture and returned it to her purse, then retrieved her drink and had a long pull. Her eye fell on Vural Bey, the old librarian, who was standing by himself on the other side of the room. "That old man is getting on my nerves," she said. "He has been following me around spying on me. One day in his library he made wild accusations. He is mad, I think."

Hoping to introduce a more pleasant note Ed said, "So, Lucie, have you bought any new rugs lately? I must say, I'm hooked."

"Hooked?" She stared at him for a moment, her mouth slightly ajar, and then said, "No. I am tired of that game." After this she seemed to lose interest in the topic. "Where is Erol? Ah, there he is. I must go and speak to him, and then I must go. Thank you very much, Ed. I am glad that we exchanged our thoughts about our doggies."

"Good night, Lucie. Thanks for coming."

Vural Bey, who had been watching them closely, shuffled over to Ed, tripping over the edge of the carpet as he came. He took him by the sleeve, listing forward, and fixed him with his eyes. "I saw you talking with that French woman. I have new information about her. She is a drug fiend! I heard it all." He looked around with exaggerated caution. "We will speak later."

At the end of the evening, when the last farewells were completed, Balkiz cleared away the debris and Ed opened the windows to let out the cigarette smoke and *rakı* fumes. He had invited Brown to stay on, but he had seemed uncharacteristically out of sorts and said he would push on. The fresh air revived Ed somewhat and he decided to pour one last rakı to drink while Balkiz finished cleaning up. He had poured himself a second drink when she came in to see if there was anything else to do. As she stood there flushed and cheerful, having enjoyed the party as much as the guests, he found her suddenly very attractive.

"Will you join me for a drink, Balkiz? To celebrate our successful party." She seemed startled and then looked more closely at him.

"OK, *efendim.*"

He poured her a light *rakı* and she sat down on the edge of a chair opposite him. *"Şerefinize, Balkiz!"*

*"Şerefinize, efendim!"*

Though they said little, there was somehow a sense of expectation. At last Ed said, "Why don't you come over here and sit next to me?"

She looked down for a moment and then got up and came over. She stood in front of him where he sat on the sofa and he put his arms around her, burying his face in her soft stomach. He felt her hands come around the back of his head, pressing him to her. Then she stepped back, turned out the light and sat down on the sofa with him. They kissed and the tension went out of her.

"At last!" she sighed.

"At last?" he asked.

"Yes. Zeynep Hanım said you would."

His relationship with Balkiz was to be a happy one. While shy at first, and embarrassed by her old-fashioned cotton underwear, she soon grew confident with him and became a most enthusiastic lover, confessing to him that her husband was "too old" and seldom came near her. Since she had to return to her house in the evenings, Ed began coming home early in the afternoon on the days she worked for him. As soon as he came in the door she would rush over to him, give him a hug, and lead the way to the little bedroom. He noticed that she had given up her cotton underclothes and started wearing more up-to-date nylon panties and bras. Ed said that he hoped her husband wouldn't become suspicious because of these innovations, but she smiled shyly and said, "No. He doesn't see. Just for you!"

The morning after his party, Ed thought that he would look in to see Vural Bey, the old librarian. He had seemed a little unsteady when he left, and Ed wanted to be sure that he was all right. He left home early, so that he could visit the library before his first class, and walked quickly to the Academy and upstairs to the former ballroom where the library was located. There were few people around, but he said hello to Mehmet Efendi, on his early morning rounds, and greeted a few students on their way to the canteen for breakfast. When he got to the library, the door was open and the lights were on. The old boy seems to have gotten a jump on the day, he thought. He entered and went to the office, but it was empty, though the light there was also on. The morning sun shone through the jars of pickles and made a colorful reflection on the opposite wall. Perhaps he was reshelving books in the stacks. He went over to the bookshelves, lined up in columns against the wall.

"Vural! It's me, Ed. Are you there?"

No reply. He began moving along the line of stacks to see if he was there. At the last line of shelves Ed found him. He was lying on the floor in a heap, his head twisted at a terrible angle, and his eyes open and staring. Beside him there was an overturned stepladder, the one that he used when he was shelving books.

Ed ran over to him, reached down and touched his face. It was cold and stiff, like a piece of marble. He was certainly dead, and had been for some time. Ed rose and stood for a moment, looking at the old man. Had he come here after the party? Perhaps decided to do some reshelving and, being unsteady with drink, fallen to his death from the ladder? Ed went quickly to Zeynep Hanım's office and told her what he had found. She came back with him and, after assuring herself that he was indeed dead, called the police. The police, when they came, were not overly concerned by the old man's death.

"Maybe a heart attack, maybe just drunk. Happens all the time."

Zeynep Hanım also seemed to take it in her stride. "Perhaps it is just as well. He couldn't have stayed on here much longer."

Vural Bey's funeral was conducted at the little mosque on the island. Most of the teachers from the Academy attended and Ali Bey said a few words about the old man's long and faithful service to the school. There seemed to be no one from his family, but there were three old men whom he used to play bezique with in a little tea garden near the school. The coffin was a plain, dark-green plywood box. Ed stood aside as the prayers were said; then the coffin was loaded onto a horse-drawn hearse and, led by Ali Bey, they followed it in a straggling procession up the hill to the graveyard. They passed the Christian cemetery, with its Greek-lettered tombs, and then into the Muslim cemetery, where the older gravestones were topped with carved representations of turbans or fezes for men and flowers for women. The hole had been freshly dug beneath a cypress tree and the burial was quickly done. The teachers didn't linger, but soon moved through the gates, lighting cigarettes and talking among themselves. The three old men stayed for a few minutes, not seeming to know what they should do next, and then finally shook hands with Ed and went away also. Ed stood for a while, thinking about his friend, who had lived so long and seen so much, but had ended up with so little. Perhaps Zeynep Hanım was right. Maybe it was just as well that it had ended quickly for him in his library, and not lying on a cot in the public ward of a hospital.

"Well," thought Ed, "I'll miss him."

# 18

It was only two days before the new term was to begin when Ed met Zeynep Hanım in the hallway near her office and she asked him to come in. He followed her and after they were seated she said, "Well, Mr. Wilkie, I hope you are happy with your house."

"Oh yes. Very."

"And Balkiz. I hope she is satisfactory in every way. As I wrote you, I thought she would be a useful addition to a bachelor establishment." Her lips curved slightly and she looked up at him through her eyelashes.

"Yes, Zeynep Hanım. She is a jewel."

Having disposed of this, she moved on. "My reason for asking you in was that we have an emergency, and I am hoping that you can help us with it. You know Mlle Leblanc, of course?"

"Yes."

"Well, she has most unaccountably and unprofessionally departed from the school, just as the new term is about to begin."

Ed was surprised. "I know that she wasn't entirely happy here, but I thought that she intended to finish out the year."

"So did we all! However, she seems to have simply left, without a word to anyone, leaving me to find a French teacher on the shortest notice."

"Did she mention anything to Erol Bey? I believe that they were..."

"He is as surprised as everyone else. It was he, in fact, who told me that she had gone. In any case, I am searching for a substitute for her, but will certainly not be able to find someone before the term begins. I believe that you speak French—from your resume.

"Well, I studied French in college and have traveled in France, but I don't..."

"Good! Then you can fill in for a few days or weeks, until we are suited with a replacement. Kemal Bey will help cover some of your English classes. You and he can work that out between you." With a sigh and a smile of dismissal, she concluded, "Well, that's settled. I appreciate this, Mr. Wilkie."

Kemal and Ed worked out a schedule allowing Ed to take on the first and second year French classes while Kemal covered several of Ed's English lessons. The first-year students worked from a little textbook called *Pas à Pas* and he was able to keep a few pages ahead of them without much problem. In the second year, however, the students were reading works of literature from an anthology, and they were able to catch Ed out repeatedly, particularly in his spoken French—where he inevitably used the wrong gender or lost control of the grammar in mid-sentence—shrieking with laughter as Monsieur Wilkie again messed up. Ed took refuge in having the boys memorize long passages of poetry, which he had them recite in class. They were good at memorizing and the recitations ate up class time effectively:

"OK, Uğur, let's hear your passage."

"Yes, sir. It is a nice poem by the famous French poet La Fontaine called 'Le Chêne et le Roseau.' La Fontaine was born in..."

"Don't bother with that. We all read the introduction. Recite."

*Le Chêne un jour dit au Roseau*
*« Vouz avez bien sujet d'accuser la Nature;*
*Un Roitelet pour vous est un pesant fardeau.*
*Le moindre vent qui d'aventure*
*Fait rider la face de l'eau*
*Vous oblige a baisser la tete…*

"What...yes. Go on." Ed had been surreptitiously looking over the next selection.

"Sir, do we really believe that the tree talks to the reed?"

"Well, yes. I mean, no. Not really. It's like..."

*"The Wizard of Oz, sir?"*

"The Wizard...?"

"Yes, sir. In *The Wizard of Oz* a tree talks to Dorothy. And then throws apples at her."

"Look. This is quite different..."

"We saw it at the cinema on Büyükada last Saturday."

"Well, this isn't like that! This is a fable. It's symbolic."

They exchanged glances: *Symbolism again!*

"And, sir. Why does he kiss his head?"

Ed started. Kiss his head? Had he missed something? He looked frantically at the text.

"Yes, sir, *'baiser la tete.'* It's right there!"

"What? What? No, *baisser,* to bow—not *baiser.* Now go on with your recitation."

Ed sometimes found himself wondering if the boys might be taking liberties with him. Was it possible, behind those innocent faces?

Ed asked Erol Demiray about Lucie's departure and he said that they had, in fact, had a more than usually stormy falling-out, but that he also was surprised that she would have left without a word, or even a note. He seemed quite upset and depressed, but asked Ed not to say anything to Zeynep Hanım about his fight with Lucie, as she would probably hold him responsible for her having decamped.

Later, Ed saw Mehmet Efendi carrying out a carton of odds and ends that Lucie had left behind in her room. He set the box down in the front hall and Ed saw an old pair of tennis shoes, a broken travel clock, a sweater with a hole in the front, some ungraded student themes. Then, in the midst of the jumble, he noticed the little folding picture holder that she had taken out of her purse to show him the night of his housewarming party. He reached down and took it out of the box and opened it. There was the picture of Pompom, her French bulldog, goggling at the camera from his blue armchair—the picture that she said she always carried with her. Was it possible that she could have forgotten it? Something that had seemed so precious to her? Or, in her quixotic way, could she have suddenly decided to discard it? Then, he found himself wondering if, by any chance, there could be any connection between the death of the old librarian and the sudden departure of Lucie. He had said that she was a drug fiend. Was it just his usual obsessive talk about the new women on the faculty, or could there have been more to it? There seemed to be so many unanswered questions. Ed put the picture of Pompom in his pocket with the vague thought that she might want it back one day.

Happily, Ed's role as a French teacher didn't last as long as he had feared that it would. At the end of several weeks, Zeynep Hanım called him to her office to meet a young woman who would be taking over the French program. She was an attractive woman in her late twenties, with a round face, rather prominent green eyes, light brown hair cut in a pageboy style, and a pleasingly ripe mouth. She was of medium height, with a slim, but solidly built body and good legs, quietly dressed in a tailored suit and low pumps. When he entered the room she was standing stiffly and, with her lips compressed slightly, nodding gravely as Zeynep Hanım spoke to her.

Zeynep Hanım turned to Ed and said, "Let me present you to Elif Ekmekçi. Elif Hanım, Mr. Wilkie."

Elif Hanım looked at him and smiled. The ripe mouth turned up at the corners, where two dimples appeared, and the green eyes widened: This woman had *It!* Ed knew this because his mother had, as a girl, been devoted to the works of Elinor Glyn, and they had discussed the quality many times.

"I can't tell you how happy I am to see you, Elif Hanım," Ed said with a slight gulp.

"How so, Mr. Wilkie?" she said, looking rather startled.

He suddenly grew confused. "I have been teaching your classes and I...that is, of course, I am happy to meet you in any case..."

"We quite understand, Mr. Wilkie," broke in Zeynep Hanım. "Elif Hanım has recently completed her *doctorat de l'université* at the University of Dijon and was able to come to us at short notice. Her father, Ömer Pasha—General Ekmekçi—is an old friend of Ali Bey's. Would you be so kind as to fill her in on her duties—tell her what you have been doing with her pupils, show her the classrooms, introduce her to some of the staff?"

"I'd be delighted. Are you free now, Elif Hanım?"

"Yes, of course. Good-bye, Zeynep Hanım. And thank you."

As he led her along the corridor, he noticed how gracefully she moved. Her voice was feminine, very clear and melodic. Ed had visited Dijon once with his mother, and remembered only a rather depressing gray city and a dull museum, in which the highlight was a group of small statues, medieval hooded figures called Les Pleurants. Obedient to the guidebook's suggestion, his mother had used the mirror of her compact so that they could look at the faces of the bowed heads. From their expressions, they appeared to be just as tired of Dijon as he was.

"We ate one evening, I recall, at quite a good restaurant," he was telling Elif. "Something like Pré aux Clercs..."

"...et Trois Faisans. Yes, a very famous restaurant," she smiled, "but much too expensive for a poor student from Turkey. I mostly ate in the student commons, or in a little cafe, or sometimes cooked on a hotplate in my room."

"Are you from Istanbul? How do you happen to have such good English?"

"So many questions at once," she laughed. "Yes, I am an *Istanbullu*. I live with my parents in Beyoğlu. I went to Robert College—a high school, you would call it—where I studied in English. But I studied French at Istanbul University."

"And Dijon?"

"I got a fellowship through the Alliance Française and studied three years for my doctorate. Just a *doctorat de l'université*. Not a *doctorat d'etat*," she said, looking at him earnestly. "I wrote my thesis on Julien Green."

"Ah yes! Green!" *Who?*

As she continued talking Ed was thinking, This is a remarkably attractive woman. I wonder if she is involved with anyone? He showed her the classrooms, took her to the library, and, not wanting to let go of her for the moment, walked her through the garden. Finally, he suggested that she might care to join him for a drink somewhere. She looked pleased by the suggestion but said that she would have to catch the next ferry for Istanbul, as her parents were expecting her. They agreed that they would have a drink another time to celebrate her joining the faculty.

Over the next two weeks Ed saw a lot of Elif and continued to be extremely attracted to her. She was very serious and earnest about her work, and about life in general. A good, well-brought-up girl, who had always loved and respected her parents and done as they thought best, she frequently quoted their good advice, particularly that of her father, the general. Most of it seemed to Ed like what Brown would have called "a load of old cobblers," but he affected to find it illuminating. She had been a good, conscientious student, which had gained her a fellowship—but to Dijon, not Paris. Ed found her genuinely, and somewhat intimidatingly, sincere and principled, but with a delightful playfulness and sense of humor. She had an unexpectedly loud laugh, which would erupt and overcome her when something amused her. It seemed to Ed that she seemed also to like him and to enjoy his company, but clearly thought he was not really serious enough about his career and had wasted too much of his life on idle pursuits. "A man without a career is only half a man," she quoted that old rogue, her father. Ed would like to have taken her out, but she returned each evening to Istanbul, so the best he could do was an occasional coffee together. Once she read his fortune in the coffee grounds of the little cup. She was very serious about it, wrinkling her eyebrows and pursing her lips, her hair falling over her eyes as she looked deeply into the cup and concentrated on the shapes formed by the grounds. He didn't remember his fortune.

# 19

Ed was in the library reading over a set of senior themes on "Bartleby, the Scrivener," and had arrived at the following passage: "...this is a reaction formation, which is a type of ego defense mechanism. Bartleby gets this mechanism unconsciously in order to keep in psychological being as a whole and also in order not to feel any anxiety in the social environment. Thus, he ends up with living in a world of his own, without caring for any other social norm or social context." Gülsen Agi's unit on psychology seemed to be bearing fruit. But what could this mean? Did it mean anything? Was it a joke? He was puzzling this over when Elif came in.

"Ah, Ed, I was looking for you. In class today there was some confusion in our lesson on La Fontaine. The boys said that you told them that La Fontaine had gotten his ideas from *The Wizard of Oz*. I felt sure that..."

"No, not at all. The boys just got mixed up and...anyway, look at this." He showed the "Bartleby" essay to her:

*"Critique psychanalytique*. Very popular today in France. I am not, however, so familiar with this story, 'Bartleby.' Maybe you should ask Gülsen," she concluded.

"Perhaps you're right. I'll do that." Then he went on to ask if she had time to have that long-delayed drink with him. "We could have it at my house. I would like to show you my garden."

She thought for a moment. Doubtless the general would not approve of an unchaperoned visit to an unmarried gentleman's house. However, she said, "Very well. Only I can't stay long. I have to get back to Istanbul."

They walked together to Ed's house. He took a roundabout route, both in order to prolong their tete-à-tete and to show her some of his favorite island sights. When they arrived, she was overjoyed by the little garden. Ed had trained honeysuckle up one wall and planted mimosa and lavender; he had also found a little marble basin, which he had placed near the grape arbor and filled with water. He suggested that they have their drinks in the garden, both because the setting was nice and because he thought she would feel more at ease outdoors. She agreed and Ed left her sitting on the bench, saying that he would return in a moment; he had laid up a bottle of vermouth and some Italian cookies against this day and planned to prepare an elegant little aperitif tray. He also took a copy of A Burning House from his bookshelf. Then he went directly to the kitchen and was reaching up to a cupboard, when he felt arms around his waist and his neck being nibbled: Balkiz!

He turned and she reached up and gave him a kiss on the mouth, while at the same time playfully pulling down the zipper of his fly. "I waited for you, *canım...*," she started to say. Ed was just trying to adjust to this new development when he heard behind him: "Ed, I thought you might need some help. Oh!"

Balkiz hopped back from Ed and said, "Shall I bring the things, *efendim?"*

Recovering rapidly, he said, "Yes, please do. We'll be in the garden."

Elif and Ed returned in silence. Following her down the steps he had the presence of mind to zip his fly up again. She sat stiffly on the bench, while Balkiz served the drinks.

"*Merhaba, efendim, hoş geldiniz.* Buyrun," said Balkiz, offering the tray of snacks to Elif.

"*Hoş bulduk.* Thank you," she replied.

After Balkiz left, Ed said, "I hope you don't think..."

"Please don't concern yourself. Your life is your own business," she replied, but he could see that she was upset. They continued to talk, but she finished her drink quickly and said that she would have to go. He offered to accompany her to the landing, but she said no. When they shook hands good-bye, he felt sure that it was over between them.

When Ed went back to the house, Balkiz was in tears.

"I am so sorry, *canım.* I hope I have not spoiled things with the lady."

"Don't worry, Balkiz," he reassured her. "She wasn't a special lady. Just a teacher from the school."

She looked pleadingly at him, as though seeking further proof that he didn't blame her. He kissed her and then led her to the little bedroom.

The next day Ed received a letter from his old teacher, Ray Collins. Ray apologized for the long delay in replying, but said that he had been on holiday in Hawaii and had just returned to find Ed's letter waiting for him. After some introductory paragraphs, he got down to Ed's question:

*As you probably have guessed, Ali and I were both involved in intelligence work, he for his government, I for ours. When I got out of that business, I decided to take up teaching—to get away from all that and do something completely different. Ali also left his official job, but continued as an independent dealer in information, using the excellent networks that he had established in his earlier career. For years he was very successful in this line and doubtless made a lot of money at it, but he must have retired long ago from all that. Ali is a very good friend and a serious and trustworthy person. If he invites you to join him in his business ventures, I think you should consider it.*

So, what was he to think? Was Ali Bey only in business, or was he still ply-ing his former trade? Who were the "business associates" Ed had met at his party?

Ed and Elif continued to see each other at the Academy, but it was clear that the relationship had changed as a result of the incident with Balkiz. Ed worked hard to repair the breach between them, but was beginning to wonder if it was a mistake to take so much trouble over so puritanical and inflexible a woman.

Meanwhile, Brown had gotten over whatever it was that had been bothering him and they continued as before. Ed told Brown about Balkiz, and Brown gave it as his opinion that Ed had fallen into a good thing: a simple, loving woman, who gave herself without reservations and with no strings attached.

"You've got the perfect setup, old boy! No complications! Just keep it that way!" he advised, drinking his *rakı* with a flourish.

"Right you are, Brown," said Ed, raising his glass. " No complications!"

# 20

Mrs. Balian's voice came over the wire. "Mr. Wilkie, I hope all is going well in your house."

"Oh yes. Thank you. I love it. I have even given a housewarming party," said Ed, guiltily thinking that he probably should have invited her.

"Good. There is something I would like to discuss with you. Do you think you could join me for dinner one evening?"

"With pleasure, Mrs. Balian."

"Say, tomorrow evening at 8:00?"

He thanked her and she rang off. He wondered off and on during the next day what she might want to discuss with him. Maybe something about the house.

The next evening Ed again put on his "good" suit and a quiet tie and went off to Yeni Hamam Street. Mrs. Balian's manner as she greeted him seemed slightly strained and he couldn't account for it, since she had seemed quite friendly on the telephone. As on the day of their tea party, she was somewhat formally dressed in a silk dress with a floral pattern. She wore a string of what looked like very good pearls and an emerald and diamond ring. Again, he recognized the scent of Habanita. Since she had said that there was something she wanted to discuss with him, he had assumed that there would be no other guests, and such turned out to be the case. In the now-familiar sitting room there was a tray with a whisky decanter and soda siphon and two glasses. She asked him to make drinks while she put our some nuts and crackers in little bowls. Remembering the previous session, he made the drinks fairly strong.

Mrs. Balian seemed in no hurry to have their discussion. On the contrary, she moved from topic to topic in a nervous way. At one point she got out a photograph album to show him pictures of the island in earlier days. Most of the photographs were of her late husband's family, beginning with formal studio portraits of men wearing fezes and stern expressions, and women posing stiffly, with little boys and girls next to them, staring unsmiling into the lens; later, there were more relaxed snapshots. Mrs. Balian shyly pointed out one photograph of a pretty young woman in a light-colored cotton dress standing next to a tall, dark, mustachioed man wearing white flannels, smiling at each other on a sunny day long ago.

"I was just 19 when that was taken."

"Your husband?"

"Yes. A happy time." She looked reflective and closed the album.

Gül announced dinner and Mrs. Balian led him to the dining room. It was of a piece with the sitting room, with heavy dark furniture and an old-fashioned dinner service. The silverware was very heavy and cumbersome, and there seemed to be lot of pieces of it beside Ed's plate. The table was long enough to accommodate a dozen people so they were seated across from each other on the two long sides. The dinner was excellent, with a creamy soup, roast lamb, mixed salad, and a delicious dessert made, surprisingly, with chicken breasts. During dinner there was the same, slightly strained, atmosphere, as they both strove to make conversation and to seem lively and interested. When they had finished,

Mrs. Balian said they would have coffee in the sitting room. There, he thought, they would presumably finally get down to their "discussion."

She settled herself on the sofa and Ed sat in a chair opposite, with a low table between them. Gül brought in the coffee things on a tray and asked if there would be anything else. Mrs. Balian said that they would look after themselves. She then turned to Ed.

"Will you have a glass of cognac with your coffee, Mr. Wilkie?"

He said he would, and she rose and poured them each a glass from a serious-looking bottle. Now the discussion? he wondered.

"Mr. Wilkie, I hope that we are good enough friends that I can speak to you frankly."

"Of course, Mrs. Balian." This sounded rather ominous.

"The matter I wish to discuss concerns your reputation. As a foreigner, you may not be aware that there are certain usages that one must observe—if one doesn't want to damage one's standing in the community. You, as a teacher of youth, in a reputed Academy, must be especially circumspect, no?"

"Of course, Mrs. Balian. But what...?"

"In a small place like this, nothing goes unobserved. What may seem to you like a small thing where you come from, here can be more serious, more complicated..."

The penny dropped.

"...Your relationship with your maid is something I blush to mention, but your neighbors have spoken to me and, as a friend, I think I should talk to you, for your own good. She is married and you could find yourself in grave difficulties with her—and her husband's—family."

Ed was mortified that his personal life appeared to be on such public display, and he stammered a reply:

"I do appreciate your frankness, Mrs. Balian. I...I had no idea. She is a very nice person and I just..."

"I quite understand. I was married and I know that men have their...needs. But please reflect, this is not fair to Balkiz and it is not appropriate to your position in life."

"I understand. I..."

"You should not be wasting yourself on a maid servant. If you wish for a liaison it should be with a discreet woman of your own class." His neck prickled, like Starleen seeing a cat. "Come over and sit by me, Mr. Wilkie." She patted the seat beside her and smiled.

The second penny dropped.

Ed sat next to her and leaned over to kiss her, but she said, "Just a moment," and reached across him to turn off the table light, leaving the room in darkness. She kissed him with surprising passion and then took him by the hand: "This way. Follow me."

She led him upstairs—the whole house was now in darkness—and opened a door.

"This is my room. You can undress in the room opposite."

This turned out to be a spare bedroom, smelling slightly of mothballs, with, Ed noticed, an old leather *nécessaire de voyage* opened on the bureau for his use—Mrs. Balian seemed to have had little doubt but that he would fall in with her plans. He undressed slowly, thinking that she would probably require longer than he, then went across and tapped on the door.

*"Entrez,"* she called out.

The lights were off, but Ed could make out the shape of a huge bed.

"This way, *chéri.*"

Ed's night with Mrs. Balian was not as spectacular as what he was able to remember of his night with Zeynep Hanım, but very satisfactory, all the same. She was more than enthusiastic, telling him that she had not been with a man since her husband had died. When the moment came, she cried out, *"Mère de Dieu!"*—briefly putting him off his stroke.

At 3:30 in the morning her alarm clock rang—she had been very methodical—and she told him that he would have to be on his way. She added that he could use the shower in the bathroom attached to her bedroom. He stepped in and was soaping up when the shower curtain parted and she joined him. They soaped each other and kissed. She looked quite appealing without her makeup and with her long hair hanging down her back. He was about to make a suggestion for a reprise, when she hopped out again, saying, "Hurry up, *chéri*. Next time." Next time?

When he got out, Mrs. Balian was in a long robe, with her hair wrapped in a towel like a turban. He dried himself and got dressed, and she led him down to the front door.

"Now, wasn't that better than your little village woman, chéri?"

She left him standing on the steps, with only a lingering scent of Habanita. Ed had to admit she had a point.

Since Ed's courtship of Elif had come adrift, the prospect of a discreet liaison with Mrs. Balian was not unappealing. While not in her first youth, she was an attractive woman with, certainly, more conversation than Balkiz. She seemed, further, to be ready to consider this an affair, rather than a serious romantic entanglement. All this, however, left Ed to consider what he should do about Balkiz. He genuinely liked her and didn't want to hurt her, but if their relationship was indeed public knowledge, then it would certainly end badly for her.

As it turned out, the situation solved itself. Several days after Ed's night on Yeni Hamam Street, Balkiz and he were in bed together. She had been especially affectionate and tender, and he was feeling sentimental and distressed about how to tell her what he had learned.

She turned to him and said, *"Canım,* this is the last time."

Her eyes filled with tears and he didn't know what to say.

"Balkiz, what...?"

"Someone said something to my husband. He doesn't know anything for sure, but says that I must leave my job with you. He says that he is being dishonored by *dedikodu*—gossip."

Ed was sorry to see this happy, loving woman go out of his life, but reflected that it was the best way. The next time he saw Mrs. Balian he told her that he had followed her advice and ended his relationship with Balkiz. She looked up and patted his cheek. "It is best thus, *chéri,*" then kicked off the covers. *"Allez, viens!"*

Later, Mrs. Balian sent a new maid to Ed to replace Balkiz, an elderly and exceedingly plain woman who spoke no English. While Latife performed her housekeeping functions admirably, Ed had no temptation to approach her carnally, which is undoubtedly just what Mrs. Balian had in mind.

When next he met Elif, Ed mentioned that he had parted with Balkiz.

"And why do you tell me this?" she asked, shrugging her shoulders and appearing to dismiss the information.

"I just wanted you to know that I felt strongly your disapproval. I knew that you were right."

"This has nothing to do with me. Your life is your own affair," she sniffed. But Ed could see that she was touched.

# 21

Brown called and suggested that they go over to Sultanahmet in the old city to a restaurant he liked, a famous place that served *hazır yemek*, old-fashioned home-style food. "Not fancy," he said, "but the food's a treat!"

They took the ferry at 7:00 and when they arrived at the Sirkeci landing, walked twenty minutes to the restaurant. It was still a little early, but the two floors were starting to fill up. The owner greeted them cordially and showed them to a table in the lower room against the wall, were they could talk undisturbed. *"Ne içersiniz?"* asked the waiter and Brown ordered a large bottle of *rakı*. When he had brought it, Brown poured their drinks, adding ice and water, and said, "Here's how, old boy!"

The waiter invited them back to the kitchen to select their meal, where they were shown various pots filled with aromatic vegetables and meats. Under Brown's guidance, they picked out a variety of these and on their way back to the table added some cold dishes to start with. When the food arrived they ate and drank in silence for a few minutes and then slowed down.

"So, Doc, how's your sex life?" asked Brown. "You still poking the little maid?"

"Really, Brown! There's no need to be so crude about it. In fact, no. Balkiz and I have parted company."

"Husband tumble, did he?"

"In a manner of speaking. I have, however, formed a new relationship." He went on to give an outline of his liaison with Mrs. Balian, not going into details, which he knew Brown would simply treat with his usual ribaldry.

"Balian, eh? Never heard of her. Nice young piece?"

"Yes, very nice," he replied, not wishing to be too precise about her age. Given Brown's irreverent comments on women, Ed was glad that he had never mentioned his ill-starred courtship of Elif.

After dinner Brown suggested that they go to a *hamam*—a Turkish bath—in the neighborhood: "A great way to relax and take out the kinks." It sounded interesting so Ed agreed, and they proceeded on foot to a small *hamam* on a nearby side street. Unlike the grand *hamams* in Galata frequented by the tourists, this was a little neighborhood place and seemed to be very old and rather decayed, with a dim electric sign over the door reading Sokollu Hamamı and a broken, dirty entrance way. Inside, however, it was more promising, with a tile floor leading to a wooden reception desk, where they were welcomed by the owner and given towels. A boy led them to changing booths, where they left their clothes, then to a room with shower stalls, where they showered off, and finally to a great domed room filled with moist heat. The dome was set with colored glass, through which daylight would filter, but in the evening it was in deep shadow. There were little basins around the wall, into which streams of water continually flowed, making an agreeable sound, and a few men sat or lay around the room with towels around their waists and shoulders. The air was heavy and steamy, with a smell of soft soap and the drowsy sound of intermittent conversation.

They settled themselves down and Brown ordered tea from the boy who had shown them in. As they drank the tea, Ed reverted to their previous conversation in the restaurant.

"So, how about you, Brown? How's your love life? Are you making do with Mrs. Akkaya's girls?"

"Actually, Doc, I was feeling a bit down for a while," he said, readjusting his towel. "There's a very respectable lady I've been seeing on the q.t. for some time. We met through a sort-of business connection. She has a position to keep up and so we get together on the sly." He took a sip of tea. "But I have the idea that she's been seeing someone else."

Ed found this rather surprising. "So, Brown, how do you know?"

"Well, Doc, as I say, I have been calling on the lady at night—by previous arrangement do you see, when she thinks the coast is clear. The last time I called on her, she turned me away. Said she wasn't well. But I had the feeling that there was someone with her."

Ed felt a tingle in his scalp. "When was this, Brown?"

"In fact, Doc, it was the night you came to see me after your beano at the school. I had been waiting for zero hour and having a few snifters. Then, you see, we had several more together. The fact is, I had more than I was planning on and fell asleep in my chair. When I woke up it was after the appointed time, but I pulled myself together and rushed over to her place and let myself in. As I said, when I tapped on her bedroom door—our usual signal—I heard a terrific crash and she came to the door. She complained that I'd made her fall over a chair in the dark. She gave me a rocket for being late and told me to buzz off. There wasn't much I could do, so I buzzed. But I still think someone got in before me!"

"Ah. Who is this lady? Are you back together?"

"Must be discreet, old boy. Lady of quality. But a firecracker in bed! Yes, we're back together, under the old arrangement. But I still have the feeling I was cut out."

"Very strange. Well, it was probably just your imagination. After all, you were a little out of it that evening."

"Perhaps you're right, Doc. But if I ever catch the bugger, I'll have his balls!"

Ed crossed his legs and pulled his towel more tightly around him.

That night, after Brown and Ed had parted, Ed returned home, to be greeted by a joyful Starleen. They had a stroll and settled down with her head on his knee and a *rakı* in his spare hand. At least he now knew why Zeynep Hanım hadn't been surprised to find a man in her room—even if it turned out to be the wrong man. A remarkably adaptable woman, he reflected.

## 22

"Hello, Ed?" a feminine voice came over the telephone.

"Yes?"

"This is Lily Blum. We met the other evening at the *Othello* performance."

"Oh, of course, Lily. How are you?"

"Everett and I enjoyed meeting you the other day and thought that you might be free for dinner one evening."

"That would be lovely."

They agreed on a date several days later, and as an afterthought Lily said, "Is there anyone you'd like to bring along—a girl, perhaps?"

"Well, there is someone I'd like to have meet you. I'll ask her and get back to you." "Good," she replied. "And, of course, do bring Starleen!"

Ed sought out Elif and asked if she would care to join him for dinner at the Blums. She hesitated and looked thoughtful. Then she said, "Yes, I would, thank you."

"Does this mean that you've forgiven me?" he asked hopefully.

She looked at him seriously. "There is nothing to forgive. It isn't my business." Then she continued in her earnest way. "I spoke to my father—in only a general way, of course. He advised me that young men must sow their oats before they settle down." She pursed her lips. "He learned this expression in America. I didn't quite understand—or approve—but I think everyone deserves a second chance."

The evening of the Blums' dinner, Ed and Starleen picked Elif up at the school. Ed was wearing his blazer; Starleen had been freshly bathed for the occasion and was sparkling white. Elif had changed into a pink dress with a matching jacket. He noticed that her hair had also been freshly washed and it was very soft and shiny and smelled delicious.

Lily gave Elif a kiss on the cheek and Everett shook hands, looking at her approvingly. Lily was in another long dress—this time in old gold—and Everett had risen to the occasion with white duck trousers and a dark blue silk shirt worn with an ascot.

"And this is Starleen!" said Lily, as they both got down on the floor to make over her.

Starleen responded in kind, bouncing around, licking their hands and barking with delight. Then she began a voyage of discovery around the house. "Let her go," said Lily, when Ed started after her. "The place is dog-proof." She showed him a picture of their fox terrier, Betty, who had passed to her reward several years ago. "The last one, I think. Three were enough."

The house was filled with what Everett called "the usual foreign service crap," brought back from their various foreign postings: African masks, oriental carpets, Indian brasses, odd bits of carving and pottery hung on the walls or scattered on tables. Ed asked Everett about the house.

"It's over a hundred years old," he said. "We spent years restoring it, but it was worth it. The color is called 'Ottoman rose.' Very hard to get just the right shade. Originally pigmented with red ochre."

"And I think Kemal said that you teach at a university," said Ed.

"I do," said Lily. "We live in Istanbul in the warm months and spend the winters in San Francisco. I teach part-time in the English language preparatory school in a university. Everett, however, seems simply to fall into a kind of trance for six months, emerging occasionally to pick a dead leaf off of one of the geraniums."

"A vast exaggeration," said Everett. "Drink?"

They had drinks in the garden and Everett barbecued steaks, while Lily and Elif brought out salads. The women were getting along very well and discussing Dijon, a city Lily seemed to know well. Dinner was leisured, and after they had cleared up they went inside for coffee and brandy.

Lily took Elif off to show her some photograph albums that she thought might have some old pictures of Dijon, and Everett and Ed settled back with brandy.

"So, are you liking the school?" he asked.

"Very much. Ali Bey is an outstanding person. I understand that he is still active in business of some kind."

"You know that, do you?" He seemed a little surprised. "Yes, he seems to have the protection of some powerful people in Ankara. Friends among the generals. Enemies, of course, also."

"Have you met Osman Bey?" asked Ed.

"Osman İlik? Yes. You know him? You know everyone."

"He approached me. Who is he, exactly?"

"Some sort of policeman. Also well connected in Ankara, I hear."

The women joined them. Lily had been telling Elif about the *Othello* evening.

"At the end of it I was in agony, but I wasn't going to use the on-the-floor toilet that I knew was lurking in the cafe nearby."

"No kidding," said Everett. "I remember once in Sultanahmet. I was waiting in line to use the public facilities. An Italian woman in front of me came out, and her friend pointed out to her that she'd peed on her stockings. She had to go back inside to change them."

Shocked, Ed tried to catch Everett's eye to indicate that this was not appropriate language to use in front of Elif, but at that moment Elif joined the conversation.

"Oh, but Mrs. Blum…"

"Lily."

"Oh, but Lily, they are much more natural than western toilets. Very good exercise for the thighs and stomach muscles. That is why we Turkish ladies find it easy to have our babies." She must have seen something in Ed's face. "You don't agree, Ed?"

"Oh yes. I'm sure you're right," he said hurriedly.

Lily gave a whoop and added helpfully, "Oh, Elif, you've shocked him! Look at his round, blue, innocent eyes!"

The two ladies snorted together, while Ed and Everett exchanged pained looks. Everett put on some music, and they listened to some New Orleans classics and old jazz. About 11:30 Ed said that they would have to get the ferry to their island. He took Elif to the Academy, where she was staying that night, and was rewarded with a chaste kiss.

"It's been a lovely evening, Ed. Thank you very much. I am glad you asked me to go with you."

# 23

Despite Ed's progress with Elif, he continued to see Mrs. Balian on a regular basis, and was thus able to maintain a balance between spirituality and carnality. Mrs. Balian seemed perfectly content with their discreet relationship, so they settled into a mutually satisfactory routine. Ed would go to her house around 11:00 at night and return home around 3:00 to finish the night alone. By taking a nap in the afternoon, he didn't find the program too taxing. One day, however, Mrs. Balian called and said that there was someone she would like him to meet, and suggested tea the next day. He readily agreed, since he had never met any of her friends and duly presented himself in his "good" suit.

Mrs. Balian was dressed, as before, in a silk dress and greeted him with formality. He was then presented to another lady, a contemporary of Mrs. Balian's named Mrs. Papas. Mrs. Papas was a plump and bosomy lady of medium height, with a round, pink face and short, curly black hair. She wore a kind of cocktail dress in a shiny material, cut low in front and showing a good deal of cleavage when she leaned forward. She said that she and "Lolly" were old friends and that their late husbands had been in business together. She had a very lively and playful manner, which, though a little young for her, Ed found engaging.

Mrs. Balian proposed tea, then added, "...or, as we have a gentlemen with us, Maria, perhaps he would prefer a drink. Would you care for a drink, Mr. Wilkie? I think you might be persuaded to have a whisky and soda," making a slight moue at him.

"Yes, please."

"Maria?"

"Why not, Lolly?"

"Why not, indeed?"

She gave them their drinks and Mrs. Balian remarked, "Maria—Mrs. Papas—is an adept, a natural adept."

"I'm sorry. I don't quite..."

"A medium," broke in Mrs. Papas. "I am able to make contact with those who have passed to the Other Side."

"One day, Maria, we must have a séance with Mr. Wilkie. I think he would be interested. Another drink, my dear? Mr. Wilkie?"

"Yes, thank you, Lolly. I agree. Mr. Wilkie seems a most sympathetic type," said Mrs. Papas, looking deeply and significantly into Ed's eyes. "Would you like to try the experiment, Mr. Wilkie?"

"That would be very interesting, Mrs. Papas." Ed nodded. "Well, yes, perhaps just one more, Mrs. Balian."

The ladies continued talking about spiritualism, a subject on which Ed had always harbored doubts. According to them, Mrs. Papas had remarkable success in summoning various historical figures, as well as less famous of the Dear Departed, through the agency of an Egyptian princess named Ramala: "Sealed alive in her tomb by her jealous husband," Mrs. Papas elaborated breathlessly.

After several more rounds of drinks, Mrs. Balian excused herself to refill the decanter. Mrs. Papas continued, "I am also something of an expert in palmistry, Mr. Wilkie. Do come over and let me see your hand. I am sure we will find it interesting." He moved over to the couch beside her and she took his hand between hers. "Ah yes. A long life line. Marriage. Just once. Two, perhaps three children. You have a great capacity for love, Mr. Wilkie." She looked up from his hand and into his eyes. "So Lolly tells me."

"I... That is..." *What on earth had she been saying*, he wondered.

"Lolly suggests that you might wish to make some of this great capacity available. Lolly is a most unselfish girl." She laid her hand on his thigh and leaned closer. There was a puff of scented powder from her corsage as she pressed herself against him. "Shall we say Thursday evening, Mr. Wilkie?" He found himself nodding dumbly.

Just then, Mrs. Balian returned. "Everything settled?" she asked brightly.

Ed's evenings with Mrs. Papas were a contrast to those with Mrs. Balian. She lived in more modest circumstances in a little house in a wood, standing at the edge of the sea. It had probably been built originally by a rich family for seaside teas, picnics and boating expeditions, in a more leisured and expansive era, for it was lightly constructed, consisting of four rooms on one level set on top of an abandoned boat landing. It tended to be rather damp and drafty, but the setting was beautifully secluded and romantic.

The first time Ed called on Mrs. Papas, she received him in what he took to be her professional costume, a sort of gypsy blouse and long full skirt, with a piano shawl draped about her shoulders. She wore gold hoop earrings and bangles, and her lipstick seemed to be a more vivid shade of red than that which she had worn the evening at Mrs. Balian's. She invited him in, in her lively, bustling way.

"How lovely to see you, my dear Mr. Wilkie! You are just on time. An excellent trait in a man. Come over here and sit by me. Mind the little table. It's a trifle unsteady. And the edge of the rug. Oops! Are you all right? Good. Comfortable? What would you say to a slight aperitif?"

"Yes, thank you, Mrs. Papas," he said from his place on the slightly damp velvet loveseat.

"Do call me Maria, my dear Mr. Wilkie."

"Yes, please...Maria."

He looked around the room, which seemed to be decorated with an eye to creating an atmosphere conducive to establishing contact with the supernatural. There were heavy drapes on the windows, wall sconces that provided a dim light reflected on the low ceiling, and a great deal of furniture covered with scarves and bric-a-brac. The room had a light aroma that reminded Ed of Sen-Sen, which he took to be incense or scented candles. He later learned that this was not the room in which she conducted her séances. Another room, used exclusively for that purpose, was sparsely furnished with a dining table and chairs. The salon simply established the mood. As they drank their aperitifs, Mrs. Papas told Ed something of herself.

"I was very young, only twelve, when I first learned of my powers. My parents were horrified. Thought I was mad and took me to a dreadful old doctor, a psychiatrist, who talked about my sexual repressions and tried to put his hand up my dress. A refill, my dear?"

Ed nodded, wondering where this was leading.

"There we go! So, I felt rather alienated from other young people at first, though, of course, the Dear Departed were company for me. Such interesting stories for a young girl to hear. I matured quickly."

"Was this in Greece?" asked Ed, thinking to contribute something to the conversation.

"Greece? No, I was born in Buenos Aires. But the big breakthrough came when I met a very great medium. In London. I was seventeen."

"In London?" Had he missed something?

"Yes. I had run away from home by then and was traveling in Europe with a little circus. So broadening, travel. Isn't it?"

"Indeed. I have always..."

"Edgar was a wonderful man. Much older than I, but very experienced. Very gentle," she glanced at him, "and able to delve deeply—into the vast Beyond." She looked thoughtful. "Eventually, Edgar and I parted. He died years ago, but we are still in touch from time to time. It was a perfectly amicable parting. After that I became a professional medium."

"And Mr. Papas?" asked Ed, still trying to get his bearings.

"My late husband—my third—was an associate of Ali Bey's"

"And how did you meet?"

"I had met Ali Bey in Vienna. He is, as you know, a man of great imagination, of vision. He was interested in seeing whether my powers could be useful to him in his activities. I met Mr. Papas while I was engaged in Ali Bey's experiment."

"And was the experiment successful?" Ed asked haltingly.

"The results were mixed." She seemed to dismiss the subject. "If you'll excuse me, dear, I'll put on some water for tea."

"Oh, thanks. Whisky is fine," said Ed, holding up his half-filled glass.

"Not for drinking, dear." She got up and bustled away.

During her absence, Ed sat reflecting on Ali Bey's curious experiment with spiritualism. After a few minutes she returned with a tray on which were a flowered teapot, a single cup, and a bowl.

"Here we are, dear, let's have a look." She sat down and poured out a cup of tea, let it stand for a moment, and then poured the tea into the bowl. She looked into the cup and studied the leaves. "Well, my dear, this is most interesting. Though somewhat confusing. I see some troubles in your life—perhaps brought on by, what would it be? A pencil or pen? Are you a writer?"

"Well, some poems. Maybe you have heard of…"

"Or perhaps it's something else. Love will come to you soon," she glanced up, "but I see a crescent. A Muslim girl, perhaps. Poor me!"

"Maybe, since we're in Turkey."

"Let's try a second cup." She got a fresh cup and poured and emptied the tea again. "Once more, rather confusing. You will meet someone who will start you off on an adventure. A woman is also involved. And...do you have a cat, a dog?"

"A dog."

"The dog is involved in some way in all this," she looked up and smiled. "Well that's it. I don't know how helpful it was."

"Oh, it was very interesting...Maria," Ed said, happy to finish with the mumbo jumbo.

"Good!" she said brightly. "So, if you've finished your drink, I think we may as well be getting to it, my dear." She got up briskly. "Come with me, dear."

She let the way through the séance room and to a small bedroom containing only a double bed, a dresser set out with toilet articles, a nightstand, and a chair. Above the bed was a reproduction of Landseer's *The Monarch of the Glen*.

"The bathroom is just opposite, dear, if you have need. Here, I'll turn out the light. You can put your things on that chair—I'm afraid I can't provide a separate dressing room," she giggled. "There we go!" She turned out the light and Ed could hear her unfastening buttons and snaps. "My, but it's chilly!"

He hurried out of his clothes and stood naked by the side of the bed, uncertain whether to get in yet.

"Hop in, dear. Lolly tells me you prefer the outside."

Several days later Elif said, "You seem rather tired and distracted, Eddy. I am rather worried about you. Are you working too hard? Getting enough sleep? You seem simply hag-ridden." She noticed his start at the appositeness of the phrase. "Isn't that right, Eddy—hag-ridden?"

"Yes, Elif," he agreed, nodding. "Exactly right!"

# 24

"Can I talk to you for a moment, Ed?" asked Erol Demiray, as Ed was returning from class. Ed had seen him regularly, but he had not been very communicative since the departure of Lucie Leblanc, seeming rather dull and wistful.

"Sure," he replied. "What's up?"

"Ali Bey asked me if you would be so kind as to deliver a package for him—to your friend Mr. Agopian. He said that it was quite urgent and he wanted to entrust it to someone he could count on. I guess it must be valuable."

"Of course," Ed agreed. "I'll take it this afternoon. I'll go right over and get it from him now."

Erol shook his head. "He has left town. He gave the package to me to give to you. He seemed sure that you would be able to undertake the commission for him. I have it locked up in my lab."

As they went to his lab Ed asked, "If it isn't indiscreet, Erol, any word from Lucie?"

He looked more depressed: "No, Ed. Nothing. I just don't understand. She was, what do you say? Up and down—extremes."

"Mercurial?"

"Maybe. We had our fights. But always made up. She was very loving. This last time, a big fight. But not, I thought, as bad as all that. Then, poof! She's gone!"

They entered the lab in silence, and once again Ed was nearly overcome by the chemical smells, which seemed even worse than he had remembered. Erol led the way through a door, which he unlocked, and into another, smaller lab. There was a workbench on which some sort of complicated chemical experiment was set up.

"What are the boys doing here?" Ed asked, looking around him.

Erol laughed. "Oh, I wouldn't let the little wretches anywhere near this. This is my own research that I work on during off hours." He went to a wooden cabinet and unlocked it. Inside were rows of labeled jars and bottles, along with a square package wrapped in brown paper and neatly tied with string. He handed it to Ed. It was fairly light and had no name or address on it.

"OK," Ed said, "I'll take care of it right away. Should I call to see if Mr. Agopian is in?"

"No. He's expecting you."

It struck Ed that Elif might like to join him and she said that she would like to meet Mr. Agopian. She could visit the bazaar and then continue on to Beyoğlu where she lived.

It was a lovely, crisp day for an outing and Elif seemed happy and glad to be with him. She let him hold her hand as they rode on the ferry to Sirkeci and eventually said, "Eddy, I was thinking. Would you like to come to visit my parents one day?" She looked down and her cheeks grew pink. "That is...I have mentioned you to them. My mother liked your poems. My father...um, would like to meet you also "

This was an unexpected and positive development. "Of course, Elif. I'd love to meet your parents."

She smiled and nodded. "We will fix a time. Soon."

When they arrived at Mr. Agopian's shop, his nephew, Ari, was lounging outside. Ed shook hands and introduced him to Elif, whom he acknowledged with a negligent smile.

"Uncle is with some customers right now. He asked me to get Ali Bey's package from you. It's rather urgent, it seems," he said, shrugging an elegant shoulder.

"Sure. Here it is. Should we not go in now?"

"Oh, it's fine. He'll be glad to see you. See you around," he said, sauntering off with the package.

Mr. Agopian greeted them warmly. *"Merhaba,* Mr. Wilkie. *Merhaba,* Elif Hanım. You are very welcome! I heard that I could expect you, but I didn't expect to have the pleasure of meeting your lovely lady," at which Elif looked down and blushed again. There was a middle-aged couple in the shop wearing khakis and polo shirts. Mr. Agopian introduced them as the Nutleys, from Springfield, Missouri. Mr. Nutley shook hands, saying, "Pleased to meet you, sir, ma'am. Mrs. Nutley and I were just looking at some of Mr. Agopio's fine carpets. Want to get something good for the living room back home."

"That's right," said Mrs. Nutley. "I know just the colors I want. Got everything matched to a 'T.' I was just showing Mr. Agopio these color swatches."

Mr. Agopian was clearly used to this approach to rug buying and said with an ingratiating laugh, "Yes, indeed. Mrs. Nutley has a wonderful eye. She spotted this fine Hereke right away," gesturing to the 6' by 8' carpet rolled out on his floor.

Mrs. Nutley beamed. "Just matches the pattern on the chesterfield!"

"Now if you good folks will just excuse me," said Mr. Nutley, "I was just going to get down and give it a real close look." He dropped to his knees and began moving over the carpet, staring at it inch by inch.

"He's a real careful shopper," confided Mrs. Nutley. "Not like me. Why, I just..."

"Got to be!" Mr. Nutley looked up. "Don't want to be sorry later. Now, Mr. Agopio, this nap seems kinda short to me. I saw a lot longer nap on another one of these."

"I assure you, Mr. Nutley," said Mr. Agopian, "the length is not what's important. It's the clarity of the pattern."

"Doesn't feel as... well, rich, somehow," said Mr. Nutley, feeling his way in unfamiliar territory.

"But, honey, the color's just right!" broke in Mrs. Nutley.

He got to his feet. "Well, Mr. Agopio, you heard what the boss said." He winked broadly and patted his wife affectionately on the shoulder. "She's the interior decorator in the family. I don't..."

"That's right, honey. What say you write Mr. Agopio a check?" she said a little impatiently.

He was shocked. "Hold your horses, Grace! It's a lot of money. What say we go discuss it a little first?"

"Yes, please do," agreed Mr. Agopian. "You should be completely sure."

"Maybe we can talk about the price a little more?" Mr. Nutley said hopefully.

"Oh, that is my last price, sir."

"Well, OK. We'll be back in a while. So long, folks!"

"But don't sell it while we're gone, hear!" said Mrs. Nutley. "Good-bye folks!"

Mr. Agopian said good-bye and then turned to Ed and Elif. "Now for some tea. What can I show you? I have some Caucasians—not too expensive, but very nice—that I'd like you to see. They were just sent to me, so you'll be the first to see them."

They spent the next two hours looking at rugs. Elif was interested also, but said that she didn't know much about them.

"My parents have old Persian carpets in our apartment, Tabriz, Nain, other names I don't remember. But I like this kind very much."

As before, Mr. Agopian's assistant rolled out rugs and they made a pile of those they liked, then went through that pile and finally came down to the two or three they liked best. Elif said, "I will take this Shirvan, Mr. Agopian. I will put it in my bedroom. I feel more comfortable with it than my parent's Persians. It will remind me of this nice day," she added, glancing at Ed and smiling.

When they left Mr. Agopian's it was still fairly early and Ed was trying to think of something else they could do to extend their time together. Perhaps with the same thought in mind, Elif suddenly said, "Would you like to see where I went to university?"

"That would be fun," Ed said, so she led him to the old arts faculty of Istanbul University. She seemed happy to be showing him her school, as she took him through the dignified, rather rundown buildings. He could imagine the eager, serious girl rushing to class to get a seat near the front of the crowded amphitheater, listening attentively to the professors, taking down their words like holy writ, laughing with her friends in the courtyard. What about boys, he wondered? Had there been boys?

In their ramblings they encountered an old man standing lost in thought, whom she introduced as Lütfü Bey, who had been one of her favorite professors, a world-famous authority on Stendhal. He shook Ed's hand, looked vaguely up at him, and said in a trembling voice, "Well, so Elif got married at last! You are a lucky boy. She's a very good girl," glancing at her affectionately.

She looked mortified. "Oh no, professor..."

He smirked and patted her hand. "You newlyweds. So shy. So, you captured a foreign boy. Like Mehmet captured Constantinople. Ha ha. 'The spider has wove his web in the Imperial palace and the owl hath sung her watch-song on the towers of Afrasiab.' There, there, dear, I must run." and he tottered off.

"Eddy, I am so embarrassed. I...," she began.

But at that moment a door was flung open and a voice said, "Hey! What about keeping it down out there. These are offices y'know." The voice was followed by its source, an intense-looking young American man with a ponytail. He wore a very wrinkled shirt and jeans, together with an indignant and aggrieved expression that seemed to be habitual. "So, what do you want here? You aren't on the faculty."

"No. I'm sorry," Ed said, falling back a step. "We were just..."

"An American! You were just snooping around, right?"

"Actually, we were just..."

"So, are you from the government?"

"The government? Which g..." Ed stammered.

"Here to spy on us, eh? Keep track of us. Well, you can just beat it!"

"Look," Ed said. "I think there is a mistake here. I'm not with the government."

"Oh sure! Like you would really say! I know my phone's tapped, mail opened. Now this!"

"But I don't even know who you are."

"Sure!"

"Well, who are you?" said Elif, getting to the heart of things. "We are teachers. Like you, maybe."

"Yeah, well..." What he was going to say remained unspoken, interrupted by the arrival of another person, a young woman.

"Randy, will you shut up!" she said. "These guys aren't from the CIA." She turned briskly to them. "Randy thinks everyone is from the CIA. Spying on him." Their new friend was a decisive-looking girl, also in jeans, with long blonde hair in braids.

"Look here, Patty...," Randy began.

"I don't know why he should think so. I tell him, Ersin Bey and Süreyya Bey tell him, everyone tells him!" she continued. "He doesn't know anything that anyone would want to spy on!"

"We were just visiting an old professor of mine," Elif said.

"Yeah, right!" began Randy, only to be interrupted again by Patty.

"We're here on Fulbright grants," she said. "I'm working on 'The New Islamic Woman' and Randy's up to some guff in the Ottoman Archives."

"That's right! Let them compromise you!" said Randy bitterly.

Patty looked at him and then at Ed and Elif. "He's really not such a dope when you get to know him—just, y'know, paranoid. Well, see you around!" and she herded Randy back into his office.

They walked away in silence, and then Elif said, "I don't understand what that was all about. He thought you were a government spy?"

"I guess so."

"But that's ridiculous. How could you be?"

"Beats me. I wouldn't even know how to begin. I guess Patty was right. He's 'just, y'know, paranoid.'"

# 25

One day Ed suggested to Elif that they go to a little island beyond Büyükada, where there was a good swimming beach. She agreed and they fixed a day during the week, when there would be few other people. The island is one of the Princes' Islands, but has been developed privately, and consists of large, modern houses set in gardens. There are no businesses, no horse carriages, nothing for tourists to see. Since the island is a part of greater Istanbul, the public cannot be excluded, but the residents expend every effort to make it unwelcoming. There are few ferries, many signs saying "No entry," "Don't pick the flowers," "No picnicking," to discourage the casual visitor. So the typical *Istanbullu* in search of a little sea and sun is much more likely to content himself with the more relaxed and welcoming accommodations on one of the other islands. There is, however, a small beach, designed for the use of the residents but accessible to the determined visitor. It includes cabins for changing clothes, a little cafe, and a pebble beach giving gradually down into the sea.

They identified a ferry that would get them to the island around 11:00 and, as he had hoped, they were among only six people to disembark. The landing was an unprepossessing floating dock, with a footpath leading up the hill to a small square with a few benches and concrete flower planters. There was a grocery shop, which was closed, and a cafe, also closed. Since it was still early, they decided to have a walk around the island before going to the beach.

Elif was wearing a sleeveless cotton dress, with bare legs and sandals. She gave Ed her swimsuit wrapped in a towel and he put it with his in a shoulder bag. He slipped his arm around her waist as they walked and eventually she put her arm around him. The silence was almost total as they strolled along the unpaved road, past the big modern houses. They were mostly closed for the season, though several had open shutters and lawn furniture on their deep covered porches. Occasionally, a resident would come out to look at them suspiciously. The feeling was very much like the off-season South of France, with mimosa, lavender, lilac, oleander, and hedges of sweet-smelling rosemary. There was a hum of insects, and bees fed on the acacia and honeysuckle.

The little road wound up and around the island, sometimes in direct sunlight, sometimes dappled with sun filtered through overhanging pine trees. They reached the summit and looked out over the smooth, sparkling blue sea. Ed's head swam with the beauty of the view, the scent of honeysuckle, and the distant murmur of seagulls. He turned to Elif and, without even thinking about it, took her face in his hands and kissed her on the mouth. She stiffened for a moment and then suddenly relaxed and kissed back. Then she shivered slightly and stepped back. Her cheeks were very pink and she seemed a little unsteady. "I think we should move along, Eddy," she said. And then she squeezed his hand, to show that she wasn't offended. As they walked back they were both silent and reflective.

They arrived back at the square and then followed a path down to the *plaj*, the beach. Again, as he had hoped, it was deserted. The changing stalls were primitive, featuring a sort of half-door, as seen in Western saloons. There was no one to supervise them, so they selected two and changed into their suits. Elif wore a modest one-piece suit in pink, but he could admire her compact body, with its small high breasts and shapely tan legs. At first she seemed a little shy, but Ed opened two Efes beers that he had brought in his shoulder bag and after a few minutes she began to relax. They put down their towels and lay in the sun, not talking, just relaxing and enjoying being together. He smelled the perfume of her hair and the slightly acid aroma of her body, sweaty from their walk.

She suggested that they have a swim and they made their way down the pebble beach and into the water. The sea seemed icy, after lying on the beach, but they quickly grew used to the temperature. Ed floated on his back and Elif did a determined dog paddle—doubtless learned in the Robert College lifesaving class—out to sea and back. Then they returned to shore, lay on their towels again, and had another beer. After a while he rolled over and gave her a kiss. This time she seemed prepared for it and kissed back enthusiastically. Encouraged, he put his hand experimentally on her breast, but she immediately sat up.

"Really, Eddy, I thought you had respect for me!"

He was surprised. "I'm sorry. I just thought..."

"I am not one of those American girls. You can't do just anything with me. You can't sow any oats!"

"Of course, Elif. I guess I just got excited." It seemed that this was going to be tougher than he'd thought, "You mean with Turkish boys you never...?"

"Not with any boys!"

"I guess I thought maybe in France—in Dijon."

"Those French boys were the worst! They have no respect for Muslim women. They think we are just...nothing!" Her green eyes were hot and wet with the memory.

He coaxed her back to him. "I do respect you. It was just a mistake." He nuzzled her neck and she smiled. It seemed he was aces again, but he now knew that Elif was a woman of principle.

Later, when she had calmed down, she said, "You know, Eddy, I came to hate the French. They talk all the time about the greatness of French culture, but it's dead. They just use it to exploit. Even the degree I earned from them is nothing, a *doctorat de l'universite*. Good enough for Africans and Arabs...and Turks! *'Bon pour l'orient'* one disgusting old professor said, laughing at me and trying to pinch my...my...to hell with them!" So much for La Mission Civilisatrice, he thought.

## 26

In due course, the meeting with Elif's parents was arranged: a dinner at their apartment in Beyoğlu. Elif had given Ed elaborate and precise directions, but he went over early, to be sure not to be late. He took the ferry to Sirkeci and then decided to walk over the Galata Bridge, across the Golden Horn, and continue on into Pera, the old European side of Istanbul. On the way, just before reaching the bridge he stopped at the Spice Bazaar, a smaller version of the Grand Bazaar, devoted to spices and herbs, dried nuts and fruits, and garden supplies. There was nothing that he especially wanted to buy, but he enjoyed the bustle, the dim coolness, and the intoxicating aroma of the open sacks of cardamom, saffron, cumin, sage, and dozens of other spices, and the rich colors of apricots, glossy brown dates, and plump purple figs piled in bins. He thought it would be fun one day to bring Elif to Pandeli's restaurant on the second floor of the bazaar.

When he came out it was still quite light and it took him a moment to get his bearings. He paused a few minutes to watch the old ladies feeding pigeons in front of the Yeni Mosque, and then continued over the bridge. The Galata Bridge was lined, as usual, with some of Istanbul's greatest optimists: fishermen, who spend every day casting their lines in the murky water, hoping to catch enough of the little fish called *hamsi*, a kind of anchovy, to make a fry for their families. Looking at the pots and jars at their feet in which a few tiny fish swam, it was hard to decide if they were the bait or the catch. There must be few housewives who actually depend on this activity to supply a family dinner. At the other end of the bridge there were men in little fishing boats like the one on Ed's island frying fish in hot oil to make sandwiches to sell to the passersby. The boats tossed in the backwash of passing ships and ferries and the hot oil slopped in the cookpots, while the cooks yelled, *"Balık, ekmek! Bak!"*

He wound his way up the steep hill, passing through alleys, looking at the craftsmen working at their trades in front of their shops. Ed stopped to watch an old shoemaker, who then invited him to take tea with him under the little grapevine he had trained over the front of his shop. Later, nearing the end of his journey up the hill, he was struck by the large shop of a *turşucu*, a maker of pick-les. Since he had, under the influence of Vural Bey, become something of a *turşucu* himself, he stopped to check on the competition. The windows were filled with large glass jars containing pickles of all kinds, from the humble cucumber to elaborate mixtures of vegetables. The shop was lit from the inside so that the jars seemed to be part of a great stained-glass window. He went inside to look around; the owner was with another customer, but he nodded to Ed gravely. The shop smelled of brine and vinegar and he noticed that on one side there was a display case with various kinds of pickles arranged in little glass dishes, like sundaes at a soda fountain. And there were round tables with chairs where customers could sit to eat the pickles at their ease. He was studying the dishes when the owner fin-ished with his customer and came over to serve him.

"*Evet, efendim. Hoş geldiniz. Ne istersiniz?*"

"*Hoş bulduk,*" he replied, thereby exhausting his conversational Turkish.

Pulling himself together, he pointed at a two-liter jar of tiny stuffed egg-plants.

"*Güzel,* very nice," he said, meaning to communicate his appreciation for his artistry.

"*Evet, efendim,*" the turşucu nodded, as he reached down the jar and went over to the counter. "*Başka, efendim?*"

Ed shook his head. The storekeeper nodded and rang up his cash register. It seemed that he had just bought a jar of pickles to carry with him.

He continued on his way, shifting the jar of pickles, which had been thoughtfully placed in a plastic bag, from hand to hand and wondering what he was going to do with it. At last, he reached Istiklal Caddesi, the main street of Beyoğlu. In the 1920s and 30s it was one of the smartest streets in Europe, and it still retains some of its former charm, with many lovely Art Deco and Italianate Art Nouveau buildings, though unfortunately now interspersed with tacky mod-ern shop fronts from the 1950s and 60s. Istiklal is a pedestrian street—which in Istanbul does not exactly mean that there are no cars, but only that there are fewer cars than on other streets—and a little tram runs on it from Taksim Square to the Tünel, the shortest and one of the oldest subways in Europe, on which you can take a ninety-second ride down to the sea front. When Istanbul was the capital of Turkey, before Atatürk moved it to Ankara, most of the embassies were in this area, several on Istiklal Caddesi itself. These have now been reduced to consulates, but they are much more elegant than the chanceries that replaced them in the middle of Anatolia. As Ed walked down the street, by the shop windows displaying expensive merchandise, the music stores blasting arabesque music onto the sidewalk, the gypsy women selling dried lavender and flowers, and the shoeshine boys clamoring for business, he passed the Italian, the Russian, the Dutch consulates, and then the great Galatasaray Lycée, the French-language high school that traditionally trained the elite of Turkey, before English replaced French as the language of science, commerce, and diplomacy—at least in the minds of everyone but the French.

Ed saw that he had forty-five minutes before his dinner engagement, so he decided to have a haircut in a barbershop he had admired on a previous visit to the area. It was like something from the heroic age of barbershops in America: sanctuaries to which a man could repair for a peaceful hour, to have a haircut and a shave, complete with hot towels wrapped around his face, and perhaps even a manicure. The clientele was, of course, exclusively male, and the solid chairs, with worn chrome and leather, could be adjusted to lean back almost to a horizontal position. A mirror ran the length of the shop behind the chairs reflecting bottles of multi-colored potions, looking like the Lucky Tiger, Polar Ice, and Lilac Vegetol that used to decorate its American counterpart. The shop had few customers and a barber was sitting in his chair reading the newspaper, a dignified older man wearing a white jacket. When Ed entered the shop the man rose and greeted him ceremoniously and then placed him in the chair. When Ed was swathed in a cotton sheet, he inquired how Ed wanted his haircut. *"Az, lütfen—* just a little,"* he said, having prepared the phrase in anticipation. The barber nodded and went about his craft, ending by massaging Ed's scalp, trimming his eyebrows, and splashing him with lemon cologne. They consulted briefly about several fascinating hair lotions, but Ed finally declined.

Ed had stopped to look at several old maps in the window of the Denizler bookstore, when it struck him that he should get a hostess present for Elif's mother. He wished that he had consulted with Kemal about this before leaving the school, having never forgotten the shocked expression on the face of a French hostess to whom he presented a bouquet of chrysanthemums—a flower used in

France only to place on graves. He came upon a florist and decided to give it a shot.

"I need some flowers..."

"Of course, sir," said the pretty girl at the counter.

"To give to my hostess," he continued with relief. "I'm going to a dinner party."

They discussed the relative merits of a potted plant and cut flowers and she showed him over her stock. Finally, he emerged with a dozen pink roses.

"Should go nicely with the *patlıcan,* the eggplants, sir," she giggled.

The Ekmekçis lived in a beautiful old building, four stories high, with elegant Art Nouveau details. He took a creaking birdcage elevator to the fourth floor and rang the bell at a door of dark, solid oak. Elif met him and smiled nervously.

"Welcome, Eddy. Please come in."

He entered and found himself in a high-ceilinged entry hall, with glowing old tiles on the floor and wood-paneled walls. She led him from there directly into a large salon with windows offering a spectacular view of the Bosphorus. As she had said, the floors were covered with wonderful Persian carpets.

An elderly couple had risen to meet him, and Elif led him over to them.

"Baba, Anne, this is Mr. Wilkie. Eddy, my mother and father."

Mrs. Ekmekçi came forward and put out her hand. "Welcome, Mr. Wilkie. Elif has told us a great deal about you." She was an agreeable-looking woman, about Elif's size, with the same rather prominent green eyes and ripe mouth, and dark brown hair pulled back into a bun. Her voice, like Elif's, had a feminine, musical quality that Ed had learned was a mark of ladies in old Istanbul families. He started to reach for her hand when he realized that he was still encumbered with his flowers—and eggplants.

"Oh, pardon me, Mrs. Ekmekçi," he improvised. "A little something for you..."

She seemed slightly startled, and then she smiled—a lovely smile, like her daughter's: "How nice! Pink roses. My favorite. And pickles, a charming idea." She looked at the label. "Ah, not your own. But a famous shop. Thank you." She took his offerings and set them down. Then they shook hands.

Elif's father was a big man, a little heavy, like an athlete gone a trifle to seed.

He had gray hair combed back from his forehead and icy blue eyes. He was dressed in formal gray and his manner was also very formal. Not unfriendly, just guarded.

"Welcome, Mr. Wilkie. It is a pleasure to meet a colleague of our daughter's." His grip was strong and hard.

During this exchange Elif had been glancing nervously from face to face. Now her mother said, *"Canım,* please put these lovely flowers in a vase, would you? And the pickles in the kitchen. We can have them with dinner. Mr. Wilkie, please sit down. What can we offer you to drink? Ömer, will you please...?"

Her husband, evidently well disciplined at home, moved quickly over to the drinks cabinet and put several bottles on a tray. "Whisky, sherry, Cinzano, gin, *rakı.* What will you have, Mr. Wilkie?"

Ed hesitated. Sherry, to suggest temperance? Whisky, to indicate manliness? Would a gin and tonic seem more chic?

"I think I'll have a *rakı*, sir, if I may."

Ömer Bey smiled for the first time. "Of course. With water? Nilgün, what will you have?"

"A Cinzano, dear."

Elif brought the roses in an old Chinese porcelain jar and was provided with a sherry. The general took *rakı* neat. The meeting was much less of a strain than Ed had expected. Nilgün Hanım was a charming and lively hostess and the general eventually loosened up and became less formal. Elif beamed at them like a mother at a successful children's birthday party.

They asked Ed about his family and he told them that his father had been a rancher in California who had died when Ed was a boy and that he had lived with his mother until her recent death, indicating that the family money, such as it was, had died with her.

"Very interesting, Mr. Wilkie," said Nilgün Hanım. "Your mother sounds like a lovely person. I can see why you miss her."

"I know your president, Mr. Wilkie...," broke in the general.

Ed was startled by this, but before he could reply Elif added, "Director, Baba, not president."

"Oh yes. Ali Bayraktar. An old comrade. He speaks highly of you, Mr. Wilkie."

"That's very gratifying, Sir. Your comrade, you say. What branch of the army were you in?"

"Intelligence. Though an American friend at Fort Benning told me that 'military intelligence' is a contradiction in terms. Ha!"

"Did you ever know a Major Collins, sir?"

"I don't think so. Maybe he used another name. Ha!"

"Well, sir, the dog barks, the caravan moves on," Ed hazarded, thinking the phrase might somehow be appropriate.

He looked uncertain and glanced at his wife. *"İt ürür. Kervan yürür,"* she translated.

"Eh?" he thought for a moment. "Ha! Yes, of course."

Nilgün Hanım had prepared a table full of *meze*, including special Ottoman dishes that one seldom saw. Ed noticed that his eggplants were also present in a pretty cut-glass bowl. The main course was lamb served with yogurt. The general and Ed continued with *rakı*; Elif and her mother drank wine. Ed asked the general about their family name.

*"Ekmek* means 'bread,' doesn't it, sir?"

"Yes, it does. But my grandfather didn't sell it door to door. He owned a bread *fabrika,* a factory, in Adana. When Atatürk required all Turks to take family names in the 1930s, he chose Ekmekçi—the bread seller. My wife, however, comes from a great family." He looked at her proudly. "Her ancestors were high officials in the Ottoman administration, Ministers of State, Governors. But she had faith in me."

After dinner they had coffee in the salon and Nilgün Hanım showed Ed a family album of photographs, so that he could see how their neighborhood had looked "in the good old days, before all these terrible people from Anatolia came to Istanbul." She then turned forward to show him some pictures of their summerhouse in Çeşme, on the Aegean coast. As she stopped on one page he saw a picture of Elif as a young teenager, looking shyly into the camera, one coltish leg, clad in white shorts, crossed over the other.

"What a sweet picture!" he said.

"Yes," said Nilgün Hanım. "She was just thirteen that summer."

"Ha! Turn back a few pages, Nilgün. I think there is an earlier picture of her on a bearskin rug," said the general, who had drunk a little more *rakı* that Ed had quite realized.

"Baba!" said Elif, and Nilgün Hanım quietly closed the album.

Ed said goodnight to Elif's parents at 11:30 and Elif took him to the door. This time he got a kiss.

"Good night, Eddy. They like you very much."

## 27

Much to his surprise, a few days later Ed received an invitation to a reception at the American Consul General's residence, in honor of a senator, a member of the Foreign Relations Committee, who was in Turkey on some sort of government business. Why he should have been invited wasn't clear to him until he got a call from Lily Blum to say that they had thought he might be interested and had asked to have him put on the invitation list.

"We always get invited, for old time's sake," she added, "but at least we'll have someone nice to talk to." He asked if he could bring Elif and she said she would arrange it.

Elif was very excited at the prospect of an official reception at the Consul General's and she and Lily had a number of telephone conferences about what she would wear. In Ed's case the decision was simplified by the limited nature of his wardrobe. He got his "good" suit cleaned and Elif bought him a silk tie from İpek.

"And do get your shoes polished, Eddy. They look like you've been playing football in them."

Ed and Elif took a taxi to the Consul General's residence, a modern mansion on a bluff overlooking the Bosphorus, and were passed through a cordon of

Turkish security guards, who took their invitations and checked their names off on a list. Several young American men with short haircuts and double-knit suits earnestly said, "Thank ya, sir, thank ya, ma'am." Ed later learned that they were marine guards in mufti.

They walked through the garden with several other guests and were welcomed at the door by the Turkish majordomo, who greeted them in English and passed them on to an eager young American woman wearing a mail-order dress and good gold jewelry ("The hallmarks of the American female foreign service officer," Lily explained).

*"Hoş geldiniz!* Hi! I'm Elaine Clifton of the consular section. Welcome to the Residence." They mentioned their names and shook hands, and she motioned them to a line of people waiting to meet the Consul General and guests of honor.

The Consul General was a correct and professional-looking man in his late fifties, with the brisk courtesy of one who has been through this drill many times.

"Good evening, Mr. Mmm. Thank you for coming. Please meet Senator and Mrs. Goff."

The Senator, who represented a large and largely empty Western state, was an imposing, almost overpoweringly genial man, with a red face and longish gray hair brushed theatrically over his ears. He had a loud voice and the wide mouth of an orator.

"Great to meet you, Mr. Mmm. And this must be your good lady! Yaas!"

"Well, actually...," Ed began, but found his hand being shaken with a technique that involved one hand grasping his as the other held his upper arm, while both moved him smoothly like a bottle of pop on a conveyer belt to the next person in line, Mrs. Goff. She was a bored, blowsy woman, with blondined hair and an irritable expression, who looked as though she had already had it with this game and wanted a drink big-time. Ed murmured his name and she passed him on wordlessly to some other consulate official, who launched him into the crowd: "Please do enjoy yourself, Mr. Mmm."

Elif and Ed flagged down a passing waiter carrying a tray of drinks. Another waiter soon approached and offered them a tray of canapés, odds and ends on limp little rounds of white bread and meatballs on toothpicks. They took some of these and circulated through the crowd. Since they didn't know anyone, they stayed together and inspected the "usual foreign service crap" displayed on the walls and bookcases—the mementos of the Consul General's thirty-five years overseas, spent, it would seem, largely in the Middle East.

Ed was starting to think that this was pretty poor fun, when he heard a whoop.

"Ed, Elif! How are you!" It was Lily, very lively and elegant, leading a glum Everett in a dark suit and looking as though his feet hurt.

"Are you having fun?" asked Lily.

"Ha!" said Everett.

"Be still, dear. These people aren't jaded." Then turning to them, "Have you met anyone? The senator is well known for..."

"...being a windbag of the first water," interpolated Everett.

"...his interest in Middle Eastern affairs," she continued. "So Tom—the Consul General—has invited officials from Middle Eastern consulates and some Arab business people. Along with the usual consulate hangers-on, who are invited to everything—like us."

"Actually," said Everett, "the Goffs are here for the same reason all the delegations from Washington come to Istanbul: to shop in the Grand Bazaar. Many of these deep thinkers actually believe that Istanbul is still the capital of Turkey. Big shock for them when they find out that they have to go to Ankara, too!"

They talked for another few minutes and then the Consul General, "Tom," gave Everett and Lily the high sign to join him at the bar, where Mrs. Goff was clamoring for a Jack Daniel's.

Ed and Elif continued to circulate and made small talk with various officials from minor consulates. From time to time Ed heard Mrs. Goff, whose voice was decisive and penetrating, telling someone about her trip to the Grand Bazaar: "Tried to cheat the pants off us, but I said..." or her visit to the Blue Mosque: "'Take off my shoes?' I said. Yeah, so you can swipe 'em, probably..." Occasionally she would signal to a waiter: "And Jack Daniel's. Not that moose pee!" Her husband, the senator, clearly accustomed to his wife's antics, moved through the crowd unconcerned, clutching hands, patting shoulders, gripping upper arms.

"Wonderful to meet you. Yaas! Very interesting. Our two nations have much in common. Business is the key. A market economy and democracy go hand in hand. Yaas!"

Elif and Ed had floated up against a depressed-looking man named Mr. Nazar, who identified himself as an Egyptian businessman dealing in farm equipment. Ed was doing his best to simulate an interest in mechanical manure-spreaders when a desperate-looking Lily arrived at his side.

"Flo, I'd like you to meet Ed Wilkie, an American—from California—who teaches at a school in Istanbul." She looked at him pleadingly, as she introduced him to Mrs. Goff, who was by now in a state of considerable disarray, her hair coming down and her eyes staring. He assumed an air of calm competence and nodded at Lily.

"How do you do, Mrs. Goff," he said in his most urbane manner. Then, motioning to Mr. Nazar, "I'd like you to meet..."

She brushed this aside. "Ed. Great to meet you! I thought I was gonna have to spend another night talking to Arabs!"

Happily, at this juncture Senator Goff, who seemed to understand that his personal intercession had become necessary, suddenly appeared.

"Well, honey! Maybe time for you to be saying good night to these fine people!" and she was led away protesting.

"You always butt in when I'm starting to have a good time! Why don't you just mind your own..."

Mr. Nazar had melted away, and Elif and Lily, who had disloyally removed themselves from the scene, were talking animatedly together across the room, pointedly not looking in Ed's direction. He assumed a reproachful expression and was about to go over to them when a voice spoke beside him.

"Well, even in the b-best regulated families."

He turned to see who his comforter was and a man stuck out his hand.

"Bill Hobson. F-foreign Commercial Service." He was a tall, stringy man with a pale face, dry mouse-colored hair, and muddy eyes. His suit hung on him like a tent, inside of which his body moved nervously and jerkily. "She's f-famous for making these little scenes. That's probably why Lily was trying to stick you with her." Ed's new friend, however, seemed diverted by the event. "D-don't take it personally. We've all been through it. Shall we have a drink?"

They grabbed a couple of drinks from a passing waiter and moved on through the crowd. "D-don't take any of those canapés," he warned. "God knows who's been handling them. They'll probably give you c-constipation—or worse."

Ed snatched his hand back from the tray that the waiter had been offering him invitingly. The noise level had reached a new peak as more guests swelled the throng, so Bill led the way to an adjoining room arranged to take the spillover, but which no other guests had as yet found. They took a couple of armchairs and he continued, "I heard Lily say that you were t-teaching at a school in Istanbul."

"Yes. I'm at the Istanbul Collegiate Academy. I teach English."

"That's Ali B-bayraktar's school, isn't it?"

"Yes. He took it over this academic year."

"I'm very interested in this private English-medium school phenomenon in T-turkey. It seems to me that English acquisition is an important element in establishing commercial relations. English is becoming the international n-nexus language and that gives the U.S. a central position commercially. T-turkey is going to be an increasingly important player in this part of the world. If Turkey and the U.S. can work together, both will benefit. L-language is the key!"

Ed didn't quite follow all this, but nodded. "I expect you're right, Bill."

"Ed, I'd like to t-talk more about this with you some time—when we can hear ourselves think. I'd like to get your ideas on this—maybe visit your school. What do you say?" The muddy eyes looked anxiously into Ed's.

"Sure, Bill. Anytime."

"Good. I'll be in t-touch with you."

He patted Ed's arm and moved off, as Elif and Lily rejoined him.

"Sorry about that, Ed," said Lily, but her words were belied, as she and Elif exchanged glances and snickered. Then, Everett came up.

"Why this untoward merriment? I was just going to suggest that if we've all had enough fun we should get out of here and get a real drink somewhere—not this moose pee. Yaas!"

# 28

Twice more over the next month Erol Demiray brought a message from Ali Bey asking Ed to take another package to Mr. Agopian.

"Ali Bey is very grateful to you," he said. "This information is hush-hush, but important for his business interests. He asks me to tell you that he has other assignments in mind for you. Maybe travel outside of Turkey."

One time Ed took Elif with him again and once he went alone, each time giving the package to Ari, who met him in front of the shop.

Ed had not seen Brown for some time. When he called the hotel, Mustafa Bey said that Brown was away on business, but would doubtless call when he returned. A few days later Brown did call and invited Ed over for drinks, suggesting that they might go out for dinner afterwards. Thinking that this might be a good time for him to meet Elif, Ed asked if he could bring a lady with him. "Of course, Doc," he said. "Add a little feminine charm to our evening." Elif agreed to join them for drinks, but said that her parents were entertaining relatives and would expect her for dinner.

Ed picked her up from the school at 6:00 and they went down to the hotel. She looked slightly apprehensive, but Mustafa Bey greeted her warmly, as did Mrs. Akkaya, who came in shortly after them.

"*Merhaba,* Elif Hanım. We all miss Mr. Wilkie at the hotel. Such a nice man. My girls liked him very much. Unfortunately one of them, Rezan, has recently left us. I am quite devastated."

Elif smiled and shook hands. As they went upstairs she remarked, "What a nice, distinguished-looking lady. I can see that you make friends easily, Eddy."

In expectation of entertaining a lady, Brown had made an effort to smarten up his sitting room with bowls of flowers and several trays of snacks. Dizzy Gillespie was going full blast and the atmosphere was decidedly festive. He ushered them in and then went over to turn down the music.

Ed said, "Brown, I want to introduce you to Elif. Honey, this is my friend

Brown, whom I've talked so much about."

"How's that?" asked Brown, fussing with his sound system. "Ah yes. Delighted to meet you. I feel I know you already."

Elif smiled. "I'm pleased to be meeting you also, Mr. Brown."

Brown settled her into an armchair and inquired about drinks: "I think you are a whisky-and-soda lady, aren't you?" Elif said no and asked for white wine. He got them their drinks and pushed trays of snacks towards them, then fussed with the music again, then finally settled down.

"Yes, indeed. Doc has told me so much about you. I know that you are a very special person to him. But, Ed," glancing at him and smirking, "you didn't do her justice. She's even younger and more beautiful than I had imagined." Elif smiled and looked affectionately at Ed, who couldn't understand why Brown was going on like this, as he had never mentioned Elif to him.

"Elif was born in Istanbul," Ed said, "and her parents still live in Beyoğlu."

"Ah yes. Many old Armenian families live in Beyoğlu, I believe." Suddenly, a terrible apprehension crossed Ed's mind and he started to open his mouth, but Brown continued relentlessly. "But, of course, your married name is Balian. Is your family also Armenian?"

She looked puzzled. "Armenian? Why, no. I am Turkish. I..."

"Ah, of course, you live on our island, Mrs. Balian. I must say," winking at Ed, "our friend is certainly lucky to have such a nice, understanding landlady. And so convenient, living so close to each other." He looked at her with an oily smile. "But let's not be formal. May I call you...what is it, Doc? Ah, 'Lolly'!"

Elif looked at Ed uncertainly. "I think that there is a misunderstanding. My name..." Then she stopped short and looked again at him with narrowed eyes.

"Oh, I'm sorry," said Brown. "I have put my foot in it!" Turning accusingly to Ed, he added, "You didn't introduce her properly, Doc." Then turning back to Elif. "You must be Mrs. Papas. Maria!"

There was a brief silence, during which Ed's ability to respond to the crisis seemed to be paralyzed. As Star would have said, he didn't know whether to shit or go blind—or maybe just kill Brown.

Elif, however, recovered and said with a small smile, "I'm afraid you have me confused with some of Mr. Wilkie's other lady friends. My name is Elif Ekmekçi. I teach French at the Academy." And then, moving briskly on to another topic, "What a large music collection you have, Mr. Brown!"

Brown instantly leaped onto his hobbyhorse and took Elif over to the book-case, where he showed her his system for arranging his recordings. Elif listened with apparent attention to his explanation, never looking at Ed. Then she commented on his collection of books, mostly mysteries.

"Oh yes, Mr. Brown, I love Maigret. The psychology of the individual, not the puzzle. And the style is very pure. Did you know that Simenon was Belgian?"

Brown nodded and grinned like a dog, while Ed sat in his chair, stiff with apprehension. At last Elif looked over at him and remarked brightly, "Well, I must be on my way. I know you two are planning dinner together. Since you've been away, Mr. Brown, I'm sure you have much catching up to do. Thank you for a most informative evening."

Brown continued to nod and grin. "Thanks for coming, Lol...Elif. Always a pleasure to have a literary discussion."

Ed jumped up. "Let me walk you to the landing, Elif. I'll be right back, Brown."

They exited in silence, Elif walking quickly with her heels clicking militantly on the floor of the lobby. When they got outside he tried to catch her arm.

"Elif, you don't understand. Brown was completely mixed up. I..."

She snatched away her arm. "I understand perfectly. You are a...a...monster of deceit! I let you make love to me. I introduce you to my parents. And all the while you are making up to another woman. No! Two other women!"

"Sweetheart, please, will you just let me try to explain?"

"No! There is nothing to explain. I forgave you for your—*divertissement* with your maid. But this is too much. Good-bye!" and she flounced away down the street. Even in the agony of remorse, he couldn't help reflecting appreciatively on what a beautiful bottom she had. Now, he thought sadly, perhaps never to be his. When she was out of sight, Ed returned to Brown's room. Brown seemed quite pleased with himself.

"Well, Doc, I thought that went off quite well. Don't you? She seemed to enjoy looking at my music collection. I think I retrieved that little slip over the name rather neatly. She probably didn't even notice..."

"Didn't even notice! You moron, she has just walked out of my life. We are through, thanks to you!"

"Well, really, Doc. You can't say it's my fault. You never told me about her. I naturally thought she was one of these other pieces you've been bonking. I mean it's lucky I didn't ask about Ramala interrupting while you and Maria were..."

"Enough!" Ed raised his hand. "I see your point. Let's not discuss it anymore."

"I mean, maybe she'll come around. Being a bit of a cad can appeal to some women." Possibly, thought Ed, but he doubted that Elif fell into this category.

# 29

Ed was drooping disconsolately around the garden of the Academy, when he was boarded by Zeynep Hanım.

"I noticed on your resume, Mr. Wilkie, that you are a sailor." The accursed resume again, thought Ed.

"Yes, I did a little sailing at one time, when I lived in California." This was true. One of his short-lived enthusiasms. "But I wouldn't say that I really..."

"Good. My father has decided that it would be useful for the Academy to have its own launch. Useful for the Academy and for his other business interests, since it would make us independent of the ferry schedule."

"Yes, I can see that we..."

"He would like you to look into this for him. A launch, he said. Capacity for around twenty people. Engine capable of attaining...well, it's all here. He wrote down his specifications, together with the maximum price." She handed him a piece of Academy letterhead with a typed list of requirements. "You might start at the Büyükada harbor. Kemal Bey can help interpret, if necessary."

"I'll get on this tomorrow. On Saturday. You can count..."

"Good. Get back to me when you've got something appropriate and I'll ask

Ali Bey for his approval."

On Saturday Ed and Kemal caught the ferry for Büyükada. Kemal had found the name of an agent who dealt in boats and had spoken to him on the telephone, so he was expecting them. Zeynep Hanım's confidence in Ed as an authority on power launches was wholly misplaced, since his experience had been confined to a small motorboat that was the nautical equivalent of a sports car. But he had learned that it was pointless to try to argue with her once her mind was set. As Kemal said, "It makes an outing. And, after all, the agent is supposed to be trustworthy. Having a boat for the Academy may turn out to be fun."

Ed hadn't been to Büyükada since he had gone with Brown for his residence permit. Kemal led the way to the harbor and then up a side street, muttering the numbers under his breath. Finally they arrived at small shop front with a sign in the window: "Cem Akbulut—Yat ve Tekne Pazarlama."

"Cem Bey knows everything for sale that floats in the whole Istanbul area," said Kemal.

They entered and were greeted by a cheerful little man seated at a battered desk that took up most of the available space.

"Welcome. Kemal Bey? And Mr. Wilkie, maybe? I speak English. I was for twenty-six years an officer in the navy. A captain. Submarine fleet. But I will find you a boat that stays on the surface—ha ha! Please, sit down."

They squeezed themselves into two visitor's chairs, with their knees pressing painfully against the front of his desk. He went on, "When I was a sub-lieutenant, Mr. Wilkie, I went for training in the USA—five of us Turkish boys from the navy. First to Annapolis. Then by train all the way across America to San Francisco. What memories! One of my friends almost got arrested for pinching a lady in a swimming pool. Of all the ladies he could have pinched, this lady was married to the chief of police! What a drama! I went with my friend and explained that in Turkey he had seen only ladies' ankles. When he saw so much lady, he just got excited. The chief laughed and let us go. A great country!"

Ed smiled and nodded at this tribute to his homeland. "Thank you, Cem Bey. I am enjoying your wonderful country, too, though I haven't yet pinched any ladies."

"Ha ha! Very good. But don't pinch any, Mr. Wilkie. A Turkish husband would not be so understanding." He then introduced a business note. "So, you want to buy a launch?"

"That is so. Here are the specifications. I think Kemal indicated the price range?"

"Yes, thank you, Mr. Wilkie. The price is rather low." He looked sad and shook his head. "But we shall triumph!" His face cleared and he regained his cheerfulness. "Damn the torpedoes..."

"...Full speed ahead!"

"Ha ha! Exactly so. Look, I've made up a short list of launches that I think might be what you are looking for. None of them are in your price range, but that is what I am for!" They looked over the list together. "Most of these aren't on this island—one at Istinye, one at Bebek, Tarabya...but there is one here that might be just right. It is not yet on the market, but I know the owner and the boat. It is about fifteen years old, fiberglass. The engine is within your specifications and recently overhauled. The cabin appointments are nice, but haven't been renewed. Zeyyat Bey's wife, Melek Hanım, says that she is sick of spending her weekends on this boat. Cooking and cleaning like at home, but more cramped. She has her eye on a flat in Alanya, on the Mediterranean coast. I think that Zeyyat Bey is about ready to cave in. This is strategy!"

"Sounds good. Now what?"

"Let's go have a look. If you like it, we can talk with Zeyyat—and Melek!"

"What is the boat called?" Ed asked with interest.

"Called? Oh, I see—Elif. Their daughter's name."

"Kısmet!"

"No. Elif."

The *Elif* was, indeed, a lovely launch, so far as Ed could judge. Very trim and fast looking, white with blue piping. The interior seemed fine—real leather, worn but not shabby. He told Cem that he thought they should proceed, so Cem called Zeyyat, who was available for discussion.

"He says he hasn't made up his mind to sell," said Cem, "but if Melek is at home, the matter may pass from his hands!" He rubbed his own hands in anticipation.

They took a horse carriage up the hill, stopping eventually before a beautiful old house that had been divided into two flats.

"His brother's family lives on the second floor," explained Cem. In the garden was a middle-aged lady looking suspiciously at a rosebush. Cem Bey brightened.

"Melek! *Merhaba.* How are you?" She looked up.

"Cem! Welcome."

"Melek, please meet my friends Mr. Wilkie and Kemal Bey. We have come to speak to Zeyyat about buying his boat." He accompanied his words with a significant look.

She arched her eyebrows. "Excellent! Please come in." She went ahead of them, calling out, *"Canım.* Cem is here!"

Cem strode purposefully into the sitting room. *"Merhaba,* Zeyyat!" The room was very bright and modern, in complete contrast to the exterior of the house. It had recessed lighting, modern low furniture of exquisite discomfort, and a long glass coffee table strewn with interior decorating magazines. Zeyyat, a tanned elderly man wearing informal weekend clothes, didn't somehow look at ease in this setting, which was probably the choice of his wife. A good sign, Ed thought.

*"Merhaba,* Cem." He turned to Ed. "Mr. Wilkie, I think? Kemal Bey? Welcome."

They sat down and Melek entered with tea things. She poured glasses of tea and offered around a plate of cookies. These formalities completed, she sat down in a determined manner. Zeyyat looked depressed.

Cem looked at Ed and said, "You will please excuse us if we speak in Turkish?"

"Of course," Ed replied.

The negotiation was long and dramatic, but Ed had little doubt of its eventual outcome. It began with a long, measured preamble by Cem. He indicated a figure that was less than their maximum. Shock and smiling disbelief from Zeyyat. More palaver from Cem and a new, slightly higher, figure was proposed. More disbelief, more gestures. Shoulders were shrugged, eyes were cast up, voices rose and fell. Finally, Ed recognized a figure that was within $1,000 of their maximum, and Cem put out his hand, palms up, lifted his shoulders, and brought down the corners of his mouth. Zeyyat, smiling and shaking his head, started to say something, rising slightly out of his chair. But at this point Melek spoke for the first time, in a tone that was not loud, but exceedingly firm. Her husband started to reply, but she broke in and continued to speak for some time. Cem kept his head down and his mouth shut. Zeyyat tried again to make a point, but Ed could see that he was a beaten man. At last, he turned to Cem and said something, to which Cem nodded gravely and Melek smiled grimly.

Cem turned to Ed. "Zeyyat will consider our last offer and will give me his decision tomorrow." They rose and shook hands, and Melek showed them to the door. As they walked down the hill, Cem said, "The deal is done!"

"But what if he changes his mind?" asked Ed.

"He will not. This is to save face. The deal is done."

Kemal agreed. "You can believe it! A very determined lady. I hope he likes his flat in Alanya!"

Ed checked with Cem the next day and he confirmed that the offer was accepted. Later, he brought the launch over for Ali Bey's inspection. Ed and Kemal rode down to the harbor with him and he looked over the Elif carefully.

"Very nice," Ali Bey observed. "Plenty of room. I very much like the leather fittings." They took the launch around the island and he had Cem open it up to full speed.

"Very exhilarating!" exclaimed Ali Bey. "I presume it can keep up this speed without overheating."

"Oh yes, indeed. Several hours," Cem assured him. Ali Bey nodded and said he was satisfied.

# 30

Several weeks later, Zeynep Hanım announced that Ali Bey was inviting the teaching staff and their families for an outing on the new launch the following Saturday, to include a picnic lunch. Since it was something of a command performance, they all accepted and duly presented themselves at the boat slip at 10:00, swimsuits and suntan oil at the ready.

Elif was also there, but pointedly ignored Ed. This, he reflected, was going to be a long day. When Ali Bey arrived they marched up the gangplank and settled themselves in the cabin and on the deck. While the guests were dressed or undressed in sports clothes, Ali Bey was as formal as always, with his black suit and dark tie. Ed noticed that he even wore his rosette in his buttonhole, a multi-colored dot in a sea of black.

"What is that order that he wears?" he asked Kemal.

"A *Mérite agricole*. Awarded by the French government. His doctorate is from France. In agronomy."

Ed was surprised and looked again at the decoration. "Do you know why they gave it to him, the French?"

"I think for work he did many years ago. With flowers."

"Flowers! What kind?"

"I don't remember. A commercially grown flower. Red."

"Roses, hibiscus, poppies...?"

He was clearly bored with the discussion. "Yes, maybe poppies."

Ali Bey announced that they would have a tour around the islands and then would land at the little island where Elif and Ed had gone together for their picnic. A friend of his had, he said, kindly lent his summerhouse for the day. Ed tried to catch Elif's eye, but she wouldn't look at him. Mehmet Efendi passed among them with tea, beer, and soft drinks, and after two hours of sailing, they stopped at their destination, where they disembarked and made their way up the familiar path to the square. They continued on a path lined by pine trees to one of the large modern houses that Ed had seen the last time. The housekeeper was waiting for them. They changed into their suits and she showed them where they could climb down to a semi-private beach. Ed was standing in the garden wondering what to do next, when he saw Elif, alone, sitting on a bench under a pomegranate tree. Could she be waiting for him, he wondered? He went over to her.

"Can I sit with you, Elif?" She said nothing, so he sat down. "Elif, can we talk? Can I try to explain?"

"What is there to explain?" She looked away.

"I was so lonely after the business with Balkiz. I didn't think I could win you back. I was just weak."

"I know. I discussed it all with my mother."

"You..."

"She explained to me that all men are weak where...ladies are concerned. Even Baba." She turned and looked at him. "I was very surprised."

"Me, too," he said truthfully.

"She told me that I could hardly expect you to be faithful before there was an...understanding between us. We talked a long time." Green eyes looked into Ed's.

"And she convinced you?"

"I think so. She also pointed out that these were not ladies of...professional ladies...street ladies. That would have been very bad!"

"So you will forgive me?"

"Yes." She nodded seriously. "But these affairs must end!"

"Of course!" He put his arms around her and kissed her. "So, we have an 'understanding' between us now, Elif?" he asked.

"We do. But don't forget. No more ladies!"

As they walked hand in hand down to the beach he wondered how he was going to terminate his relationship with the "other ladies."

# 31

Ed was finishing up his American literature class with "The Snows of Kilimanjaro." One of the boys was giving an explanation of the concluding passages.

"So a hyena came up to the man's bed and bit him and he died. Then the plane came..."

"Wait," Ed interjected. "A hyena didn't bite him."

"Oh yes, sir. See, it says right here that it put its head on the foot of the cot."

"But this isn't a real hyena, Mehmet," he explained patiently.

"But, sir. It *says!*"

"This is a symbol. A symbol of death."

"A symbolic hyena, sir?" Mehmet looked around significantly: *Allah! Here we go again!* The boys settled back for another symbolic tussle.

As Ed walked out of the classroom, buffeted by the eddies of departing pupils, he was arrested by a small, sharp-eyed boy whose name he had temporarily forgotten.

"Telephone call, sir. You can take it in the hall!" He went to the hall and found the receiver off the hook.

"Hello. Ed Wilkie here."

"Hi, Ed. This is B-bill Hobson." At first he was at a loss and then he remembered his acquaintance from the consulate party.

"How are you, Bill?"

"Great. You know that evening I m-mentioned my interest in talking with you about private education in Turkey. I wonder if you might be free sometime this week—maybe for dinner—c-courtesy of the U.S. government."

A free dinner sounded all right. "Sure. When do you suggest?"

"Let's say Thursday. Why don't you meet me at the b-bar of the Pera Palas Hotel. We can have a drink and go on to dinner."

"Thursday is fine, thanks."

"Good. Let's say 7:00 at the Pera Palas, then."

When Ed mentioned this later to Elif she said, "So you made a good contact at the party. Maybe this will lead to other opportunities for you." She patted his lapel affectionately. "And be sure your suit is pressed."

The Pera Palas is one of the most famous—though far from the most luxurious or comfortable—hotels in Istanbul. In its day it was the premier hotel of the European quarter, and the destination of the first-class passengers on the Orient Express; its salons were filled with elegant ladies and distinguished gentlemen. Today it trades on its past, with faded curtains and creaky furniture. People continue to patronize it for the associations of its glorious past, and they pay for this pleasure—for it is certainly not cheap. The bar, like the rest of the hotel, exudes both atmosphere and discomfort, and the service is slow, cranky and expensive. Ed arrived early and settled himself down on a slightly unsteady chair by the window, noting that "Don't Be Cruel" was, rather incongruously, being piped over the sound system. Eventually, a waiter drifted up and asked his pleasure. He ordered *rakı* and after some time the waiter returned with a glass of beer. Ed pointed out his error and he replied indignantly, "But you said beer!" "No. I want *rakı*." Ed replied, and the waiter went away muttering about foreigners. When he finally returned with the drink, Ed asked for ice. "No ice!" he said with satisfaction and left Ed alone with his thoughts.

As Ed sipped his drink he saw a man come in whom he thought he recognized, but couldn't think from where. The man looked over and smiled and waved. Ed remembered: it was Mr. Nutley from Mr. Agopian's shop. He came over.

"Well, well. How's about this for a coincidence!" he said, pumping Ed's hand. He was dressed in what used to be called "Full Cleveland": wine-colored blazer, white double-knit trousers, and white patent leather loafers with gold hardware. Ed inquired after Mrs. Nutley.

"She's not so good today," he said. "The bed collapsed last night and she's spent the day lying down. I mean it just collapsed! This old furniture they got here must have come off the Ark! I told Grace, next time the Hilton. I'm not staying in any more of these picturesque places!"

Hobson arrived a few minutes later. "S-sorry to keep you waiting. A last-minute call. The consulate's just next door, you know. I came over as quick as I could." He looked just the same, with his mousy hair and muddy eyes. The ill-fitting suit even looked the same. He ordered a whisky and they chatted for a few minutes.

Hobson said, "You know, I f-forgot to give you my card the other evening. Here." He handed Ed a card with an official U.S. Government seal on it, giving his name and the title "Consul for Commercial Affairs." Ed gave him one of the cards he had had made advertising him as an "Instructor in English Language and Literature." Hobson fell silent and seemed abstracted; then he said, "Well, if you've finished your drink, let's leave these gay s-surroundings and go on to dinner."

They walked a short distance up Istiklal Caddesi and then down a little side street, almost an alley, passing several shops, including a book dealer specializing in curiosa." Then Hobson led the way up a short flight of steps, through a creaky pair of doors and into a shabby foyer. He must have seen something in Ed's face, because he said, "I know it looks like kind of a d-dive, but it's an interesting historic place and the food is well cooked."

"It's good, eh?" said Ed hopefully.

"Not exactly. It's well cooked. No microbes. Not after this cook gets done with it. I've inspected the kitchen p-personally."

He led Ed into a large, high-ceilinged room, paneled in dark wood. There were booths around the wall, tables and chairs in the middle, and a sort of gallery at the end with more seating. The lighting was dim and, as it was still early, there were few other customers. He pointed out a table against the wall with a dinner setting for one person.

"That was A-A-Atatürk's table. It's always set that way. Not available for other diners."

A waiter came up and Hobson said that he had reserved a booth in the corner. They settled themselves and the waiter asked about drinks. "We'll start with lemon vodka," said Hobson, "A t-tradition of this place." A bottle of Turkish vodka with lemon peel floating in it was placed on the table and Hobson poured a couple of glasses. Ed tasted it: it was icy cold and very good. They had several and eventually ordered *meze*. Hobson advised piroshkis to follow, and then either beef stroganoff or chicken Kiev. Though Hobson's description of the food had lead Ed to expect burnt offerings, it actually turned out to be pretty good.

Hobson became more talkative. "They say this place was opened originally by some b-ballerinas who escaped from Russia after the Revolution. At least, some people say ballerinas. Other people say another p-profession."

Ed looked around the room. At the back there was an old lady sitting at a table, making out bills and giving change to the waiters. She seemed very old, but surely not that old. By now the place had filled up and there was a steadily rising level of conversation and cigarette smoke around them. Ed began to wonder when Hobson would introduce the topic he had invited him to discuss. At last, he seemed to come to a decision.

"Ed. I know that you are a l-loyal American."

This seemed like an odd beginning, but Ed agreed, nodding his head. "Yes, of course, Bill."

"G-good. I know. We had you checked out."

"Checked out? Why? What for?" He wasn't sure he liked the sound of this.

"Ed. The c-card I gave you earlier isn't quite accurate. The Commercial Service is a cover. I work for a different organization—also attached to the American mission to T-turkey."

"The CIA?"

He nodded. "S-something like that."

Ed was at sea, not being able to imagine what the something like the CIA could want with him. Not discuss private secondary education, presumably.

"So, what's this about, Bill? It is Bill, isn't it?"

He smiled. "Yes. That's my name. The c-commercial job is my cover. My reason for meeting with you is that I would like to ask for your h-help. In the name of your country."

Surely this wasn't possible. "You mean you want me to be a spy? But I don't know anything," he replied, suddenly thinking of the Fulbrighter, Randy, at Istanbul University.

"No, Ed. Not a spy. Nothing that dramatic. We are investigating an intelligence network organized by a foreign g-government, and you are in a position to supply us with some pieces of information."

"I still don't see what I can tell you. I'm just a teacher at the Istanbul Collegiate Academy." Suddenly, he had an odd feeling in the pit of his stomach.

"You don't mean something about the school? About Ali Bey?"

Hobson nodded. "S-so you already had suspicions?"

"Not suspicions. I just heard that Ali Bey had once been involved in some kind of intelligence work." Ed gulped.

"And s-still is. Work that is helping the enemies of your country and its allies."

"But, really, I can't believe that Ali Bey...look, in any case, I don't want to get involved in anything like this. This is your business, but I'm just a foreigner here. I might be arrested."

"No, Ed. It's n-nothing like that. This isn't James Bond we're talking here. Just a few pieces of information to fill out the picture. No danger. No risk. We'll make it worth your while."

"It isn't that. I just don't know."

"Look, Ed, I know what you're thinking. This is s-sudden. I won't say anything more right now. Give you a chance to get used to the idea. I'll g-get back to you later when you've thought about it. But let me stress, you are in a position to help us, to help the United States, at no risk to yourself. You'll have the p-protection of my organization."

"OK, Bill. I'll think about it. But I still don't know..."

"That's all I ask, Ed. You think. We'll meet again and I can g-give you details that I think will convince you that it's your duty. Your patriotic duty. And your efforts would not go unrewarded."

As Ed returned on the ferry after saying good-bye to Hobson, he thought, "By God! I've been recruited as a spy!" He wondered what Ray Collins would say to his spying on Ray's old friend.

Over the next few days Ed's thoughts kept returning to his conversation with Bill Hobson. It had all been so vague that he wasn't even sure what he was really proposing, and he decided that Hobson had simply been feeling him out to see how he would react. Well, he thought, how did he react? What, if anything, would he be willing to do "for his country" and against a person who had been kind to him? He supposed that he could only wait to see when—or if—he was contacted again, to learn more about what Ali Bey was accused of. He would have liked to discuss it with Brown or Elif, but he had promised Hobson, before they parted, to keep this to himself. Besides, what did he know about Brown, really? Nothing much, he realized. Whenever they talked it was always Ed who gave all the information. He didn't even know Brown's nationality. And Elif's father was a friend of Ali Bey and a former intelligence officer himself. Ed felt very lonely.

# 32

In addition to his quandary about Hobson's mysterious accusations, Ed was faced with the need to extricate himself from his liaisons with Mrs. Balian and Mrs. Papas. Elif had been very pressing in her demand for assurances that these relationships had ended. Needless to say, he had given these assurances, and now he understood that he had to make good on them. Ed continued to be very fond of both of them, for they were kind, emotionally undemanding, and discreet. And, of course, they also provided an outlet that he could not expect in his more serious courtship of Elif. In the meantime, he still saw both of them, though with a growing uneasiness. If Elif found out that he had lied to her, it would go badly for him.

Ed's indecision was ended for him in a curious way. He was sitting in his garden with Starleen, having an after-school *rakı* and trying to decide what to do with his evening. He thought about his day's classes. Why, he reflected, had he been so mad as to read the boys that poem by John Donne. All that confusion between the Holy Ghost and Caspar the Friendly Ghost. He wished that the boys didn't spend so much time at the movies on Büyükada. Elif had returned to Beyoğlu for the night and it was not one of his regular evenings with the other two ladies. The phone rang and when he answered it he was surprised to hear Mrs. Balian's voice.

"Ed, *chéri*. Do you think you could come over this evening? There is something I need to discuss with you."

He thought this odd, but said, "Of course, Lolly, when should I come over?"

She thought for a moment and then said, "About 10:00 would be good." He agreed and rang off.

Ed presented himself at Mrs. Balian's door a few minutes before 10:00. The hour he found unusual, since it seemed late for a social call and yet earlier than his other regularly scheduled appearances. The porch light was on, so it was clearly a public visit. He rang and Mrs. Balian opened the door. He noticed that she was wearing one of her silk figured dresses, rather than the less formal attire he was used to seeing her in during his regular visits. She asked him to come in and, after she had closed the door, gave him a kiss and a pat on the cheek.

"Welcome, *chéri*. Come in. Maria's here."

They went into the sitting room and, sure enough, Mrs. Papas was waiting for them. She was also dressed in the afternoon tea style of their first meeting. She came forward and also gave him a kiss and a pat.

"Good evening, dearest. Come in and sit down."

He sat down and noticed for the first time that the room seemed more dim than usual and that a card table had been set up with three folding chairs around it. He wondered: Were they going to play three-handed bridge? Canasta? Strip poker?

Mrs. Balian, without asking, brought over the whisky decanter and made him a drink. He saw that they already had half-finished glasses, which she freshened from the decanter. "Cheers," she said and they all raised their glasses. Ed had a stiff swig, bracing himself for whatever was coming.

"*Chéri*, I'm afraid that Maria and I have some rather distressing news. News that concerns us all," said Mrs. Balian.

He looked at Mrs. Papas, who nodded sadly and said, "Yes, darling, from the Other Side."

Suddenly it became clear. The spirits were horning in for some reason.

"Please, Maria, tell me about it," said Ed. "I can't imagine what objection...I mean, does Ramala...?"

"Not Ramala, dear. She has always been very fond of you. Very fond. This is another voice from the Other Side. One that I am hearing for the first time: a voice of warning!"

"Does the voice have a name?" asked Ed, puzzled.

"Bazat, a former priestess of the Cult of Sibyl, in ancient Carthage. She seems a most reliable person, but, you know, very serious. Last night I woke from a sound sleep, being alone," she looked at him fondly, "and heard a faint voice telling me that I and two dear friends, who were linked in love, were in danger. I got up and put on a robe and went to my special parlor, where I lit a candle and composed myself for communication. I fell into a trance and Bazat spoke, telling me who she was and repeating her warning. She said that the three of us should meet tonight and she would return."

This was certainly a fresh development. Ed knew, of course, that Mrs. Papas was a medium of repute and had a considerable clientele. Also, there had been a certain amount of spirit "presence" during his visits to her, but this had been more a matter of atmosphere, of incidental music. He had never participated in a formal séance—if that was what they were going to do.

Mrs. Papas continued, "I told Lolly and she agreed that we must heed this warning."

"So, Maria, let's finish our drinks and see what Bazat has to say," interjected Mrs. Balian briskly.

They gathered around the table and Mrs. Papas lit a candle, which she placed in an eggcup in the center. "Ready, Lolly." Mrs. Balian turned off the lamp at her side. The room was now dark, except for the candle flame and dim moonlight coming through the drapes. "All join hands."

The room was quiet and they sat perfectly still, holding hands. After a few minutes he became conscious of their breathing, and a slight regular creaking, which he eventually identified as Mrs. Papas' corsets. His nose began to itch, but he hesitated to "break the chain" by releasing his hand to scratch it. The tickling had become almost unbearable, when he saw Mrs. Papas' eyes close and she fell back in her chair. The back of his neck began to tingle and then suddenly there was a kind of cool earthy dampness around them, like mist rising from a graveyard. He heard Mrs. Papas' voice: "Is that you, Bazat?"

He felt Mrs. Balian's fingers tighten and they all waited. The cold dampness increased in intensity and Mrs. Papas repeated, "Is it Bazat? Do you have something to tell us?"

More silence. He began to relax, and then a disembodied whisper: "Yes. It is I." He looked at Mrs. Papas, but her lips were closed. Then she said, "Bazat, I have brought the two you asked for. Speak!" Again the whisper, a sound that seemed to have no source, but surrounded them:

"The three of you are joined in a chain of love. But that chain must be broken. The fates are spinning a web in which you will be caught—will perish. The man among you is being pulled by his...affections. True love has found him. He will soon be plunged into danger and mystery. I see death and destruction. It is better that you part."

"Is there more, Bazat?"

"Heed my warning! Farewell."

"Bazat?" And suddenly the cold dampness was gone. Mrs. Papas slumped forward onto the table.

"Maria, are you all right?" asked Mrs. Balian, turning on the light. Mrs. Papas' eyes opened and she shook herself.

"Just fine, Lolly. But I could use a drink!"

Mrs. Balian topped up their glasses and turned to Ed. "So, chéri, have you found true love?"

"I think I have, Lolly," he replied sheepishly. "She's a wonderful person. A teacher at the Academy."

"Well, we always knew that this couldn't last forever. But it has been nice, hasn't it, Maria?"

"Oh yes, indeed, dear. Such fun."

"But what concerns me are these portents of death and destruction," continued Mrs. Balian. "What do you think she meant?"

"There is no telling, Lolly. We must wait and see. The only thing that is clear is that we should disentangle our lives."

"Um. How quickly do you think, Maria?" asked Mrs. Balian, cutting her eyes at Ed.

"Oh, I should think another time—or two--couldn't hurt. Would you?"

"Not at all. So we are agreed?"

Ed nodded dumbly. A voice from Beyond had solved his problem for him, or so it seemed. Soon afterwards, he said his good-byes and left his friends in the sitting room. As he reached the front gate, he thought he heard the sound of laughter.

# 33

Though Ed was, in some ways, sorry to give up Mrs. Balian and Mrs. Papas, the renunciation allowed him to enter into a more relaxed relationship with Elif, relieved of his feelings of deceit and fear of discovery. She seemed to sense this and became even more loving and solicitous. Ed visited her parents again, where he was now received as a family friend, and Elif and he spent more of their free time together, though she still returned nightly to Beyoğlu. She noticed that he seemed more rested.

"You're not looking so hag-ridden now, Eddy. Are you getting more sleep?"

"Yes," he replied, "much more."

The weather was growing warmer and Ed suggested to Elif that on the following Saturday they take a hike through the pine forest to the center of the island, where he had found a pond with a secluded shore, and have a picnic. The pond didn't seem suitable for swimming, being fed by rainwater and appearing to have many submerged branches and tree stumps beneath its surface, but he thought it would make a nice setting. She agreed and said she would bring a picnic from home. He said that he would bring beer.

The day was up to his hopes: a blue bowl of a sky, bright sun, a light breeze, and a flat sea sparkling below. They hiked up the hill and into the woods and he led the way to the path that went to the pond. It was cool and dim under the pines, as they walked first up and then gradually down, towards the center of the island. They weren't actually very far from the school, the island being small, but it seemed remote from civilization. He put his arm around her waist and she nuzzled his neck. Then they had to walk single file, allowing Ed to admire her swaying bottom. He gave it a pat and had his hand slapped—but not hard.

When they reached the pond he was pleased to see that it came up to his expectations. Recent rains had filled it up to its banks and a little beach of pebbles looked inviting. Elif exclaimed, "Oh, how beautiful! How perfect!" and turned to give him a kiss.

He spread the blanket on the bank and they sat down and watched the surface dappled by the light breeze. He opened two beers and Elif unpacked a sandwich lunch. When they had finished eating, Elif put things away and Ed walked over to throw several stones into the center of the pond, to see if he could gauge its depth.

They lay down on the blanket and put their arms around each other. Elif said, "This is so peaceful. I can't imagine anything ever spoiling this moment for us!" Ed sighed in agreement. As they lay there looking at the shimmering water, he noticed a slight disturbance towards the center of the pond, a fish, perhaps, come up to feed. Then, before their eyes, a form rose and broke the surface. It appeared to be a log, probably wedged in the mud below and disturbed by the stones Ed had thrown in. As they continued to watch, it rolled over and Elif screamed. It was the body of a human being, green with slime, bloated and unrecognizable.

The next hours were a nightmare: first running back along the path through the woods, Elif hysterical and crying; bursting into the Academy and telephoning for the police; then, when the police came, leading them back to the pond, while Elif lay down at the school, calmed by Zeynep Hanım. The police captured the body with poles and ropes, wrapped it in blankets, and brought it back to a waiting ambulance, which transported it to a clinic on the island for an initial examination. By the time all this had been done, it was evening. Zeynep Hanım had deputized Kemal to act as Ed's interpreter with the police and he gave a preliminary statement of how they happened to find the body. At the conclusion of the statement, the officer closed his notebook and spoke to Kemal, who translated: "He says that this will do for tonight. Tomorrow you will be interviewed by his superiors, from Büyükada." Ed went to look for Elif, but Zeynep Hanım said that she had put her to bed with a sedative. "She was very upset, poor girl. You can see her in the morning. It was unfortunate that she had to see this thing, but at least it has nothing to do with us. So after she gives her statement to the police tomorrow she can try to forget about it."

# 34

"We think that it is possible that it may be the body of the French teacher who left the Academy several months ago," said Osman Bey. That morning the local police had collected Elif and Ed from the Academy and taken them to Büyükada. They went not to the police station where Ed had got his residence permit, but to another building where Osman Bey appeared to be organizing the investigation personally. He greeted Ed like an old friend.

"Ah, Mr. Wilkie. We meet under less auspicious circumstances, I fear."

"How do you do, Osman Bey. I'm surprised that you are handling this. I thought you weren't a policeman."

"No, I'm not exactly. But we think this may call for something more than the local police can provide. You know, an American colleague told me, 'If ever you want to commit a murder, do it in a small town.' He told me about a case in a small town in Northern California, where a body of a person who had died of natural causes had, for some reason, to be exhumed. When they turned the body over, there were bullet holes in its back."

"Very instructive. But I still don't see..."

"If the body is that of Lucie Leblanc, then this must be taken quite seriously. There may be wider implications."

"I see." He didn't see.

"The body is that of a woman. After so long in the water, her features are, of course, unrecognizable. But she appears generally to fit the description that Zeynep Hanım gave us. She died by drowning. Her legs were tied to heavy stones and she sank in the middle of the pond. Over time, the ropes had rotted and when you threw in the rocks she floated to the surface.

"So, was it murder?" Ed had the feeling that he had said this before, and then remembered the story of the Maiden's Tower that Mr. Agopian had told him when he first arrived in Istanbul.

"It isn't certain yet. All we know is that she drowned. The body doesn't show any obvious signs of violence, but of course it is badly decomposed."

"Is it realistic that she could have drowned herself—I mean in a shallow pond?"

"The pond is shallow on the edges. In the middle it drops suddenly and is quite deep. She could indeed have waded out and plunged in with the stones tied to her feet."

"But it still doesn't see likely to me. I mean, there are so many other ways..."

"We don't know for sure. We can only continue our investigation. Sift the evidence."

Osman Bey led them again through the story they had already told to the local police the day before, and a uniformed woman stenographer took down their words. Then he continued his questions:

"How well did you know Lucie Leblanc?"

"Fairly well. As a colleague. We saw each other socially from time to time."

"Did she have any special friends at the Academy?"

"She seemed fairly close to Mr. Demiray, the science teacher. I saw them together often."

"Did she have any enemies that you know of?"

"No. I don't think so."

"Did she and Mr. Demiray seem happy together? Did they have fights? Problems?"

From this question Ed suspected that he had already heard about the rather stormy nature of the relationship. "They seemed sometimes to have what I thought of as lovers' quarrels. She was very passionate—mercurial."

"I know. Mercurial, a nice word. Like mercury in a thermometer? Up and down?"

"Yes. I guess so."

He went on to question Ed in detail about the other members of the staff and their relationships with Lucie, but he was able to tell him little more than that she had done her job well and had had no particular friends except Erol Demiray. Finally, he stood up and stretched.

"All right, Mr. Wilkie, that does it for now. I guess there won't be any need for the rubber hose—this time," he said with a wink. Then they shook hands. "Please call me if anything else strikes you."

Elif and Ed left his office. In the waiting room outside they found Erol sitting with a policeman. He looked up and smiled wearily, before being motioned into Osman Bey's office.

After two days the body was confirmed as being that of Mlle Leblanc. Medical and dental records had been dispatched from Lyon, which checked out, and her parents and sister were advised of her death. The investigation, now definitely focusing on the Academy, went into high gear. The police interviewed all the staff and Ed volunteered the picture of her dog, Pompom, that he had retrieved from the box of things that she had left behind. "Not much to go on, I'm afraid," said Mr. Kuvvetli, whom Osman Bey seemed to have deputized as his man on the scene.

They dragged the pond but found nothing except old bottles, waterlogged condoms, and other irrelevant debris. Erol seemed to be the prime suspect, but nothing definite could be laid to him. He admitted that he and Lucie had grown friendly soon after her arrival, that after a few weeks they had become lovers. He considered it a casual affair, but said that she had begun to take it more seriously. She made demands on him, created scenes, and eventually forced things to a climax, telling him that they couldn't continue this way and that she was going to leave him. She was, she added, going to return to a former lover who was still in the background, though who or where he didn't know. He had, he said, not taken all this seriously, since he had been through this sort of thing with her before.

Ed braved the noisome stench of Erol's lab to commiserate with him on his ordeal. He seemed grateful after his extended interviews with Osman Bey.

"I appreciate this, Ed. I must say, you are the only person who has shown any understanding or sympathy. Most of them treat me as though I had already been proved guilty and we were just waiting for a new noose to arrive."

"I suppose people are confused by all this. They don't want to be involved. You look tired. Why don't we go out for dinner to help you get your mind off this. I'll ask Elif."

"No. Thank you very much, Ed, but I wouldn't be good company. Maybe I'll try working on my experiments again. I've been letting them go since this mess started." Ed remembered the complex-looking equipment in the private lab, locked away from the clumsy fingers of his pupils.

"Well, OK, Erol, but the offer is always open when you're feeling better." He left him looking more depressed than ever.

# 35

The alarms and excursions associated with the discovery of Lucie's body had caused Ed to forget for a while his meeting with Bill Hobson. However, he called one evening as Ed was preparing dinner, a simple macaroni and cheese that he fixed sometimes as a change from the Turkish food he ate in restaurants.

"Hi, Ed. I h-hope I'm not interrupting anything. I heard about the body turning up at your school. This makes what we had talked about even more urgent. I'd like to meet you tomorrow. Are you free for l-lunch?"

Ed said that he was, but had to be back to the Academy later in the afternoon. Hobson thought for a moment.

"OK. I have to be on the Asian side in the morning. There's a n-nice, very clean little kebab place off Bağdat Caddesi. You can take the ferry to Bostancı and walk or take a taxi. OK?"

Ed agreed, and Hobson gave him the address of the place. This was just what he didn't need, but Hobson's sense of urgency intrigued him.

He took the 10:00 ferry, thinking that he might as well walk around a little before his appointment with Hobson. In recent years, as the European side of Istanbul became more crowded and polluted, the middle classes began to look to the Asian side for less congestion and fresher air. As a result, the Asian shore has developed from a relatively empty area with a few small villages into a newly congested and polluted area of modern apartment blocks. The atmosphere is different from old Istanbul, having a sort-of plain vanilla international look: stucco buildings, tree-lined streets, luxury shops selling all the international brands, and a tangle of traffic that includes many late model BMWs and Mercedes. Like every Turkish town, there is an admixture of poorer buildings and neighborhood shops, illegal structures tucked in here and there, and a kind of hustle that you don't see in most Mediterranean cities. Bağdat Caddesi is the main artery, running roughly parallel to the coastline, but several blocks inland. On it you find some of the nicest shops, good restaurants, upscale hairdressers, imported books and magazines. You also find in astonishing numbers some of the classiest, prettiest girls in Istanbul, wearing the shortest skirts and the tightest jeans, swinging down the street arm in arm, fingering merchandise, and relaxing from their shopping exertions in cafes over pastries and tea.

Ed had been floating happily for a half hour in a sea of fancy merchandise and female pulchritude, when he saw a back he thought he recognized.

"Everett!" he shouted, and sure enough Everett turned and smiled.

"Greetings, Ed. What brings you to Bağdat Caddesi? Why are you 'standin' on the corner watchin' all the girls go by,' rather than on your island misinforming Turkey's future leaders?"

"I have an appointment over here. I'm just killing time till then. And you?"

"I have been engaged as a *hamal* for the day. That is, Lily is on a shopping expedition—her present wardrobe is, she tells me, nothing but a collection of stained rags, fit only for a bag-lady. The new season approaches and she must get the jump on the other women. My assigned role is to stand around—as I am presently doing—while she indignantly rejects the overpriced crap that the shops try to foist on her; provide counsel, advice and encouragement; carry an increasing accumulation of bags, as she finds some few acceptable items; and provide lunch. My only consolation, as I watch my miserable pension poured into the boutiques, is looking at the girls who are drawn to them like butterflies to a field of flowers." He seemed to be on a riff, and would doubtless have continued, but at that moment Lily joined them.

"Hi, Ed," she said, giving him a peck on the cheek. "How are you? How's Elif? You having some boy-talk about what a drag it is to go shopping with a woman?"

"Hi, Lily. Fine. Fine. Yes. In that order."

"Are you going to join my bond servant and me for lunch? I can show you all my purchases, including a pair of really smashing silk lilac undies."

"Eh, how's that?" said Everett, with sudden interest.

"Down, boy! We'll have a fashion show later." Then turning to Ed with a vulgar wink, "You might want to get a pair for Elif."

"I don't think Elif would consider them—be they ever so smashing—an appropriate gift. She was most carefully brought up. Your lunch suggestion sounds good, but as I was telling Everett, I have an appointment for lunch."

"How about a drink, then?" suggested Everett hopefully.

Lily looked at her watch. "Yes, we have time for a quickie—a quick drink I mean. How about here?"

She led them to a cafe and they ordered beers.

"So, who's your lunch date?"

"Oh, just a guy from the consulate. I met him at the party at the Consul General's house. He wants to talk about English teaching in Turkey. Something like that."

"Extraordinary," said Everett. "Why would anyone want to talk about anything so boring? Who is this guy?"

"Named Bill Hobson. Foreign Commercial Service."

"I don't think we know him, do we, Lil? Maybe he's new. That would account for this odd enthusiasm. Looking for a gimmick."

"Maybe," said Lily. "Still..." She looked thoughtful.

Ed almost decided to go ahead and tell them what Hobson had said. But he remembered his promise. If it seemed really serious, he thought, he could talk with them about it later.

"Well, I'd better get rolling. Can't keep someone waiting who's giving me a free lunch."

"They say there's no such thing," said Lily.

When Ed arrived at the restaurant Hobson was waiting for him. They shook hands and he suggested that they take a table in the garden. "It'll be more p-private there. We can talk without being disturbed." The garden was nice and, as it was still early, they were the only customers. They ordered beer and İskender kebab—sliced lamb with tomato sauce and yogurt.

Hobson was, as before, nervous and jumpy, moving his skinny body around in his suit, which hung on him like a toga.

"Have you thought about what we t-talked about, Ed?"

"Well, yes, Bill. But, you know, I still don't have much to go on. You didn't tell me much. I just don't see that I should get involved."

"Yes, yes. I understand c-completely. You're right to be cautious. But, as I told you, the death of the Leblanc woman makes things more urgent."

"How is that, Bill?"

"Because it fits together with the rest of our investigation." He glanced around him. " L-look, Ed, here's the story. Ali Bey has for years dealt in intelligence. He d-does this as a free agent for a small group of select customers through a network he has developed. He used to operate out of Beirut, later Damascus, and most recently, Paris. He had a p-problem while he was in Paris—a piece of intelligence he sold turned out to be a d-dud and he had to return quickly to Istanbul. He has a lot of friends among the g-generals in Ankara and in the Turkish intelligence establishment, so he was permitted to have s-sanctuary—and protection— on the understanding that he would d-discontinue his operations and retire. He did shut down most of his network—some parts had already been compromised by the P-paris mess—but one part of it he kept going. I won't go into d-detail, except to say that his customer is an enemy of the U.S. and the information that he was able to provide has been damaging to our interests. Because of the p-protection he enjoys in Turkey, we weren't able to do much about it, but more recently we have f-found his weak spot. Shall I go on?"

"Yes. Please do!" Ed was agog.

"Since many sources of income had dried up, he became d-desperate for money. He owed d-dough to men it would be dangerous to put off. Men who wouldn't wait." He paused.

"And?"

"He made a mistake. The mistake of a guy in a tough spot. He went into the d-drug trade."

"Drugs. But how...?"

"He used his c-contacts in the underworld to create a network for manufacturing and shipping heroin from Turkey to Western Europe. He has sources for the opium in Anatolia. This is brought to the island—we're not sure how—and m-manufactured into heroin. It is then taken to a distributor in Istanbul who moves it West—p-probably to the port of Marseilles."

"But this is incredible. Where...?"

"At your Academy. We think he must have a laboratory for this somewhere on the p-premises. The technician is a man called Demiray, whose cover is teaching science."

"Demiray! My God, I can't believe this." Then he remembered the "experiment" he worked on behind locked doors. He also suddenly knew how the opium came to the island: on the water ships that Erol was so interested in.

"You can believe it all right. We have all the p-proof we need. The point is, this is a small-time operation—like a cottage industry—but it gives us our hook to catch Ali Bey. The Turks can tell us to get lost on the intelligence side, but when we p-publicly expose his heroin operation, they'll have to act. And then we'll have him, or at least be able to shut him down. We want you to help us. Help us to get the evidence we need. F-from the inside."

Ed was so surprised he didn't know how to react. It seemed impossible, and yet it made sense. Still, he didn't want to get involved.

"I'm sorry, Bill. I just don't think I can help you. I'm not the right kind of person."

Suddenly, Hobson looked much less friendly. "I'm s-sorry too, Ed, because I don't like having to insist."

"Insist?" What, Ed wondered indignantly, made him think he could force him to do something against his will?

"Yes. Insist. You see, y-you are already involved."

"With the drug business? I don't think so!"

"You were a c-courier. Not once but several times. We have photographs and recordings of the deals."

"That's impossible! I've never seen any drugs. You're crazy!"

"Four t-times you took packages of pure heroin from the laboratory of the Academy to the agent in Istanbul. An agent who has a legitimate p-product that he ships West—for instance to Marseilles."

"Mr. Agopian!" Ed's head reeled.

"Bingo! You're in this up to your neck. So l-let's work together."

"And if I still refuse?"

"That's your funeral, Ed. When we t-take down Ali Bey you can either be our valued collaborator who broke the ring, or you can be a d-drug-runner caught in the net with the rest of them. That's the choice, boy."

"Hobson's choice."

"Huh?"

"And Lucie Leblanc? How does she fit in?"

"She was our f-first agent. She fell for Demiray and got careless. A real shame, but that's the way it goes."

When Ed left the restaurant, with the kebab sitting heavily on his stomach, he found that he was an accredited agent of the U.S. intelligence community. As Hobson had pointed out, he had no choice and he even sweetened things by naming a sum that he was empowered to offer Ed in recognition of his service. His task was to penetrate Erol's lab and get evidence on the manufacturing plant. He also gave Ed a package from his briefcase containing, he said, a miniature camera and information on the manufacturing process, so that Ed could recognize the elements when he saw them.

"It's very clear. In layman's language," Hobson said. "R-read it carefully and burn it. And for God's sake, don't worry. This is going to be a piece of c-cake!"

Later, on the island, Ed trudged up the hill from the ferry landing, feeling very much alone and helpless. Once at the top, he strayed from the path and headed across a field to have a look at the sea. As he walked, his feet crushed the sweet-smelling herbs beneath: *adaçayı*—sage. He breathed in the delicious aroma and, Proust-like, the doors of memory swung open: the dry brown hills of Southern California, where as a boy he had walked in the summers through the sage, his sneakers crushing the dry herb, and the aroma rising to his nostrils, a more woody aroma than the flowery *adaçayı*, but the same feeling, the same silence. Then he remembered those same hills in the spring, after the rains, not dry now, but dark green, dancing with bright spots of color, blue lupines and red poppies. The memory recalled something more recent to mind. Another bright spot of color on a dark surrounding. Yes, Ali Bey's *Mérite agricole,* awarded for his work in agronomy—on poppies.

# 36

For the next several days Ed was like a hunted man. He realized that he was going to have to develop a plan for getting into Erol's private lab and finding the evidence that Hobson was demanding. He had opened the package and studied the camera. He was not much of a photographer, but it seemed simple enough— a tiny apparatus with a built-in flash. He had been told that he was to photograph the equipment from various angles and take close-ups of the important elements. The two typed pages on the heroin manufacturing process were a little more technical than Hobson had suggested, but he got enough of the gist to know more or less what to look for.

He burned the papers, as directed, but hiding the camera became an obsession. He put it in a drawer under his socks, behind his books, in a coffee can, under a cushion. Starleen noticed his activities and decided that it was a game, following him around and then staring for hours at the place where he had hidden the camera. Finally, in desperation, he took to carrying it around with him in his briefcase, but was constantly nervous that he would forget and leave it somewhere.

Elif became aware of his nervousness and asked if he were having insomnia again. She said, "Maybe you should try taking a long walk. That will relax you and help you to sleep."

"Actually," said Ed, anxious to deflect her curiosity, "I took one several days ago and I had a Proustian experience. This will interest you!"

"Oh yes, Eddy. Tell me." She looked at him brightly.

"I was walking through a field. I was crushing sage under my feet..."

"Not sage, Eddy. *Aubépine*—hawthorn. There is no sage in Illiers. I visited it once. A literary pilgrimage."

"No. I mean this was *adaçayı*. And I remembered..."

"It was linden tea—*ıhlamur*—that he was drinking, Eddy, not *adaçayi*."

"Yes, with *madeleines*. I know..."

"Actually, it was fingers of toast. But later, in *À la Recherche*, he changed it. I'm not sure why. But I can try to find out if you are interested."

"No thanks, sweetheart." He squeezed her hand. "That isn't necessary." She sighed happily. "It's nice that we have literary discussions together, isn't it? A very interesting experience. I'm glad you told me." She stroked his cheek. Then, a moment later, she added, "Why don't you come over for tea tomorrow? My mother invites you. Then you can take me to an early movie and we can have something to eat. That will relax you."

Ed had, by this time, become quite familiar with the Beyoğlu apartment. The Ekmekçis had invited him for meals several times and he was becoming almost like a member of the family. After some initial resistance to the notion of an American boyfriend for their daughter, they seemed to have accepted the idea. It was clear, however, that the relationship had to be an honorable one, according to their—and Elif's—lights. This could not be a dalliance; their daughter's feelings were engaged. Ed felt that they were moving to the point where he would have to declare his intentions formally or give her up. He was certain that he loved her, but it was more complicated than that. He had no real career, no real prospects. Was he willing to stay in Turkey? Could he offer her anything in America?

Both Elif's parents were on hand for tea. Elif was dressed to go out later in a light blouse and skirt. As they drank their tea, Ed asked Nilgün about various old Turkish customs that he knew she loved to remember and describe. She talked about the old ways of matchmaking and turned to her own marriage.

"My husband's mother was very old-fashioned. She invited my mother, two of my aunts, and me to a *hamam* where we would spend the day talking, drinking tea, and getting to know one another. She came with some ladies from her family. One was a very old lady who sang. And even one of my aunts sang also." She closed her eyes and sang, in a beautifully pure voice:

*Üsküdara gideriken aldı da bir yağınur,*
*Katibimin setresi üsün eteği çamur,*
*Katip uykudan uyanmış gözleri mahmur*
*Katib benim ben katibin el ne karısır,*
*Katibime kolalı da gömlek ne güzel yarasır.*

Elif came over and sat beside her mother, holding her hand as she sang. She looked at Ed and explained, "It is a very famous old song, Eddy. A lady sings about her lover, an official in the Ottoman administration—a *katip*. It is unusual because the old Turkish love songs were mostly from the man's point of view."

When Nilgün had finished she said, "It was very embarrassing for a young girl. All eyes on you as you served tea—would you drop the tray? Of course, one reason for the bath was for the boy's mother to get a good look at the potential bride undressed." She smiled at her husband. "Those Turkish mothers knew how to look after their boys' interests."

"She certainly looked after mine!" he replied, and blew his nose.

Ed thought of the scene she had described, of the ladies in the bath, looking over their prospective in-laws. He wondered if his own mother were still alive might they have arranged a similar event for her? He tried to imagine her lolling naked in the bath with Elif and her mother. Would she have been expected to sing? They used to sing "Release Me" and "Home on the Range" together, but neither somehow seemed appropriate.

After tea, Elif and Ed went to a movie. Unfortunately, it was in an art house, an old film called *Five Fingers,* about a spy in Turkey during the war. As James Mason reached his final agonies at the inevitable discovery and retribution, Ed's nerves were jangling. For dinner Elif suggested that they go to a restaurant she liked near the fish market off of Istiklal Caddesi. She led the way past the more famous restaurants in the flower market and down a bustling, crowded, covered alley where fish and vegetables are sold; past stands selling kebabs, fried mussels, and other snacks; then down another alley and into a little street lined with *meyhanes*. They were doing a lively business and happy eaters spilled out onto the street at tables, with waiters diving in and out like swallows; men selling lottery tickets threading their way among the tables; and others offering almonds on crushed ice, cigarettes, and candy, calling their wares.

They passed through the street, waiters shouting to them to come in, and Elif selected a place near the end, a famous one favored by journalists and intellectuals. A smiling old Greek man welcomed them, inquired after her parents, and showed them to a table for two outside. After they were seated Elif said, "You still seem nervous, Eddy. I thought you would like a movie in English." They talked about her parents and Ed said that he liked them very much. "And they like you, Eddy. Very much. That is important for a Turkish girl." He squeezed her hand. Prospects be damned.

After dinner they walked back along Istiklal Caddesi to her parents' flat. They were talking together, not paying much attention, and turned up a street too soon by mistake; however, they continued on, thinking to cut over at the next corner. The street seemed darker and longer than he had expected, with small bars every few yards. He suddenly noticed that women were standing in the doorways and realized that they had wandered into one of the areas where prostitutes are tolerated by the police. Elif noticed too. She squeezed his hand and giggled, "Don't worry. They won't approach you when I am with you. I am your protector!" Then he remembered that she was near home and would certainly be aware of the area.

As Elif had said, the girls just looked at them and said nothing. They were a varied lot: dark Arab-looking women, Greeks, Africans, some obvious transvestites, and Russian Natashas, bold-looking women with red or blond hair.

Elif said, with an assumed sophistication, "An American friend told me that these Russian girls take to prostitution just like dogs to water."

"Ducks," said Ed.

"What, Eddy?"

"Ducks. Like ducks to water."

"Ah, perhaps that's what she said. Eddy, why is that girl waving at us?" He looked to where she was indicating and thought: This could not be! This was not going to happen!

"Mr. Wilkie! Great to see you!" He felt Elif stiffen. "You know I have leave Mrs. Akkaya. Work for myself now!" She turned to Elif. "All the girls love Mr. Wilkie. So polite man." Then back to Ed. "You see how good now I speak English? Not like when we were together at Grand Otel!"

He recognized her as Rezan, one of Mrs. Akkaya's girls, though it was not easy to recognize her in her new guise. At Mrs. Akkaya's she had always been dressed in demure costumes with ladylike makeup and had spoken in quiet, polite tones. Here she had clearly taken on the coloring of her surroundings: bleached hair teased high, startling false eyelashes and a slash of red on her mouth, a blouse that concealed nothing, and a skirt that was, as Brown would have said, "right up to the handle." Her English appeared to be courtesy of the U.S. Navy.

Elif asked evenly, "So you and the other...girls knew Mr. Wilkie on the island?"

"Natch!"

"And Mrs. Akkaya. She was...is...?"

"First-class madam. But too strict. So, you his girlfriend now?"

"No!" She grabbed away her hand, gave Ed a withering look, and flounced off around the corner before he could think of anything to say.

Rezan looked after her and then continued conversationally, "So, Mr. Wilkie. Your girl left you. Want some ficky-fick? Free, for old time sake!"

# 37

The weekend was agony. Now in addition to his enforced assignment by Hobson, he had seemingly lost Elif—again. He realized that Mrs. Balian and Mrs. Papas, and of course Balkiz, were one thing, but Rezan was in another category entirely for Elif and her mother and certainly beyond the pale. He tried calling her at her parents' the next day. When she answered the phone he said, "Please don't hang up. Just listen to me. I never had anything to do with that girl!"

"Really. How stupid do you think I am? She spoke to you—by name."

"I know. But we never...I mean, I didn't even know that she was a...I thought she was Mrs. Akkaya's daughter!"

Frozen silence. "She does not look like anyone's daughter."

"I know, now. But then...." He was speaking to a dial tone. It appeared that his career prospects were not so important after all.

The solution to getting another look at Erol's lab, however, was resolved in an unexpected way. As Ed was coming out of a class Erol met him in the hall and said, "Ed, I've been looking for you. Could you give me a few minutes?"

"Sure. What can I do for you?"

"Let's go to my lab. If you won't find it too revolting." They went down to the science rooms. He continued, "Ed, Ali Bey asked me to see if you could run over to Mr. Agopian's for him again. Later this week."

This was perfect, thought Ed. He would surely find a way to get the evidence he needed. "Of course. I'd be glad to. I have a rug I've decided to return."

"Good. In any case, he said that this would be the last time. It seems that the business with Mr. Agopian is almost finished."

Almost finished? Did this mean that they were closing down the drug business? Ed wondered.

Erol took out a bunch of keys held together with a piece of string from the pocket of his lab coat and unlocked the door of his private lab. They went in and Ed was relieved to see that the 'experiment' was still set up. He walked over to it.

"What is it that you are doing with all this stuff?"

"Oh, just some work on alkaloids. An idea I'm trying out..."

He went to the cupboard, selected another key from the bunch, and opened it. Once again, Ed saw the rows of bottles and jars. He started to reach in when they were startled by a muffled boom, followed by an overpowering stench and the tinkle of broken glass; then, shouts and laughter of increasing volume. An excited little boy rushed in and yelled, "Ibrahim just blew up his experiment! It's all over everything!"

Erol looked distracted. *"Hay Allah!* I leave them for one minute..." and rushed to the door and down the hall.

*Kismet!* Ed was alone with the 'experiment' and the little camera was in his bag. In a moment he took it out and tiptoed over to the equipment. He remembered Hobson's instructions: a shot from each side and close-ups of the working parts. He looked at it more closely and saw how cleverly it had been assembled, with many extraneous and complex pieces of tubing to conceal what was in fact a simple process. He selected an angle for the first shot, stood back, put the viewfinder to his eye, and focused it. Perfect. He pushed the button—nothing. Again—nothing. He looked at the camera with mounting anxiety and noticed for the first time that it was covered with little dents—tooth marks! Starleen had seen him put the camera in its final hiding place.

He was going to have to come back again, but this sort of opportunity would not present itself again. How would he get in? He looked around. There were Erol's keys hanging from the cupboard door, but he had no way of making an impression, even if he had known how to do so.

There were several windows around the room about six feet from the floor, covered with heavy curtains to exclude the light from the back garden. He pulled aside a curtain and saw that they were protected by steel grills secured with padlocks. He thought: padlocks have keys! He rushed over to the cupboard and grabbed the bunch hanging from the lock and went back to the window. He pulled over a chair and got up on it. The padlock seemed fairly new, so it was possible that a key for it might be in his hand. He tried them feverishly one by one. At one point in his haste he dropped the bunch and had to start over again. At last, with the sweat dropping from his face, a key fit and turned, and the lock opened in his hand. He reached through the grill and found the catch on the window, which he released. Then he turned the hasp of the lock so that it was ready to close, but didn't push it home. He got down from the chair and looked. If you checked carefully you could see that the lock wasn't closed, but the probability was that Erol wouldn't be looking closely at it. In any case, he had no other choice. He ran back to the cupboard and replaced the bunch of keys. When Erol returned a moment later Ed was sitting on a chair innocently looking over the lesson for his next class.

"I'm sorry to leave you like that," Erol said. "Fortunately, no real damage was done. Just a big stink. Which is probably what the little devils intended anyway."

The lab was now prepared for Ed's next, solitary, visit. But he would need a new camera. He would tell Hobson when he called for his progress report.

## 38

"Your d-dog ate the camera! Is this some sort of joke?"

"No. She didn't eat it, exactly. She just chewed on it. She thought it was some sort of a game."

"Well, dammit, that c-camera was expensive! Can it be fixed?"

"Maybe. But I think we need another one. In any case, I have to work quickly if they are going to shut down the operation. He may take apart the equipment—or notice the padlock on the window."

"OK, OK. I'll g-get another one. More damned paperwork! Meet me on the Asian side tomorrow at 5:00. Do you know Göztepe Park, in Caddebostan?"

"No, but I'll find it."

"I'll be there. By the Atatürk statue."

Ed looked up Göztepe Park on his map and decided that he and Starleen could walk to it from the ferry landing. The streets were fairly crowded, but, as always, the crowd parted as Starleen proceeded on her way. They got to the park a few minutes early, so Ed bought them each a *simit*, a kind of circular bread roll covered with sesame seeds, and stationed himself on a bench near the statue.

A few minutes after 5:00 Hobson arrived, walking jerkily with his suit flapping around him. He looked at Starleen with disfavor.

"So this is the g-guilty party? Let's see the camera. My God! It looks like you put it through the garbage disposal!" Starleen sniffed at his leg with friendly interest. "Hey! Keep her off. I don't want my l-leg to look like this!"

Ed pulled her back. "I'm sorry, Bill. She didn't do it on purpose. Anyway, what's done is done."

He seemed very grumpy. "Easy for you to say. You don't have to fill in r-requisitions for the equipment. I've been running around all afternoon. S-say, what are you eating?"

"*A simit.* You want one? I got it from that man over there. Here, have a bite," he said, offering it to him. Hobson could not have looked more offended if Ed had handed him a dog dropping.

"You bought it off the street! It's probably covered with g-germs. You had a hepatitis shot?"

Ed reflected that for a spy Hobson was an excessively fussy and finicky man, but then he didn't know any other spies to compare him with.

"So, Bill, do you have the new camera for me?"

"Yes, yes. Here, sit down and I'll show you. It's a d-different model. A more expensive model," he added pointedly. He showed Ed how it worked. "There. You really need to get c-cracking on this Ed. We've confirmed that the g-good doctor is about to close down. We've got to get the evidence quick if we want to n-nail him."

"I'll do my best, Bill."

"You'd better, friend. R-remember, we still got you!" He gave Ed an unpleasant smile.

"So, shall I call you as soon as I have something?"

"No! I told you, never call me at the c-consulate. I'll call you at regular intervals from a secure phone. Well, I g-guess that's it!" He nodded and walked quickly away, his trousers flapping on his thin legs.

Ed sat on the bench trying to plan his next move. The important thing seemed to be to return to the lab as quickly as possible—at night—to take the pictures, gather any other evidence he could find, and get away. Then, when Erol gave him the package for Mr. Agopian he could try to open it unobtrusively and extract some of the heroin for additional evidence. That should be enough to get him off the hook. He got up and walked back to the landing. On the way they stopped and got another couple of simits to eat on the ferry—another dose of hepatitis to keep them in trim. On the ferry he met Brown, who said he had been in Bostancı taking care of some business deal.

"So, Doc, I spotted you on the boulevard earlier today, but you seemed to be in a hurry somewhere. Something important?"

"Not really. A meeting with a guy from the consulate."

"Visa problem?"

"No. The commercial guy. Name's Hobson. He's interested in English teaching."

"Seems odd, but no accounting for tastes. Is this the thin chap, Hobson?"

"That's the one. You know him?"

"Eh? Not really. Must have met him at some do. Rather rum. Speaking of which, what say to a drink at my place?" But Ed was feeling distracted and asked for a rain check.

An hour later Ed was letting himself in the front door of his cottage when he heard the phone ringing. Could Hobson be checking on him already? He ran over and answered, Starleen helping by running between his legs.

"Wilkie here."

"Hello, Eddy. This is Elif."

His heart stopped. "Sweetheart, what..."

"Eddy, I have been calling all afternoon. Where have you been?"

"Sweetheart, I..."

"I have misjudged you. I have called to say that I am sorry."

"But Elif, that's wonderful! But how did you decide that you had misjudged me?"

"Rezan explained everything to me."

"That's great, I...Rezan!" Ed's mind went blank.

"Yes. I decided that it wasn't fair to condemn you without seeing if you were telling the truth. Though, you know, Eddy, you must admit that it looked very bad."

"I see. Yes. Very bad..."

"So I went back and found Rezan..."

"You mean on that street! You..."

"...and we went and had tea together. She explained about the Grand Otel and Mrs. Akkaya. She thought it was very funny that you thought they were Mrs. Akkaya's daughters. She thinks you are very sweet, very *naif*. We talked for a long time. She is from Adana, like Baba's family. She talked about her mother and sister at home. We cried."

Ed was stunned. Clearly he didn't understand women. Maybe no man ever really did.

"So, we are back together?"

"Of course, Eddy."

"I love you, Elif."

"Of course you do, Eddy. But you have taken a very long time to say so. It seems I have something to thank Rezan for. Goodnight, Eddy."

He poured himself a *rakı* and sat down in his comfortable chair. The sky was bright again. Starleen sensed his lightened mood and came over to lean against his leg. He took a sip of *rakı* and sighed. Then he remembered Hobson.

# 39

The next day Ed met Elif after classes. They took a walk overlooking the sea, where he had had his Proustian experience. She was very loving.

"You must understand, Eddy. I thought you had deceived me with that kind of woman. I thought I had lost you."

"I understand. It looked terrible. But I will never be unfaithful again."

"Yes, I know." Green eyes held his.

"Elif, I feel so lucky that I found you. How can it be that a wonderful woman like you was not taken away by another man long ago. You must have known other men that you liked."

"No. This is *kısmet*. You were the man whom fate had prepared for me."

*"Kısmet.* Yes, it's like *kısmet.*"

"Mrs. Papas explained it all to me."

His mind shut off. "You mean the Mrs. Papas, the island Mrs. Papas?"

"Yes. Maria Papas. Mrs. Balian introduced us."

"Mrs. Bal..."

"Yes. I called her after we had our conversation. I wanted to see what sort of a person she was, and to determine—discreetly, of course—that you had broken off your relationship with her. At first, she was..."

"But, I mean, wasn't she surprised..."

"...a little surprised by my visit. But when I explained, she quite understood. She is a very nice lady, very *cultivée*. She said that you had told her that you had met me and that you and she would have to part. It was very sad."

"Then I visited Mrs. Papas. Also a very nice lady…and so understanding. She told my fortune with Tarot cards. So exciting! Maria explained that our meeting was kısmet. That is why I had never been in love before."

"You mean that you are in love now?"

"And then I met Ramala. Some day Maria is going to have a séance and invite me. She said that she and Mrs. Balian were planning one, but it was already fully subscribed."

"Yes, fully subscribed. But, then, everything is all right?"

"Oh yes. I think you showed good taste in your choice and you did end the relationships when you met me. Besides, as Maria pointed out, she taught you a lot."

"My God! She said..."

"So later you can show me everything you learned."

"Everything I..."

"Yes. She said she even gave you a set of Tarot cards."

"Ah, so she did." He gave her bottom a pat. This time his hand wasn't slapped.

After he saw Elif off at the ferry landing he felt at loose ends so he thought that he would look in on Brown at the Grand Otel. Everything remained the same, including Mustafa, who came over with a smile.

"Mr. Wilkie. Welcome! How have you been?"

Ed filled him in on his activities. "Oh, and I met Rezan the other day."

Mustafa looked serious. "Yes, very sad. I was sorry she left us, but she and Mrs. Akkaya couldn't get along. How is she?"

"She seems very happy. Likes being in business for herself."

"Yes. But not good. Dangerous. Here she had Mrs. Akkaya to see to her interests, to protect her. A nice, refined clientele." He shook his head, "Everyone told her. Well, the dog barks..."

"He certainly does. Is Brown in?"

"Yes, he came in an hour ago. Go on up."

Brown seemed glad to see him. "Hello Doc! How's it hanging? You look like a man in need of a drink."

"You're a mind reader."

He poured them each a stiff *rakı* and put out a little bowl of nuts. "How's your beautiful lady?"

"Elif is fine. I'm thinking of asking her to marry me."

"A big mistake. Responsibilities. Children. Debts. Better just to keep banging the old ladies."

"But I love her."

"Rum idea, love. It never happened to me—at least I don't think so." He rubbed his face and took another swig. "Never had time, I guess."

"What about your mysterious lady friend?"

"I don't know, Doc. Everything is rather confused now. I may be moving on sometime in the not too distant future."

Ed was surprised, having come to think of him as a permanent element in his island life. "I'm sorry to hear that, Brown. What...?"

"Changing business climate. I'll let you know when I know, Doc. I've enjoyed knowing you."

"Me too, Brown."

# 40

Ed had decided that he would try that night to get into Erol's lab to take his photographs, as there seemed no point in putting it off. He reflected for the first time that if he did, in fact, succeed in helping Hobson "take down" Ali Bey, he would not have a job, since the school would presumably go down with him.

Could he get another job in Istanbul? Could Elif? There seemed no point in following this line of thought. He had little choice, and besides drug trafficking was a dirty business. He shivered and set his alarm clock for 1:00 in the morning.

Setting the alarm proved unnecessary, since he was unable to sleep. He tried reading, made himself a drink, thought about Elif, but he was keyed up and could neither concentrate nor rest. Hobson had described this as a "piece of cake," but he had no doubt but that if he got caught he would be dealt with as Lucie Leblanc had been. He wondered who had done the job: Erol? Zeynep Hanım? Someone else on the staff? How had it been done? He thought about the path to the pond. Was she forced to walk along it at gunpoint? Was her unconscious body carried there in the night and submerged? He shivered again.

At 1:00 he checked the camera and put it, together with his flashlight, in a book bag and let himself out the front door. He had changed into sneakers, jeans, and a dark sweater. It was slightly chilly as he walked through the dark silent streets, with just an occasional dog bark or seagull cry in the distance, and the familiar shape of the Academy was soon before him. No lights were on in the residential wing, so the last paper must have been graded for the night.

He made his way around the side of the building and into the back garden, then along the wall of the old house until he found the windows at ground height that he knew led down into the private lab. He couldn't remember which one he had unlocked, so he would have to try them in order. The heavy curtains made it impossible to see whether the lights were on in the room and it struck him that Erol might be working in his lab. It was an unsettling thought, but he would just have to chance it. He reached down and pulled gently on the first window. It didn't move, so he went on the next. He pulled and it swung open with a muffled creak. He froze, but there were no sounds from inside. So he stooped down and reached through the open window, putting his hand through the grill and feeling for the padlock. It was there, and still open, so he quickly unfastened it, put it in his jeans pocket, and pushed open the grill. Then he seated himself on the window ledge and slowly drew back the curtain. The room was dark and silent, so after a moment's hesitation he jumped from the ledge and into the darkness. Stage One accomplished.

Checking to be sure that the curtains were again securely closed, he turned on his flashlight and tiptoed over to the workbench where Erol's "experiment" was set up. He fully expected it to be gone, or disassembled and lying in a jumble of glass tubing on the table, but there it was, just as he had seen it last. He set down his flashlight and took out the little camera. What about light? It had a flash, but that might not be adequate for what he needed to do. He decided to risk putting on the light for a few minutes.

When he turned on the wall switch he was momentarily blinded, and then, following Hobson's instructions, he moved around the equipment, taking the general shots to show it in its setting, then close-ups to show the working parts. In all, it took perhaps ten minutes. He then went over to the cupboard, but it was, as he had expected, locked. He looked elsewhere around the room, but there was nothing that looked like evidence, so he shut off the light, put the camera and flashlight into his book bag, and moved back to the window.

When he got to the window he looked up and realized that he hadn't taken into account the fact that the windows were six feet off the ground. He pulled over a chair to stand on, so that he could get onto the ledge. If Erol notices it tomorrow, he thought, it just can't be helped. He eased himself onto the ledge, and wiggled through the window. Then he closed the grill, relocked it with the padlock, and pushed the window closed, hearing the snick of its spring lock. He stood for a moment, weak with relief, and noticed that his heart was pounding. He looked up again at the building, still completely dark. So he moved back around the wall, into the front garden, and out the gate. He walked briskly for a few minutes and then he heard a sound behind him and turned and saw a figure moving quickly towards him on the other side of the road. He slipped into a doorway and waited for it to pass. As he stood there a cat, seemingly disturbed by his passage, came over and stood in front of him, looking up with interest.

The figure on the other side continued to move toward him, then stepped into the light of a street lamp and moved on. It was Brown, on his way home from the embraces of Zeynep Hanım. When he was out of sight, Ed came out of the doorway and started down the road for home. He would hide the camera in the cottage and wait for Hobson's call.... But he didn't have the camera. It was in the book bag, lying on the bench in the lab, where he had set it down when he moved the chair to the window.

# 41

The following morning Ed was in an agony of impatience to get to school and recuperate the camera from Erol's lab. The one positive thing was that it was in the book bag, so if he could get to Erol early enough he could claim that he had left the bag when he visited the lab yesterday. But it was essential that he get to him before he noticed and opened the bag. The purpose of the little camera was too obvious to be explained away.

Ed was at school by 7:00, since there was no way to know how early Erol might start his day. He rushed to the science room, but Erol hadn't yet arrived, so he stationed himself on a bench in the garden where he would have to pass to go downstairs to his lab. Mehmet Efendi noticed Ed and came over to say good morning and point out the new flowers starting to come up. Time passed and a trickle of pupils arrived and began playing football before classes. Several sleepy-looking teachers arrived and stopped to pass the time of day. Still no Erol. Ed looked at his watch. It was 8:45 and in fifteen minutes he would have a class to teach. He couldn't remember if Erol also had a 9:00 class.

It was now 8:55 and he could barely sit still. Should he cancel class? Then he looked up and saw Erol coming through the front gate. "Erol!" Ed shouted, and he looked over and smiled. Ed ran over to him.

"Thank heaven you've come. I left my bag in your lab yesterday. There is something in it I need for class!"

He seemed puzzled. "You did? I don't remember seeing anything when I closed up."

"Maybe I'm wrong, but could we have a look?"

"Well, it's almost time for class. Is it really urgent?"

"Yes, I'm afraid so. I'd appreciate it."

He nodded and led the way to the lab. "No, I don't see anything."

"No, not here. In your other lab."

"You were there? Oh yes, you're right." He unlocked the door and Ed rushed in ahead of him while he turned on the lights in the main teaching lab. There was the bag on the table. He gathered it up then went over and took the chair from beneath the window and replaced it against the other wall.

"Well, find it?" asked Erol, coming into the room.

"Yes, it was here. I was sure it was," holding up the bag. "Thanks loads. Now I have to rush off to class."

The rest of the day Ed was palpitating with anxiety to get in touch with Hobson and rid himself of the camera and its contents. He still didn't like the idea of being his cat's paw, but he reasoned that, after all, when the bust came he had to be on the right side. Since he was presumably going to be out of a job, the sum Hobson had mentioned would do to tide him over.

It was difficult for him to concentrate on his classes and, of course, the boys sensed this and took full advantage. The day ended with a literature class, where they were finishing "The Fall of the House of Usher."

"So as you can see, boys, Poe's narrator is slowly brought to take the point of view of Roderick. He also participates in Roderick's obsession, and the two of them believe that they see the Lady Madeleine risen from the dead. Poe does this by presenting..."

"Please, sir, you mean she doesn't come back to life?"

"No, no. It's a study in abnormal psychology. You know, like you learned about in your psychology lessons with Gülsen Hanım."

Thirty pairs of eyes exchanged glances. *Hay Allah! Gülsen Hanım, the well-known crackpot!*

Then after a silence, "But, sir, maybe they just didn't nail the lid of the coffin down tight enough."

What the hell, he thought: "Yeah, maybe that's it. Class dismissed."

He came out of class wondering if, perhaps, it weren't just as well that he would shortly be leaving the teaching profession, when he saw Ali Bey and Osman Bey coming out of the front of the building in deep conversation. Osman Bey was speaking intensely as Ali Bey slowly nodded his head. Then Ali Bey spoke for a moment, making chopping motions with one hand, while Osman Bey looked down at his feet. They stopped at the gate and shook hands and Osman

Bey continued down the road, while Ali Bey walked back through the garden with an abstracted look on his face. As they were coming towards each other Ed said, "Good afternoon, sir."

He started and looked up. "Oh, good afternoon, Mr. Wilkie. It's been some time since we spoke last. How are you doing?"

Ed told him that he was getting along fine and that they were reading Poe. Then he said, "I saw you with Osman Bey. How is the investigation coming along? Any progress?"

Ali Bey looked at him and then away. "I'm not sure. It seems to be taking a new direction."

Ed noticed that there seemed to be something different about his somber clothing today. "Ali Bey, you aren't wearing your *Mérite agricole.*"

He looked down. "That's odd. You're right. I forgot it. I think I'm a little distracted by all this."

"I understand that you were originally an agronomist."

"Actually a botanist. I did research at one time at the Jardin des Plantes in Paris. Long ago."

"And specialized in poppies, didn't you?"

"Poppies?" He seemed surprised. "No, Atatürk flowers. What do you call them in English—poinsettias. Named for an American diplomat—Poinset. A terrible diplomat, but a good botanist for his day."

"Well, sir, I know you are busy and I won't keep you. I'll be ready to take the new package whenever you say."

"Package?"

"To Mr. Agopian. Like the other ones."

He looked at Ed sharply. "I'm sorry. I don't understand."

"The packages you asked Erol to give me. To take to Mr. Agopian in the Grand Bazaar."

"Ah, I see. Those packages. Thank you very much for your help. Erol Bey will contact you, in the usual way. Good day, Mr. Wilkie," and he went off at a brisker pace.

It seemed odd, Ali Bey's reaction to his reference to the packages. Had he somehow given something away? He went over the conversation in his mind. He couldn't see anything, and yet clearly he had tipped him off to something. He was pondering this, when Elif interrupted his thoughts.

"Eddy, why have you been avoiding me all day? Is something wrong?"

"No, sweetheart. I've just been a little upset. I need to talk to someone at the consulate. I have to give him something, but he's told me not to call him there. I'm not sure when he'll contact me."

"But that's silly! Why can't you call him?"

"He said not to. It's sort of..."

"Look, Eddy, I will call. I will tell his secretary that I am your secretary and that I need to speak to him. When I get through to him I will ask for an appointment so you can give him whatever this is."

"I'm not so sure..."

"Wait here. What is his name? Hobson? I will go right now," and she marched away.

She came back in a few minutes. "Nothing easier, Eddy. His secretary put me right through. I said you wanted to see him urgently to give him something and he said you could see him at 7:00. He is working late and then going to a reception."

"He wants to see me at the consulate?

"Yes. He said that he'll give your name to the marine guard. See, wasn't that easy? Men always want to make a lot of fuss and bother. It is all quite simple."

If Hobson were willing to see him at the consulate it must be because things had reached the point where secrecy was no longer so important. Strange, but all Ed wanted was to be free of the camera.

Ed said that he would go over on the ferry with Elif and then continue on to the consulate. They sat outside holding hands and then took a taxi to Taksim Square. As they walked together to her parents' apartment he was thinking about his upcoming interview with Hobson. Suddenly Elif spoke.

"Eddy, I think I may have misled you a little about the toast fingers."

"Toast?" Was he losing his mind from the strain?

"Yes. When I said that Proust was originally eating toast fingers I didn't mean for you to think..."

"Proust? Sweetheart, what are you talking about?"

"Well, Eddy, if you are going to be huffy because I know more than you do about Proust, then I think it is very silly. Your specialty is English literature." She pursed her lips.

"No, you're right. I was being ridiculous." God knows what this was all about.

"You are just on edge, Eddy. We will talk about the toast fingers and madeleines another time." She patted his cheek, like a kind auntie comforting a fractious child, and kissed him good-bye.

# 42

It was a little before six when Ed arrived at the consulate. It stood in a compound, surrounded by a high wall, with a sort of booth by the entry gate with a marine in uniform seated in it. When Ed gave him his name, he said, "Yes, sir, Mr. Hobson is expecting you. I'll call up to his secretary." Ed waited while he spoke to her on the phone. "She's coming down. Do you have some identification?" He passed over his passport and was given a badge with a number on it. "Please just fasten that to your jacket, sir." He let Ed through the gate where he was able to study the consulate building. It was a pretty, though surprisingly small, 19th-century building of classical design. There was flight of steps up to a portico with three arches capped by lions' masks. He noticed a plaque set into the wall and learned that the United States had established diplomatic relations with the Ottoman Empire on October 3, 1831. It appeared that the first ambassador was one Commodore David Porter. Why a commodore, a navy man? The plaque had been placed there by the American community in Constantinople on the 4th of July, 1922.

A few minutes later a tired-looking, middle-aged woman arrived. "Mr. Wilkie?" she smiled. "That's me," he replied and she led him across a parking area to another building, worked a cipher lock, and took him up in an elevator. They entered a door marked "Foreign Commercial Service" and she took him through that, past her own desk, and to a private office marked "Mr. Hobson."

"Bill, this is your visitor, Mr. Wilkie."

Ed thanked her and entered. A gray-haired black man was seated at the desk. He smiled and got up.

"Mr. Wilkie?"

"Yes," he said, shaking hands. "I'd like to see Mr. Hobson. I have something for him."

"Well, you're looking at him. We don't know each other, do we? I only arrived at post a few months ago."

"I'm sorry, but...you are Bill Hobson?"

"I am." He looked slightly offended. "What's this all about?"

"But the Hobson I met at the Consul General's residence was a different man."

"Well, I'm the consulate's full complement of Bill Hobsons. What is it you want?"

"I'm very confused. As I said, I met a man at the Consul General's house, at a party. He said that he was Bill Hobson and gave me this card." Ed handed it over. "He was a tall, thin man with brown hair. He stuttered slightly."

"Yeah. This is my card. He was white, I take it."

"What? Oh yes, white, with brown hair and eyes—very thin." Ed found himself babbling. "A party for Senator Goff. And Arabs."

"Oh yeah. Goff. I missed that one. Look, let me keep this card. I'll need to report this to security."

"But why did you give me an appointment if you didn't know who I was?"

"Well, your secretary said it was urgent. I thought that this private school of yours might have some sort of commercial angle. I was going to be here anyway."

"Well, I won't bother you anymore. Just a mistake, I guess."

He took Ed's name and telephone number ("Security will want to look into this") and the tired-looking secretary took him back down and handed him over to the marine, who said, "There you go, sir. Here's your passport back. Have a good one!"

Ed walked away from the consulate with his head in a whirl. What did all this mean? He felt the camera in his pocket. What should he do with it? He finally stopped off at a cafe and sat down to think things over. He knew now that the man who had contacted him was not Bill Hobson, but who was he? He had said that he was in "something like" the CIA, so perhaps he didn't work out of the consulate. Maybe the consulate didn't know about him. Was that possible? Had Ed blown his cover? On the other hand, maybe he wasn't a U.S. government agent, but if not, what was he? Why would someone want to blow open Ali Bey's drug racket? A rival gang, maybe? It suddenly struck him that Brown had called Hobson "that thin chap." Said he had met him. But the real Hobson was black. Was Brown, then, also involved in some way?

It was all very confusing, and Ed didn't know where to turn. He thought of Elif, but she was, after all, Turkish, and if the faux Hobson was legit Ed shouldn't expose him. Maybe when the security man called him from the consulate he could talk to him about it. But then the faux Hobson had some sort of evidence that Ed was a drug courier. How would that play with the consulate? If only there were someone...then he thought of the Blums. Surely they could advise him. They had been in the diplomacy business, but were no longer. They could advise him as friends. Revitalized, Ed hopped up from his table and asked the waiter where there was a phone. Ed found a phone token in his pocket and called the Blums' number. No reply.

He took the ferry back to the island and went home. Then he tried the Blums' number again at intervals throughout the evening. At last, a little after midnight, Everett answered.

"Ah, Ed. We just returned from a little festival that Lily got us roped into: Dhrupad singers, if you can believe it! At the Indian consulate."

"Everett, I..."

"It was an eternity of torment. As I sat there on my butt-numbing folding chair I felt like those dead chieftains in *King Solomon's Mines*, left in limestone caves, with the water dripping on them over the centuries, and slowly becoming like human stalagmites, their rigid features, caught in the rictus of their dying agonies, becoming blurred and indistinct as the mineral deposit covered them up."

"It sounds bad, Everett, but..."

"The torment was not even relieved by the solace of alcohol. They served— are you listening—mango nectar! Well, we're remedying that, at least!

"Everett! Will you listen!"

"Well, I thought a friend would be interested in my sufferings," he said in an offended tone.

"I need to see you! Right away."

"Sure. No more boats tonight, but why don't you come tomorrow. It's Saturday. Come for breakfast. Can Elif come?"

"Thanks, Everett. No, Elif won't be joining me." Ed rang off and poured himself a *rakı*.


# 43


It was overcast the next morning when Ed caught the first ferry for the Blums' island. When he arrived at their house the Blums were still in their dressing gowns. He started to apologize, but Lily said, "Don't be silly. We're just making a *grasse matinée* after our evening with the Indian rock-and-rollers. I couldn't drag Everett away!"

Everett refused to be drawn. "Bloody Mary, Ed?" He accepted gratefully and they settled down in the living room.

"So, what's the big mystery, my friend?" said Everett, "Why this sudden anxiety for our company—delightful though it may be—at this hour of the morning?"

"I seem to have got myself into some sort of bind, and I was hoping you could advise me."

"Sure. What are friends for? A small loan can always be arranged, at only slightly above the prevailing rates of interest..."

"No. It's nothing like that. It's some sort of...international intrigue."

"Tell us about it," said Lily. "Take your time."

Ed didn't know exactly how to summarize his problem, so he just began with the Consul General's party and worked his way through the events leading to his visit to the consulate the day before, and the discovery that Hobson wasn't Hobson. The Blums listened carefully, occasionally asking for clarification or amplification of his points. At last he wound it up and stopped.

"Wow," said Everett. "You've been a busy boy."

"But what does it all mean?"

"I don't know," said Everett, looking at Lily, "but the faux Hobson, as you call him, is certainly not a Company man. I mean, they would never recruit someone like that and simply trust to his discretion. They would have their own people already in place. They wouldn't need you." He looked at Ed quizzically. "Don't you ever go to the movies?"

"Try to be serious, Everett," said Lily. "But you know, Ed, he's right. This guy isn't a U.S. government type. But who he is and why he's trying to get at Ali Bey I don't know."

"I also think that my friend Brown may be involved in some way," said Ed. "I'm afraid that he's working with Hobson."

"That's bad," said Everett. "How much have you told him?"

"I'm not sure anymore. But what should I do?"

"Sit tight," said Everett. "I'll get in touch with the station chief and see what he thinks."

"Talk with Ted, too," said Lily. "The head of security," she explained, looking at Ed reassuringly. "They may have a better idea of what this is about. It may be something for the Turkish police."

"Right," said Everett. "Presumably nothing will happen until you've turned over your pictures and they've been processed. They must be the key element in whatever this is. Wait for the faux Hobson's call. See what his next instructions are, and then let me know right away. Depending on what our guys think this is all about, they may want to grab him, or have the Turks do it. But under no circs go to any meeting with him without telling us, so we can make arrangements to have you covered. Also, be sure that any meeting is in a public place—not by a pond in the woods."

"You see," said Lily, "I told you there was no such thing as a free lunch."

The Blums gave him pancakes and then they agreed that he should go home to wait for the faux Hobson's call. He felt better now. Their sensible and knowledgeable advice seemed to have cleared his head. They were setting things in motion that would take this awful mess off his hands and let him get back to Elif. But he didn't much like Everett's reference to the pond in the woods.

When he got back home it was early afternoon and the sky was growing darker. His cottage looked especially cozy and inviting, nestled in honeysuckle with the lavender blooming. He took out his key and turned it in the lock, but the door was already unlocked. He couldn't remember if he'd locked it, but he did forget often enough. Wound up as he was, he thought about Everett's warning—only in a public place where he could be covered. He listened: nothing. Then, as he stood there, he heard a slight creak. Someone was standing on the other side of the door. The perfect setup: whoever it is could kill him, take the camera and be away, with no witnesses. He cautiously began to turn, intending to tiptoe back down the steps. Then, the door sprang open.

"Surprise, Eddy!"

He thought he would throw up with relief. "Elif, sweetheart, what are you...."

She put her arms around his neck and kissed him. The feel of her breasts against his chest and the scent of her hair were intoxicating.

"I thought it would be nice to spend the day together, Eddy," she explained. "You were gone and I was so sad. You had left your door unlocked—you must be more careful Eddy—so I came in. I am afraid that you are rather messy, so I straightened things up and washed the dishes. It is a lovely cottage. Also, very useful to have a *sarnıç* to catch the rainwater. I opened it. See, I left up the cover in the hall floor. It is dry now, because the downspout from the roof was plugged up. I unplugged it. So, with the next rain you will have a nice full tank." She walked over to the *sarnıç* to show him, allowing him to admire how gracefully she moved in her full-skirted dress.

"That's great, honey."

"So, I was just looking at your cute little camera, when I heard your key."

"My little camera? How did you find it?"

"Starleen was staring at the bookshelf and I thought maybe you had put one of her toys there. So I looked, and I noticed that the roll had been finished. You must take it to be developed...I hope you don't think I was snooping!"

"Not at all, sweetheart. We have no secrets. I tell you everything."

"Yes, eventually, Eddy. You never told me about that girl who sent you the postcard."

"S-s-tar?"

"Yes. Mehmet Efendi told me."

"Ah… have you written to her...called?"

"Of course not, Eddy," she laughed, then seriously, "I hope you don't think I pry into your personal life."

"Never. The thing I want most in the world is for there to be nothing separate about us, forever."

"Are you asking me to marry you?" The green eyes opened wide.

He felt a little confused. "Yes, I guess I am. Yes, I am!"

"But, of course. It is *kısmet*. I already told you."

"Then, will you...?"

"Before I answer you, I must tell you something. Something about myself. A confession."

"Yes, sweetheart?" His heart sank a little.

"I wouldn't want you to find out later and think that I had deceived you."

"Don't worry, Elif, nothing matters. I haven't exactly been…"

"My two front teeth are false."

"Your...teeth?"

"Yes. It is a bridge. See?" She opened her mouth wide for his inspection.

"Well, they look very natural. I would never..."

"They were perfectly good teeth. They got knocked out playing field hockey. At Robert College. I was seventeen. Would you like to see the bridge?"

"No, sweetheart, it's not necessary. I would love you even if all..."

"We were playing Üsküdar Girls High School. Very rough girls. Terrible cheaters!" She brooded for a moment. "So, Eddy, you don't mind?"

"Of course not."

"Then I will marry you. Give me a kiss."

One kiss led to another and after some time they were lying on the sofa in each other's arms. He looked into her deep, deep green eyes. They reflected dreamily back at him, holding something older than Byzantium. After a final hearty kiss and nibble, she sat up.

"You know, Eddy, I don't think we should wait too long to get married." She studied his face. "Eddy, you should grow a mustache."

This was unexpected. "A mustache? Why a mustache?"

"A married man should have a mustache," she explained, holding her finger horizontally under his nose. "Yes, it will look very nice."

"But your father doesn't"

"Baba is a soldier. Turkish soldiers never wear mustaches. Atatürk's rule. But you are a civilian."

"Well, I don't know. We'll see."

"Yes, Eddy," she said, kissing his cheek. "We'll see."

To get away from the mustache theme he said, "Elif, I'm afraid that I proposed rather awkwardly."

"Yes, you did. But I found that reassuring. I could see that you had no previous experience proposing to girls."

"Should I speak to your father?"

"Of course, Eddy. He will expect it."

"Do you think he will approve? What about your mother?"

"Oh yes! I have explained it to them, that it is my *kısmet*. My mother was very interested in Mrs. Papas' ideas."

"You told her about Mrs. Papas!"

"Of course. She agreed that you had not really been unfaithful. Actually, she seemed to find it rather amusing. 'Practice makes perfect,' she said." Elif turned green eyes on him as she spoke.

Then, he suddenly remembered his predicament. "I'm not sure how I will be able to support you, Elif."

She laughed. "Eddy, you are so old-fashioned. We will both work. Here at the Academy. I can move into your cottage, then someday Baba will give us an apartment in Beyoğlu."

"But maybe the school will close."

"Why would it close? Ali Bey just opened it. Are you keeping something from me? After what you said?"

He bit his tongue. Why on earth had he mentioned this? Then he thought, she's right, he should tell her.

"OK, I wanted to spare you, but here goes."

She listened as he gave his second recital of the day, though, unlike the Blums, she didn't interrupt. At the end, she said, "But it is impossible!"

"How do you mean impossible?"

"Ali Bey would never deal in drugs. He is a gentleman. He is Baba's friend!"

He tried to reason with her. "But, Elif, he was desperate for money. He gave me packages of dope to take to Mr. Agopian. There is proof."

"It is impossible. It is some kind of trick. I will call Baba."

"Look, please wait. We can trust the Blums. Let's at least ask them if we should speak to your father."

"Very well, I will discuss this with Lily. I will call her now," she said firmly. Ed began to wish that Elif were not quite so decisive, having a feeling that the Blums would not be best pleased that he had spilled the beans to her.

Ed said, "I'm waiting for Hobson's call. As I said, I'll insist on a public place, a safe place where..." As he spoke he looked out the window and saw Hobson rounding the corner and starting up the path of the garden.

## 44

Ed whispered, "My God, Elif, here he is! Hide yourself. I don't want him to know that you're involved!"

She understood immediately. "Where? The house is so small, if he searches." Her eye fell on the open *sarnıç* cover. "Perfect. I'll hop down there. Close the lid and put the rug over it. There's plenty of air from the downspout."

Before Ed could object, she had lowered herself into the reservoir and was crouching below. Hobson knocked on the door and shouted, "Ed, I know y-you're there. Open up!" Ed shut the *sarnıç* cover and pulled the rug over it. He opened the door and Hobson stood panting on the step.

"That's a l-long haul up the hill, Ed. I'm bushed." He came in. "N-nice little place. Mind if I look around?" Before Ed could reply, he went into the bedroom. "Very cute," he opened the closet and looked under the bed, then moved on to the kitchen. "Nice. A little old, though. Get b-bugs through these old walls." He looked under the sink. "No pantry, eh? What are these jars of vegetables? You could give yourself b-botulism, you know. So, that's it. Small, but c-cozy for one—maybe two."

He went back to the sitting room and sat down. "Do you suppose I could have something to drink? I'm p-parched."

"Sure, a beer?" Ed was feeling calmer.

"That'll be f-fine."

Ed brought two beers and sat down. Hobson took a sip of his. "So, you got the p-pictures." It was a statement, not a question.

"Yes."

"Tell me about it. T-take your time. I hear the rain starting. I didn't bring an umbrella, so I'll wait till it lets up. Dangerous to get wet when you're h-heated." He settled back.

Rain! Ed thought of Elif in the reservoir. How quickly would it fill up? Could she drown? "I have some things I have to do, Bill."

"F-forget them. This is the most important thing right now. Do I have to remind you that you're in up to your ass? I'd better l-like what I hear."

"Oh, very well." As quickly as he could, Ed ran over his visit to the lab and opening of the padlock, the nighttime visit, the forgotten camera, the visit next day to recover the camera. In the background he heard the rain beating on the roof.

Hobson listened carefully, occasionally sipping his beer. When Ed had finished he nodded. "That's quite a story, Ed. You must have been shitting in your p-pants when you saw you'd left the camera behind. I'd l-love to have seen that!" He shook his bottle. "Guess I'll have another of these. R-raining harder than ever now."

He had been sitting almost an hour. What was happening in the *sarnıç?* Ed got him another beer and decided that he would allow another fifteen minutes and then he would open the *sarnıç*, regardless.

Hobson broke into his thoughts. "OK, Ed, let's have the c-camera."

"Look, Bill, I just don't know..."

"What d-don't you know? Hand it over, I said. I don't want to get rough, but…" He reached into the side pocket of his voluminous suit jacket and took out an automatic pistol, which he pointed in Ed's direction. "Hop to it!"

There didn't seem much point arguing, so Ed went to the bookcase and took the camera from behind the two volumes of the *Norton Anthology of American Literature* where he had hidden it and handed it to Hobson.

"No t-tooth marks this time. Good," he said and put it in his pocket. "So, that's it." He continued to hold the gun. "Well, the rain seems to have let up, so I'll be r-running along. I'll be in touch." He backed to the door, gave an ironic bow, and let himself out.

As soon as the door had clicked shut, Ed ran to the *sarnıç* and tried to pry it open, but the cover was flush with the tile floor and he couldn't get a purchase on it. "Elif, Elif!" he cried. "Are you all right?" But there was no answer. How could he have let her go down there? He rushed to the kitchen and found a bread knife, then came back and worked it into the crack between the cover and the floor, but the point broke off. He tried again, twisted it, and the cover started to move. He levered it up and got his fingers under it and pulled. He looked in and saw Elif lying on her back on the floor.

"Elif! Speak to me!" he cried. She shook herself and sat up.

"Ah, Eddy. Is he gone? I fell asleep."

Elif, ever equal to the moment, had closed the downspout again and settled down until he opened up the cover. He reached down and grabbed her arms, then pulled her up wriggling out of the hole.

"Eddy, be careful! I am losing my..." When she was out, she said, "Turn your back, please." And he waited while she made some adjustments to her clothing. Then he turned and gave her a kiss.

"Thank God you're all right. I was so worried, but I'm afraid he got away with the camera. He had a gun."

"But what about the film, Eddy?"

"Isn't it in the camera?"

"No. I took it out." She looked at him seriously. "I told you the roll was finished. You really need to be more methodical, Eddy."

"So, what should we do now, I wonder?"

"We should certainly leave the house quickly," she said. "That man may look at the camera and see that the film is gone. Then he will come back for it."

"Where can we go?"

"We can decide. But let's go, and take the film with us. If he comes back he will search the house, for sure."

Ed put Starleen on a leash and locked the door behind them. He looked up and down the road. The rain had stopped and the coast was clear.

"OK, Elif, let's head down for the village. At least there he can't pull his gun on us."

They walked quickly down the hill, saying nothing to each other. When they got to the seafront they still hadn't decided where to go, but he looked up and saw that a ferry was just pulling up to the landing.

"The ferry to the next island! Let's get on it and we can go back to the Blums. They may have made contact with the security guy at the consulate."

"Good, Eddy. Let's run!"

The made it with plenty of time to spare and went up to the second deck. Elif said, "This is good. We can discuss this whole business with them. I know that it is not possible for Ali Bey to be involved in such a thing. I will tell them." Ed still had a feeling that they would not care for his lapse of security.

# 45

The ferry landed and they joined the crowd pushing their way onto the landing. They decided to walk to the Blums' house, so they took the main street up the hill that led to their road. After twenty minutes they turned into their road and saw the big reddish-brown house, set in its garden. Ed had been worried that they might have left, since he had not had time to call, but as they approached the gate he heard Dixieland coming through the open window. They knocked at the door and after a few moments it was opened by Lily, who had by now changed into a cotton dress, her hair caught back with a ribbon.

"Ed! And Elif. What brings you back so soon? Welcome. Come in." She and Elif kissed and she called out, "Everett! Come down. Ed's here with Elif." Everett came down, still wearing his dressing gown.

"Well, if it isn't the poor man's George Smiley!"

Elif looked puzzled and Lily said, "Pay no attention. Everett is just being cute—he thinks."

Everett shook hands with Ed and gave Elif a kiss. "Ah, words from my greatest admirer and severest critic." He gestured towards Lily. "How are you? When are you two getting married?"

"Everett!" scolded Lily, but Elif looked at him seriously and said, "You are psychic! You should meet my friend Mrs. Papas. Eddy asked me to marry him today. I have accepted—though, of course, he must speak to my father."

"Oh, how wonderful, Elif!" said Lily. "I'm so glad. Congratulations, Ed."

"Yes, indeed," added Everett. "But remember, Elif, this boy needs a firm hand." She nodded. "How about some champers to celebrate this..."

"...or any other occasion," said Lily tartly. "But of course let's have champagne. Are we the first to know about your engagement?"

"Yes, you are," said Elif, "but we really came about the business that Ed told you about this morning."

Everett looked over at Ed and raised his eyebrows. "Ah yes?"

"Yes," he said defensively. "Things have taken a new turn. The faux Hobson came to my house. He took the camera from me—at gunpoint."

"Then, the pictures are..."

"No. I have the film. Elif had taken out the roll before he got the camera from me. We got away after he left. But it won't be long before he discovers that the film is missing."

"So, where is the film now?" asked Lily.

"It's right here," he said, taking it out of his pocket and putting it on the coffee table. "Were you able to talk to anyone at the consulate?"

"Yes," said Lily. "We talked to Ted—the security chief.

"And?"

"And he said that there wasn't anything that he could do until he had talked to you personally. Even then, he says, it's probably a job for the Turkish police. He is trying to get hold of the Drug Enforcement Agency guy in Ankara, to see if they know anything about this. They can check with the Turkish narcotics people. He seems to be out of town, however."

"In other works, the sap doesn't know much," added Everett. "His big concern was that this faux Hobson got through his defenses at the Residence. We probably aren't going to be able to do much today."

"What do you think Elif and I should do?"

"Well, I suggest that you stay here for now. You're safe with us and you can hide your film here until we can organize the consulate people."

"That is very kind of you, Everett," said Elif, "but I want you to know that it is not possible that Ali Bey could be involved in this."

"You know, Elif, I have a feeling that you may be right. But I still don't get it."

Lily said, "We have to go out for several hours. The wedding of a Turkish friend's daughter. You two stay here and maybe we'll hear something by the time we get back. Answer the phone if it rings and, if it's Ted Richie, tell him we'll be back by 6:00.

Everett poured champagne and the Blums drank to Ed and Elif's happiness. "All you have to do is be as happy as we've been," said Everett. "But we have to go get dressed. You continue here. We can make spaghetti or something when we get back."

Ed and Elif saw them off a half-hour later, and then settled down on the sofa with the rest of the champagne and put on some jazz.

"When shall I speak to your father, Elif?"

"Let's get this business behind us first, Eddy. Then I will invite you to our apartment and you can speak to Baba."

"You have made me very happy, sweetheart. Give me a kiss."

After a few moments she said, "Mmm. That was lovely, but would you excuse for a moment. The champagne." She rose and left the room.

He sat by himself thinking about Elif and his upcoming ordeal with her father. It was so old-fashioned. What would he say exactly? He found myself trying phrases aloud, "Sir, I would like to ask you for the hand of your daughter in marriage."

"Sure. It's j-jake with me!"

"Hobson! How did you..."

He was smiling unpleasantly and the gun was in his hand again. "I j-just came in through the French windows—the burglar's friend. I noticed that the film was missing and was just about to come back for it when I saw you heading for the ferry. I t-took the chance that you had the film with you."

"Whatever you're involved in is about to be looked into. My friends the Blums have spoken to the security chief at the consulate."

"Shame about that. I j-just have to work that much faster. OK, enough chitchat. Hand over the f-film."

"I don't have it. I left it at the house."

"Something t-tells me you're not being quite truthful with me. I'd better just have a look around."

"Go ahead," Ed said, feeling sure that he wouldn't look in the African mask where Elif had put it a half-hour before.

"On second thought, let's start with a b-body search. If necessary, we can include your lady friend upstairs, but frankly I'd prefer that we didn't meet. Up to y-you."

Ed was trying to think of his next course of action when Starleen, hearing voices in the living room, came in to make friends. "That d-damned dog again!" said Hobson. Not one to be offended, she grinned up at them. What were her two friends doing, she seemed to wonder, standing there so stiffly? Was it some kind of game? Ah yes. Like before. She began looking around the room, her dark, alert eyes darting everywhere. She went over to the African mask and stood in front of it, looking up and wagging her tail. Then, she barked once.

Hobson had been watching her with distaste. "OK, let's get on with..." Then his eye followed her gaze to the mask. "Well, I'm d-damned!" He walked over and took it down. "Good doggie!" Starleen grinned up at him with pleasure. "Well, I g-guess that does it," he said. "Adios!"

"You mean you're leaving again?"

"You bet. Catch your act!" he said, and disappeared through the French doors.

"Well, easy come, easy go," Ed said to himself. "I just do not understand what he's up to."

"This is terrible!" said Elif, causing him to jump several inches.

"How long have you been there?" he asked, seeing her at the head of the stairs.

"Long enough to hear what he said. Do you think he would really have searched me? We have to get to Ali Bey and warn him right away!"

"Let's wait till the Blums come back. Maybe the security man will call. It's only fair to get their advice before we tell what we know to Ali Bey."

After another hour the phone rang and the voice on the other end said, "Everett? This is Ted."

"No," Ed said. "This is Ed Wilkie, the guy Everett told you about."

"Right," he said, "can I talk to him?" Ed explained that the Blums would be back by 6:00 and he said that he would call back then.

When the Blums returned from the wedding they were in high spirits.

"We picked up a lots of tips for you guys for your wedding," said Everett. "I thought it was particularly effective when the maid of honor stepped on the bride's train and tore it off."

"Oh no!" said Elif, her hand to her mouth.

"Pay no attention, Elif," said Lily. "Nothing of the kind happened. It was a very nice wedding."

Ed broke in. "Look, the faux Hobson has been back—here. He held me up and got the film back." He preferred not to mention Starleen's role in the debacle.

"Damn!" said Everett. "He came here? How did he find you?"

"He followed us on the ferry."

"And he just took the film and went away?"

"Yes. He said he was going to have to work fast now. Said I was involved in his program. I didn't understand."

"Me neither. Maybe we'll understand better if we have a drink. There was only sweet pink wine at the wedding reception." He poured a round of drinks.

"Oh, I forgot to tell you. Your friend Ted called. He said he'd call back later."

Lily said, "You two must be hungry after all that. Let's go in and see if we can piece together a little supper. They followed her into the kitchen and she sort-ed through the refrigerator. "What do you say to spaghetti with fresh tomato sauce? We've got lettuce for a salad and some pears and cheese for dessert.

"Sounds wonderful, Lily," Ed said. "I'm famished."

"Me too," said Elif. "Let me help, Lily."

"OK. You boys go get bread from the *bakkal*. And some of those nice olives to go with our drinks, Everett."

Later, during supper, Ted Richie called and Everett spoke to him for a few minutes. When he came back he said, "Ted confirms that there's nothing to be done right now. We'll have to work on it with the Turkish police. They've been in touch with Osman Bey, it seems. Osman Bey thinks it must be some sort of sting operation. An attempt to implicate Ali Bey in something. He says that he reckons that the trail has been laid from here to Marseilles. Probably Hobson's people have tipped off the French police, who will then contact their Turkish colleagues in Istanbul. The pictures you took are likely going to be sent to the Turkish narcotics police—probably also leaked to the press, so it can't be covered up. You will be implicated, if they have pictures of you as the courier."

"But, Everett, even I can see that this is full of holes. Why did they need me to take the pictures? Why didn't Erol just do it? Or why didn't they just tell the Turkish police about the equipment and have them raid the place?"

"Briefly, I don't know. My guess is that they thought pressure might be brought to suppress any evidence found in a raid. I think they probably needed you for the pictures so that they would have an independent witness. You can bet neither Erol nor Hobson would willingly allow himself to be interrogated by the Turkish police."

"But I would just tell them what happened. They couldn't..."

"I don't know, Ed. Maybe you could prove your innocence, but Ali Bey would still be damaged."

"And Erol?"

"Long gone I would guess."

"What about Mr. Agopian?"

"I can't say. But from what you've told us, I would imagine that it was his nephew who was the point man. You always gave the packages to him, right?"

"Yes, that's right." Ed felt relieved for his friend. "So, what now?"

"Well, I think that by tomorrow things will have cleared up more. Osman

Bey may have more information by then."

Lily said, "Why don't you two just stay here tonight? You must be exhausted. We can easily make up two beds or..."

"...indeed, one, if that's preferable," interjected Everett.

"Everett! Don't be crass," said Lily.

"Thank you, Lily," said Elif primly, "but I must get back to my parents. They will be worried."

Ed had thought Lily's suggestion—or even Everett's—an excellent one, but Elif was firm. So they had a quick coffee and went down to catch the ferry that stopped at each of the islands and then returned to Sirkeci. The Blums walked down to see them off.

"I'll call you as soon as I hear from Ted. Just sit tight," said Everett as they shook hands.

# 46

They got onto the ferry and Elif said that she wanted to sit on the main deck. "But I thought you liked to sit upstairs," he said. "We can look at the stars."

"Because I am getting off on our island."

"You are! Why?"

"Because I exposed the roll of film that Hobson took away with him."

"You destroyed evidence?" He was aghast.

"Yes. I wasn't going to allow this to be used against Ali Bey. I am certain that he is innocent."

"And now? Why the island?"

"I am going to tell Ali Bey about this. To warn him. Now that the evidence is gone, Hobson may try something else-to harm him. You don't have to go with me."

"Of course I will. I just don't know if we're doing the right thing."

"We are."

In a few minutes they were landing at the island. They decided to walk to the Academy and set off at a brisk pace up the hill, neither of them saying anything. Elif had made up her mind and he thought probably her instincts were right. After twenty minutes they were at the Academy. It was mostly dark, with only a few windows showing light. As they approached, Ed saw light coming through the front door as it was being opened.

"Elif," he whispered, "let's get in this doorway. We can see who it is."

"OK, Eddy," she replied, and they huddled together.

A figure let itself out of the door and closed it again, leaving the porch in darkness. Then it crossed the garden and came through the front gate and into the light of the street lamp. It was Osman Bey. He looked once back at the school and then up and down the road. Seemingly satisfied, he turned in the opposite direction from where they were hiding and walked quickly down the road and out of sight. They looked at each other.

"What do you think this means?" he asked.

"I don't know," said Elif. "Let's go in." They crossed the road and went through the gate and up to the front door. Ed tried it but it was locked, so he took out his key and let them in. The hall light was on, but there were no sounds in the building.

"Let's go to his office first," Elif suggested. They went upstairs to the office marked "Director." There was no sound, but Ed could see a light under the door. He knocked, but there was no answer, so he turned the handle and the door swung open.

Ali Bey was seated at his desk, seemingly deep in thought. He was dressed with his usual formality, but Ed noticed that his clothes were wrinkled and his face drawn and tired.

"Ali Bey?"

He looked up and seeing the two of them in the doorway, looked puzzled. Then he said, "Please come in." He rose courteously and came towards them. "Good evening, Mr. Wilkie, Elif. And hello, Starleen. Please be seated. What can I do for you?"

Ed started to speak, but Elif interrupted him. "Ali Bey, we think there is a plot against you. A plot to involve you in drug dealing. We came to warn you."

He shook his head. "You, too. I have just received another warning on the same subject."

"Osman Bey?" Ed asked.

"Yes. What do you have to tell me?"

"I was approached by a man posing as a CIA officer. He met me at the Consul General's residence, so it seemed bona fide. He told me that you were involved in heroin trafficking, that you were manufacturing it here at the school." Then, for the third time Ed went through his story, explaining how damning the evidence had seemed and how he had been implicated by acting as a courier.

"Yes, I can see how you were brought into this, Mr. Wilkie. It looked very bad, indeed. In fact, I had an idea that something like this must be happening when you told me about the packages that Erol Bey gave you. You and Mr. Agopian were both used by them—he, unfortunately, by his own nephew. The effect was to look as though we were making the heroin here and moving it to Marseilles in Mr. Agopian's rug shipments. In fact, it appears that they have, indeed, been trying to reestablish their supplies from Turkey, using this route with the nephew as courier, but he is a careless boy and the police had his description. They nearly caught him several times."

Ed suddenly recalled his encounter with the police when he disembarked from the ship in Istanbul and remembered that all the men being interviewed were in their early or mid-thirties—like Ari and him. Mr. Agopian had been expecting Ari, but Ari must have spotted the trap and gone on to meet him at the Kadıköy ferry landing instead.

"But why is Hobson doing this?" Ed asked.

Ali Bey looked thoughtful and then shrugged his shoulders. "For many years I have dealt in information—of a specialized kind. Your old teacher was an early associate. When I decided to retire from the trade, some of my friends in Turkey agreed to give me sanctuary, on the understanding that my information business was well and truly finished. Like my friend Ray Collins, I decided to return to education and I bought this school. I also am involved in a variety of other businesses, in Turkey and elsewhere. You met some of my business partners at my party.

"You make enemies in the information business. Just before my retirement I provided assistance that helped expose a particularly nasty organization, one protected by a country that your country considers a rogue state. They were funding their activities through the manufacture and distribution of illegal drugs. They wanted revenge and selected this stratagem to make it seem that I was doing something that Turkey could not countenance. They could, of course, have killed me, though I am well protected, but it would have been a sweeter, indeed poetic revenge to disgrace me, even have me sent to prison for drug trafficking. Turks take drug dealing very seriously and the laws are harsh. The man you know as Hobson is an independent agent who can be hired to handle this sort of job. A very nasty fellow. Very unstable—perhaps insane even. When you gave me the hint that something was not right with Erol Bey, I went to confront him, but he had taken his equipment to pieces and vanished—probably the morning you recuperated your camera from his lab. Interestingly, it turns out that he was involved in the drug trade that I helped expose, on the manufacturing side. He was, in fact, a former teacher—they called him the Professor. Now, Osman Bey thinks that very soon this business will be made public and will be hard to control. My agents are presently working with Osman Bey, trying to find Hobson, but predicting his next move is difficult."

"But the pictures have been destroyed," interjected Elif.

"Ah!" said Ali Bey, with new interest. "Then the case is altered. How so?"

"I exposed the film. It is worthless."

"That was very intelligent of you, my dear." He smiled at her. "This certainly changes things. I will need to talk to Osman again."

"So, everything is all right now, isn't it?" Ed asked.

Ali Bey considered this for a moment. "I'm not sure. It seems that the stratagem has failed, but that may not be the end of the game. My enemies will still want their revenge. I will have to be on my guard for the next blow. My only real concern is that this...Hobson may do something irrational. It is always hard to protect yourself against irrationality."

"But don't you think that when he sees that the plot has been exposed he'll just go away?"

"It would seem so, yes. On the other hand, he may decide simply to kill me. It would be foolish, because I have friends who would make it their business to hunt him down, but not impossible. We shall see."

Just then, the door opened and Zeynep Hanım came in. "I thought I heard voices. Ah, Mr. Wilkie and Elif."

Ali Bey said, "Yes, my dear. They have been giving me some information that confirms and expands on what Osman told us. It looks as though we will, indeed, have to act as he advises."

Zeynep reflected on this for a moment. "Mr. Wilkie, if you can spare me five minutes I'd like to speak to you. I hope you don't mind, Elif."

"Not at all," said Elif, and Zeynep led Ed to her office.

It was lit only by the desk lamp and the air was heavy with cigarette smoke. She shut the door and came over to face him.

"After what we've heard, I think it is likely that my father and I may need to leave Turkey for a time, to look after other interests."

"So I understood."

"Since we will not be seeing each other for some time, I thought that I would try to explain about that night. I don't want you to think that I am naturally promiscuous. There were circumstances difficult to explain. I think you have been, will be, discreet?"

"Of course."

"Good. And what are your plans?"

"Elif and I are to be married."

"I am pleased for you. She is a lovely girl."

He thought about his suspicions of Brown and it struck him that perhaps he should give her some warning.

"I think you are acquainted with my friend Brown."

She looked at him sharply. "Yes…slightly. Why do you ask?"

"I have an idea that he may be involved in this plot against Ali Bey. I thought that I should say something."

She looked startled for a moment, then, recovering quickly, smiled and said, "Thank you Mr. Wilkie. I had a feeling that he might not be quite what he appeared." She seemed to dismiss the thought. "Well, we can't worry about what is past. It is the future that is important. Again, congratulations to you." She sighed, and looked at him thoughtfully. "I know you'll make her happy. Well, good-bye."

To his surprise, she leaned towards him, smiled and turned up her face for a kiss. Her eyes closed and he kissed her. Then there was a tap at the door and she sprang back from him just as Elif entered. Elif must have noticed something in their attitudes, for she arched her eyebrows slightly and pursed her lips.

"All finished with your business?" she inquired brightly. "We must be off, Eddy."

Later, as they were descending the hill, she said, "I hope one woman is going to be enough for you, Eddy."

"Please don't get the wrong idea about Zeynep Hanım, sweetheart. It was just..."

"Don't worry, Eddy, you can tell me all about it later."

"You are the only woman I want, will ever want."

"That is wonderful to hear." Then, following some private train of thought, she added, "Besides, mother has been giving me some excellent tips. I must say, I was very surprised by some of them." She looked at him appraisingly. "Very!"

When they arrived at the ferry landing, Mr. Kuvvetli was waiting for them. "Osman told me to escort you home," he said.

They rode back on the last ferry, almost alone on the upper deck, with Mr. Kuvvetli seated discreetly several rows behind them. Elif, exhausted, put her head on Ed's shoulder and after a few minutes began to snore in a ladylike way. At Sirkeci they took a taxi to Elif's home and he kissed her goodnight.

"Well, sweetheart, a big day. An engagement and international intrigue-packed adventure."

"Mmm," she said sleepily. "You see, I was right." Then more businesslike, she said, "I will speak to Baba tomorrow about us. Is your good suit pressed?"

# 47

Mr. Kuvvetli and Ed got back into the taxi and he said, "It's late, so I think we may as well go to a hotel for the night. We can talk to Osman in the morning." He took Ed to a small hotel on one of the side streets off of Taksim Square. "It is a simple place," he explained, "but clean and not expensive. Osman is very strict about expenses." They paid off the taxi and walked towards a sign for the Paris Oteli. "Well, here we are," he said.

As they started to go in, a well-known voice called out from the shadows, "Hi, Mr. Wilkie. Long time no see! Who's your cute buddy?"

Mr. Kuvvetli looked amused. "You seem already to be familiar with the neighborhood."

The Paris Oteli was, indeed, a simple place, but the night clerk greeted Mr. Kuvvetli as an old friend.

"At one time I worked for another branch of our service, not far from here," he explained.

After some discussion, the clerk agreed to admit Starleen and Ed and Mr. Kuvvetli took two rooms next to each other on the third floor. The hotel did not have an elevator, so they climbed wearily up the stairs. Ed was completely exhausted and Mr. Kuvvetli also looked played out, so they shook hands and went to their rooms.

The room made the Grand Otel look pretty luxurious, but the single bed called out to Ed. Floor space being at a premium, he folded a blanket and put it in the closet for Starleen. Then he pulled off his clothes and slid naked between the sheets.

He had been asleep for some time when he fell into a familiar dream, one that had recurred regularly since he was a boy, especially when he had been under strain. In it he was running down a long, brightly lit corridor, which stretched forward into the distance, farther than he could see. On both sides of the corridor there were closed doors, and he found himself rushing from door to door, frantically pulling them open, desperately trying to find someone—he never knew who. As he opened each door he looked at a blank wall and, weeping with frustration, called out, "Where are you? Where are you?" Suddenly the light became even more intense and the corridor and doors melted away.

"Here I am, Mr. W-wilkie!"

Hobson was standing by the closed door, one hand on the light switch, the other holding the now familiar automatic pistol. Ed noticed that it now had a short cylinder attached to the end of the barrel. A silencer?

"G-get up, Ed, don't be shy."

Ed started to get up, but realized that he was naked and covered himself with a pillow. Hobson looked amused.

"Sweet d-dreams, I guess." Ed said nothing and Hobson continued, "So you exposed the film. You b-bastard! You—a dope like you—blew the whole thing!"

For the first time, Hobson didn't seem in control of himself. Ed looked at his tired, strained face with its muddy-brown eyes, which now seemed strangely unfocused, and at his trembling hand, and thought of Ali Bey's description of him as unstable, perhaps insane. Ed thought maybe he could calm him down.

"But why did you need me, Hobson—Bill? You had the equipment all set up. You could have just..."

He looked at Ed and his face seemed to go slack. "The equipment was a s-setup. We didn't really make heroin at the school. Too many risks. No point. Wouldn't have stood up to expert inspection." It was as though he were talking to himself. "It was set up for your b-benefit. Demiray said that you were so d-dumb he thought you'd never be able to do it. And when you left your bag behind I thought he'd g-go nuts." A smile passed briefly over his face. "So when you finally got your b-bag and your ass out of his place, he took things down and b-beat it. The whole thing was jinxed from the s-start. First we tried the frog bitch, but Demiray got into her p-pants and when they had a bust-up she said she was going to talk. Then the old bastard in the library heard something, or thought he did...ragged her about it. So we had to s-snuff them both and start all over again—with you!" He refocused his eyes. "So now I'm s-stuck with you. The only witness. The only one who can identify me. Not good for a f-failed job. My employers won't be happy. Won't p-pay."

"There's a policeman in the next room. You wouldn't dare shoot!" warned

Ed.

He laughed. "There's a policeman d-dipping his wick across the street. Your f-friend, the girl who spoke to you when you came in, made a big impression. Still, they won't take too long, so I'd better g-get this done," he said, lifting the gun and leveling it at Ed with trembling hands.

As he was speaking, Ed noticed out of the corner of his eye the door of the closet behind Hobson begin to open softly and a white muzzle emerge. Starleen, hearing voices, had decided to join the company. Ed saw her taking in the situation. Then she grinned: she saw her playfellow from yesterday. Was he hiding something from her? She walked over. Where could it be? His hip pocket, maybe? She stuck her nose up under the back of his voluminous jacket, and nudged him to see.

The effect was electric. He jumped into the air and the gun went off in his hand, missing Ed but shattering the bedside lamp. Starleen, sensing that all was not well, began barking and growling. There was the sound of footsteps running in the corridor and someone began throwing himself against the locked door. Hobson, looking confused and wild, turned and fired at the door, which was violently thrown open. Mr. Kuvvetli, blood spreading from a wound on his shoulder, pointed a gun at Hobson and shot him through the chest. Hobson gave one cry and then fell to the floor and lay still.

Mr. Kuvvetli looked at the body ruefully. "Osman is not going to like this," he sighed. Then he looked over at Ed. "You are fine? Perhaps you would be so good as not to mention that I was with...your friend for a few minutes."

Ed nodded. "It's between us. How about you?"

Mr. Kuvvetli looked relieved. "It is just a scratch, thank you. If you will wait here, Mr. Wilkie, I will go and call Osman."

Ed waited for a moment and then walked over to the window. In the doorway opposite he saw Rezan in urgent conversation with a new client, his back to Ed. Then the client nodded and looked up at the Paris Oteli, turned and walked quickly away. It was Brown. He must have been with Hobson, thought Ed.

The next few days were a whirl of activity. Ed met Ted Richie from the consulate, who was still concerned about the security breakdown at the party. "Got to check through all the procedures" and "Y'know, you should have suspected something when he bought you dinner. Can't use U.S. government funds to pay for a meal for an American citizen. It's all in the regulations. Here, I'll show you..."

Osman was more to the point. "This has ended better than we had expected. The French, astonishingly enough, even managed to make a pinch in Marseilles. Hobson's people must have tried to save money on bribes. They got your friend Ari," he glanced at Ed with a grin, "but missed the Professor. Unfortunately, we now have a mess to clean up. Two murders at the school and now Hobson killed at the Paris Oteli—rather publicly. I'm afraid it may be necessary for Ali Bey to move on, at least for a while, until all this dies down. My superiors in Ankara will decide."

## 48

Elif reminded Ed of his unfinished business with her father. "You can't compromise a Turkish girl and then not follow through, Eddy. Last night I saw Baba in his study cleaning his service revolver." She smiled and there was a sparkle of green. "You are invited for tea on Sunday."

When Ed arrived at the appointed hour, Elif met him at the door and gave him a kiss. Then she looked him up and down approvingly: shoes shined, suit pressed, new tie, hankie in the breast pocket, flowers for Mama. Check. She smiled.

"They are waiting for you."

He went with her to the sitting room and was welcomed by Elif's parents. He gave her mother the flowers and shook hands with the general.

"Merhaba, Ed. Elif says that you have something that you wish to speak to me about."

"Yes, sir." Ed felt his cheeks burn.

"Come with me to my study. We will have tea later."

The general looked very serious and imposing in his dark clothes, sitting opposite Ed in a deep leather armchair. There was no service revolver in evidence.

"Yes, Ed?"

Remembering his ill-fated rehearsal at the Blums, Ed blurted out, "Sir, I would like to ask you for the hand of your daughter in marriage."

"Yes," he replied gravely. "Elif told me that you had reached some sort of understanding. Very different from my day. Still, times change, and I know she's a good girl."

"Oh yes, sir. And I love her very much," said Ed, relieved that the worst was over.

He smiled. "That's good. But what are your prospects? Can you give her the kind of life she is used to?"

"Sir, I honestly don't know. At the moment the situation at the school..."

"Yes, I know." He nodded.

"I told Elif that we might have to wait for some time. But she seems sure that we can get jobs in Istanbul. She says..."

"Yes, I know. She has confidence in you. Like her mother had in me." He looked thoughtful. "Well, I have talked to Ali. The school will not close. It seems that he will be taking a sort of sabbatical—is that the word? But the school will remain open. In fact, I believe that he will be offering you an improved position at the school. A sort of wedding present. You are to talk to him tomorrow."

"Oh, sir, that's good news." Then it struck him. "Wedding present. Then you agree...?"

"Yes. Her mother and I think this will be right for her. You are a good man and she says she will have no one else."

They shook hands and went in to join Elif and her mother. The tea idea was tacitly abandoned and the general poured drinks.

"Not real champagne, I'm afraid. Turkish champagne. But a festive drink, I think."

Later they all shook hands and Elif took Ed to the door. She kissed him luxuriously and patted his chest.

"We will get married after the end of the term. Mother and I are planning it.

Will Everett be your Best Man?"

"That's wonderful. Everett? Well, I guess so."

"And sometime before then you can tell me about Zeynep Hanım." She sighed. "Well, as mother says, 'practice makes perfect,'" and the door closed.

# 49

The general had told Ed that he should talk to Ali Bey the next day, so at 10:00 he found himself once again walking with Starleen up the hill to the Academy. He thought about everything that had happened to him over the last year: his life in California, his mother's death, the Academy, Hobson. And Elif.

On impulse, he turned off and went into the Grand Otel. Mustafa met him at the front desk and he inquired for Brown.

"I'm sorry, Mr. Wilkie, I thought he would have told you. He left very quickly yesterday."

"Did he say where he was going?"

"No, Mr. Wilkie, it seemed to be a very sudden decision. Perhaps he will write to you."

"Perhaps, but I suspect not. Thank you, Mustafa Bey." So, that was that, thought Ed. Brown had infiltrated the school through his affair with Zeynep Hanım and had been working with Hobson all along. Ed hoped that at least he had not been involved in the deaths of Lucie Leblanc and the old librarian.

At the Academy, Ed knocked at Ali Bey's door, and he called out to him to enter. He was sitting at his desk where Ed had seen him last, but the atmosphere was completely changed. Morning sunshine was coming through the window, reflecting brightly on the big brass telescope, and he looked alert and rested.

Zeynep was seated opposite.

"Good morning, Mr. Wilkie," he said. "I believe you are to be congratulated."

"Thank you, sir."

"I have known the general for years. A fine family. You are a lucky man."

"I feel that very much, sir. I will certainly do everything I can to make her happy."

"I am sure you will, Mr. Wilkie," purred Zeynep. "I think you have a real capacity for giving happiness to a woman." She smiled demurely.

"How's that?" said Ali Bey. "Well, yes. As you know, Mr. Wilkie, I find that it is a convenient moment to take a break from my educational pursuits. Osman Bey has urged it most strenuously, for the sake of my health."

"We'll miss you, Ali Bey. Zeynep Hanım will be in charge?"

"No, Zeynep will join me. In fact, we are leaving almost immediately."

As he spoke, Ed looked around the room and saw that many books had been taken from the shelves and were stacked on the floor in neat parcels.

"Then, who...?"

"I have decided to deputize you to run the school in my absence. I have been impressed by your initiative and your...sincerity. I think you will do well. Elif can attend to the more...practical details."

"Thank you, sir! I will try to be worthy of you. But where will you go?"

"That I cannot reveal for the moment, but I will contact you later. Zeynep will give you some necessary information, and later my lawyer will call on you with some documents for you to sign that will regularize the arrangement. And now, I must continue with my packing. We are taking the launch at 2:00, to meet a ship on its way from...the Black Sea."

"And what will you do while you are away?"

"I am thinking of doing some more work on poinsettias," he said, glancing down at his *Mérite agricole*.

Zeynep and Ed went over some details together. When they had finished she looked at him and said, "You seem a little depressed, somehow. Is anything wrong?" He had, in fact, been thinking about Brown.

"Not really, thanks, Zeynep Hanım. I have recently lost a friend."

"That is very sad, but you are after all gaining a dear lifetime friend," she replied.

Ed had never heard her speak in this sentimental way before; perhaps she felt she could let down her defenses now that they were parting. She looked as though she was going to say something else, but then seemed to change her mind and smiled and pressed his hand. As she left she said, "Ali Bey asked me to tell you that he is leaving the telescope from Yıldız Palace for you. You will find it in his—now your—office."

"Thank you. Please tell him how much I appreciate it. I'll take good care of it."

Ed called Elif with the news and she was delighted.

"I thought Baba had something up his sleeve. This is a very practical solution, isn't it, darling?"

"Yes, it is."

"Did you hear what I said?"

"Yes. A very practical solution."

"No, not that. I mean, I called you 'darling.' How did it sound?"

"Wonderful, but..."

"I think it sounds nice. Very American. I have been starting a guest list. Would you please make one up also? We can go over it later today."

"Guest list? Oh, I see. Yes, sweetheart."

"Good-bye, darling."

At 1:30 Ali Bey and Zeynep were in the hall, surrounded by baggage. He wore his usual black, plus an odd traveling cap of antique design, and she was dressed in slacks and a tweed jacket. Mehmet Efendi was assembling the pieces of luggage and taking them out to the gate, where there were four horse carriages waiting. Finally, when everything was stowed away, Ed shook hands with them and they rattled off down the hill.

Suddenly everything seemed very quiet, after all the excitement. Ed looked down at Starleen and she wagged her tail. After a few minutes, they walked back to the building and stood in the hall, empty now of baggage, with only some pieces of wrapping paper and a roll of twine left behind. Ed remained there aimlessly for some time and then went up to the Director's office—his office now, it seemed. Would Elif have Zeynep's office? Elif would decide. He went in and sat at the desk, with Starleen at his feet. He had brought his mother's sapphire and diamond ring and was planning to give to Elif later that day. He took it out of its little blue velvet box. Yes, it would be just right for her. He ran his finger over the unfamiliar prickles of his newly emerging mustache. The room was quiet and smelled familiarly of leather and good cigars. He remembered Zeynep's parting words and walked over to the window where the big naval telescope stood—Ali Bey's farewell gift—and admired its heavy solid brass gleaming in the sun.

He tried to look through the eyepiece, but could see nothing. Then he noticed that there was a cap covering it—to keep sunlight from entering the lens and burning a hole in the carpet. He took off the cap and looked, twiddling the ring to bring it into focus. He found himself looking at the little harbor. As he observed it more closely, he saw the four horse carriages pulled up in front of the landing where the Academy's launch was docked. Ali Bey and Zeynep were there, directing the loading of the baggage by Mehmet Efendi. Beside Ali Bey stood Osman and Mr. Kuvvetli, the latter's arm in a sling, apparently come to see them off. Finally, the last pieces of baggage were stowed on board, but they seemed still to be waiting for something.

Suddenly, into Ed's field of vision walked another figure: Brown. He shook hands with Ali Bey and then kissed Zeynep and put his arm around her waist. They talked for a moment and then Ali Bey pointed up in Ed's direction. Probably he had seen the sunlight reflecting off the lens of the telescope. All three looked up: Ali Bey lifted his cap, Zeynep waved, and Brown laughed. Ed smiled: so, Brown had been Ali Bey's man all along—one of his "agents," as he had called them. That would explain his presence at the Paris Oteli. Ed was pleased to see that he and Zeynep would be together.

Ali Bey replaced his cap and made a sign for them to file onto the launch. In a few moments the gangplank was pulled in and the launch headed out into the Sea of Marmara, on its way to its rendezvous with the ship from the Black Sea. As he watched it disappear in the distance, Ed realized that Starleen was barking. He smiled to himself: "The caravan moves on."